ANGEL

SAGE

HEX

Book design by Inkstain Interior Book Designing
Text set in Cochin LT.

ISBN-13: 978-1499242195
ISBN-10: 1499242190

THE EVOLUTION SERIES, BOOK 2

EVOLUTION:
SAGE

S. A. HUCHTON

To the Fierce Four.
Sometimes family chooses you.

swore to myself, that I would never, ever do? I killed him, Gabe. I ripped the water out of him and killed him. I could have... I could have..." Silent sobs shook her, her words forcing her to relive every agonizing moment of that night. "I shouldn't have left him. I should have stood by him."

"Candace..." Gabe's voice was low, forcing its way through his own emotions.

"Just go," she whispered. "Please. Let me be. I don't want any of this. I'm not a superhero. I don't deserve to be."

"Candy, you—"

"Just go!" she cried, burying her face in her pillow.

It took him a minute, but she heard the soft squeak of his wheelchair again, retreating. The door opened.

"He nearly killed me, Candy. And for what it's worth, it was only a matter of time before someone would have done what you did. I know you don't believe that, but maybe you'll understand that someday."

Finally, the door closed.

It was quiet at last.

DRIFTING IN and out of sleep, Candace felt like she was finally making progress on her plan to waste away to nothing. A week after Gabe's visit, people stopped trying to coax her into a conversation. She overheard them in the hall outside her door, arguing about who had Candace duty that day and complaining how some of them got stuck with it more than others.

"Where is he anyway?" Dina hissed, the sound carrying

through the propped open doorway. "He hasn't had to do this once. It's not fair."

"Yeah, you wanna explain that to him?" That was one of the Pryor twins, Candace was pretty sure. "I'm sure he'll understand if you put it that way, and he'll come running to take a shift."

Dina sighed. "Of all people... I mean, he was there. If anybody would be able to get to her, I'd think it'd be him. If nothing else, maybe he'd piss her off enough to make her bathe or something."

He chuckled. "Now there's motivation for him. Who wouldn't love being stuck in a room with an unwashed, unresponsive body for several hours?"

"You two should be more careful with your conversation," another familiar voice said. Candace felt her insides contract, as though someone punched her. "She can hear you, you know."

Dina and the Pryor twin lapsed into silence, and Candace heard the door close. For a second, she hoped she was alone, but then the bed sank under someone's weight.

"Candace," Deborah said. "I know you're awake."

"No, I'm not," she grumbled.

Deborah sighed. "They miss you. So do I."

Which totally explained why the empath was absent for the last three weeks. Right. She missed Candace that much.

"It's hard for me to be around all your hurt, sweetie. Why do you think Chloe hasn't been in? The poor girl moved into Andrew's room because she can't be within two hundred feet of you. She tried her best, but it's crippling for her."

"And yet, here you are."

"You're starting to settle, and I've had more practice with compartmentalizing. She'll get there. So will you."

"I don't want to."

Silence.

"You should know," Deborah said. "There's been talk of medicating you. Forcibly, if necessary. I don't want it to come to that, so that's why I'm here."

"They can't make me take pills."

"I didn't say pills."

Candace drew out her own conclusions, thinking about the different things the doctors might do to her, inject her with. They'd turn her into a vegetable and do who knows what to her while she was trapped in her body, tormented in her own personal hell until they decided they were done with her. At least, that was where her brain went. Would they go that far?

"Further," Deborah said. "You don't want to know, and I don't want you to find out."

Candace tried to care. Tried to make herself sit up, put her feet on the floor, stand.

She couldn't. She no longer knew how.

"I know this is hard, Candace. I do. I'm actually glad you're scared now. It means there's something in you that still wants to live."

Was there? She wasn't sure.

"Think about it, okay?"

She nodded weakly.

"I…" Deborah stopped and took a few deep breaths. "I want to stay, Candy. I do, but—"

"It's fine," she interrupted. "I know this sucks for you more than most. Go ahead."

She stayed a moment longer, but not much beyond that. Deborah left the room quicker than she came in. Candace didn't blame her. She didn't want to be around herself either.

DEBORAH'S WORDS struck a chord, for sure, but it wasn't enough. The most she could muster over the next few days was responding to some of the conversations with her fellow ANGELs, and there was little in the way of eye contact when she did.

Not only on Candace's part. Her visitors barely glanced in her direction when she spoke. Did she look that terrible, or was it something else?

It was six days after week three when it happened.

"This is a goddamn waste of time," he said, loud enough for her to hear even before the door opened.

"The rest of us have training to catch up on, Jackson," Hector said. "Unlike you, we've put that aside to try to help her."

"A lot of good it's done you." He snorted.

"It's your goddamn turn. She can't be left alone. Suck it up."

Silence.

The door opened. A sudden panic crept over her. Jackson was on watch? What the hell? Who was the genius that thought that was a good idea?

The door latched closed, and Jackson took a few steps into the room, stopping before he got close.

"Yep, no surprises here," he said. "So what now, Sugar

Plum? Wanna talk about your feelings?"

"Go away."

Jackson snorted. "Oh, if only I could. See, everyone else here seems to think you need to be watched, and they're tired of doing it. So, today I have to drag my ass in here because you can't get your shit together. And why? Because your boyfriend lost his mind, and you took care of business, but now you can't pull up your big girl panties and deal with it."

Candace gritted her teeth. As if her life didn't suck enough, she had to put up with his abuse too?

"Did you think being a superhero was going to be some walk in the park where the bad guys look like bad guys, and you always know what's right and wrong? Funny, because I thought you were smarter than that."

God, she hated him. Couldn't he see it was all *because* she thought she was doing the right thing? Using her own "good judgment" brought her nothing but misery.

"A piece of advice, Sugar Plum? You've got two options here. You can either drown in this thing, or accept that it's part of who you are. That's it. They both fucking suck, but that's what it boils down to."

"I didn't ask for your advice," she whispered, trying to contain the overwhelming urge to punch his stupid face.

"No, you didn't," he said. "But since I have to be here, you're going to listen to it. This pity party you're currently attending is ridiculous. This isn't who you are, Sugar Plum. This weak, needy bullshit looks terrible on you. I get it. You killed someone you loved. Join the fucking club."

She blinked. The club?

"But it's no reason to make everyone else as miserable as possible."

"Seems to work for you," she said through bared teeth, barely audible.

"Nice response. I think your interpersonal skills need some work, though." Shit. He heard that? He sounded even more pissed. "I didn't come here to be berated by someone who can't even take a bath."

Candace wasn't about to apologize.

"You know what, Sugar Plum? Screw this. You wanna off yourself, do it. Don't be a coward about it." The door swung open, hitting the wall with a bang. "I'm done trying to rescue a princess who clearly doesn't want me to."

The door slammed closed.

She didn't move. She didn't breathe, listening intently. Was she actually alone? Had Jackson seriously walked out on her? After a minute or two of stunned disbelief, Candace rolled over.

The room was empty.

She sat up, unable to fully process what happened.

Absentmindedly, she reached for the glass of water on her nightstand. His words replayed in her head over and over as she brought the drink to her lips.

The first sip was all it took to send shockwaves rippling through her. She downed the entire cupful, shuddering as the liquid coursed down her throat, spreading quickly through her system. Her legs moved of their own accord, racing to the bathroom for a refill, which she drank quickly, followed by a third and fourth.

Candace collapsed on the bathroom floor, quivering as her body absorbed the fluids. Ignoring her thirst seemed so easy before, but... She needed more. She couldn't stop herself.

After ten refills, she couldn't handle another. Her knees couldn't hold her up, weakened by the intense pleasure of rehydrating, but she managed to drag herself to the tub and turn on the tap.

What was she doing?

She leaned an arm on the edge of the tub, laying her head on top of it, watching the water level rise.

"You wanna off yourself, do it. Don't be a coward." His words rang in her ears.

Did she want to? Could she? As many times as she wished for death the last few weeks, it should be an easy question to answer. It was her opportunity. There was no one to stop her.

"Drown in it, or accept it as part of you," she said to herself. "Like it's that fucking easy." She flicked her fingers through the water. "Asshole. How would he know, anyway?"

She peeled her clothes off, sure she would probably have to burn them later; the buildup of body odor and grime would never wash out. The bath was nothing short of heaven, and she soaked it up for a good ten minutes before washing the layer of filth from her skin. Even as she rinsed out the shampoo from her hair, she wondered why she even bothered. If all she was going to do was crawl back in bed anyway, why put in all the effort?

However, she didn't crawl back into bed. Something more powerful was pulling at her, calling to her, nearly yelling it was so loud. How had she been able to ignore that need?

She changed into her suit and, for the first time in weeks, left her room.

CHAPTER 2

WELCOME HOME.

The emotions overwhelmed her as she slipped into the pool, sinking to the bottom.

Home.

Belonging.

Acceptance.

Comfort.

Candace didn't know if she deserved to feel any of that, but there was no arguing with her connection to the water. It didn't care about her mistakes. She had been missed.

She swam, moving back and forth through the water, soaking up more and more of the solitude and unexpected peace. Closing her eyes and floating, she turned inward, pushing past all of the hurt, all of the guilt, all of the loss, and drifted in a sea of calm. In the back of her mind, she knew the relief was only temporary. Eventually she would have to return to her other existence, the one where everyone wanted — expected — things from her.

Where she expected things from herself.

Jackson was right, of course. As much as she hated to admit it, his words were the slap in the face she needed. Once again, Candace was in his debt.

She frowned. There was a strange back and forth between them, an ever-shifting imbalance of helping one another. Funny, considering he was such a jerk otherwise. If he were consistently nice, maybe it wouldn't sit with her so uncomfortably. As he ran more cold than hot with her, she never knew where she stood or what to expect. It was frustrating. Jackson Lawrence was not easily categorized or pinned down. Honestly, she couldn't say with any amount of certainty whether or not she detested Jackson or kind of liked him, although the thought of liking someone as unlikable as him disturbed her on multiple levels. Did she have that much self-loathing that she'd attempt to spend more time with him?

She shivered. No. Definitely not. She more or less hated herself, but wasn't about to hang around people who made her feel worse.

She took a breath and dove backwards, under the surface again. Life was too complicated. The water was simpler. Maybe she could hole up there and no one would notice.

Swimming to the far end, she emerged at the side of the pool to catch her breath.

A crowd of people waited for her. She stared back at seven shocked faces.

"What?"

Jackson shook loose from the grasp of two armed soldiers. "Satisfied? She's fine. Can I go now?"

"You're still in trouble, Jackson. Shut the hell up." True stepped to the edge and crouched down. "You scared us, sugar. What are you doing here?"

"Um… swimming?" Candace said. "Sorry. I didn't know I wasn't allowed."

True shook her head and grinned. "Didn't you hear the alarms? We've been looking for you for thirty minutes. Why didn't you tell someone?"

Candace shot Jackson a sidelong look. "There was no one to tell."

Amir Jones rubbed his face and sighed. "Yeah, we noticed."

Dina was silent, but shifted nervously. Hector was also quiet, but looked more pissed than nervous.

"You all right, Candy Cane?" True asked. "If you want some company, I can suit up and—"

"No!" Candace interrupted. "God, no. Sorry, True, but all I really want is some peace and quiet without people constantly talking to me. No, I'm not okay. I probably never will be. But, holy hell, if I have to deal with one more day of everyone treating me like a broken doll I might actually consider drowning myself just to avoid it."

True grimaced. "You know we're all trying to help you, right?"

She sighed. "I know, I know. But, seriously. I can't think with everyone hovering like this. I just… I can't. I appreciate what you guys tried to do. Really." She pushed back from the side, treading water. "No one else can fix me, True. I'll figure it out."

She dove under again, blocking out everything but her connection to the water. The next time she came up for air, they were gone.

S H E   C O U L D N ' T sit in the dining hall at dinner. The looks of shock, curiosity, and pity were more than she could handle. Instead, she took her food outside, avoiding the side of the Quad where she used to sit with Adrian. That was the worst part of all of it; the constant reminders of him were everywhere.

She found a tree far from prying eyes and set about tucking in to her first full meal in weeks. Even though she was starving, Candace could barely finish half of it.

As she flicked small pieces of bread at the sparrows in the grass nearby, she heard someone giggle. She recognized who it belonged to immediately.

Ella. Was she still messing around with Jackson? Odd. She didn't think they'd last so long together. Maybe he did actually care about her.

But when Ella finally came into view, she wasn't with Jackson. Emerging from a break in the trees, Candace was surprised to see her clinging to the arm of a veteran ANGEL: Tobias Sokol. Nicknamed "The Falcon," he was known for his amazing tracking abilities and speed. An old urge rose up in her. She'd love to find out how his abilities worked. There was speculation he had telescopic vision and was sonar receptive, amongst other things. He came from the fourth generation of Supers, but quickly became one of their most valuable resources in uncovering dirty genetic evolution labs in cities around the country.

As Candace watched them draw near, Ella finally noticed her. Her expression shifted from a coy smile to surprise to uncertainty. She turned to Tobias and whispered something, then slowly approached Candace.

"Hi," she said. She dug at the grass with her shoe, toeing a rock buried there.

"Hey," Candace said. "So, you and Tobias, huh?"

She blushed and nodded, then met her gaze, biting her lip. "It's, uh, nice to see you, you know, out of your room."

Candace did her best to smile. "Thanks."

Ella was quiet for a minute, then took a deep breath. "Look, I owe you an apology."

"You do?"

She nodded. "I've been a real bitch to you, and that was stupid. It wasn't even your fault. So, I'm sorry, okay?"

Candace frowned, not really sure what to say. "Well, apology accepted, I guess. Can I ask what happened? I mean, we were cool and then, well, I dunno. Did I say something to piss you off?"

She shook her head, her cheeks flushing again. "No, it wasn't anything you did. It's kind of embarrassing though, so…"

It made absolutely no sense. Candace hadn't actually done anything to warrant her anger or the silent treatment that followed? And what was so embarrassing about the reason for all of it? "Uh, okay. It's fine if you don't want to tell me. You're sure it wasn't something I did, though?"

"Yeah, sorry. It was… Never mind. I'm just sorry I let it happen."

Candace decided to let it go. "Well, if you get mad at me again, I'd rather you tell me why, all right? I missed your face."

Ella grinned. "Which one?"

Chuckling, Candace shook her head. "Yours, silly. You know what I mean. Anyway, you and Tobias. How long? And what happened with Jackson? You finally get tired of hanging around an irritable jackass all the time?"

"Let's not talk about Jackson," she said, grimacing. Her smile returned when she glanced at Tobias out of the corner of her eye. "And about two weeks ago. He's really nice, Candy. He likes me for me, not for what I can do, or do for him."

"Good," Candace said. "I'm glad you found someone that cares for you." It was exceptionally difficult, but she did her best to be happy for her friend.

Ella's smile faded into a concerned expression. "How are you, Candy? Honestly. I mean, it's great to see you're out and about again, but…"

Candace shrugged. "I'm…" What could she say? She wasn't fine. She wasn't okay, either. "I'm figuring things out."

"Well, for what it's worth, I'm sorry I wasn't a better friend to you. If you need anything, let me know. I want to make it up to you."

"Thanks," Candace said, picking at her salad.

Ella cast a glance over her shoulder and sighed. "I hate to run off on you, but we were about to go get dinner. I had to talk to you, though."

"No worries," she said. "You guys go ahead. I'm kind of enjoying the quiet anyway."

Ella grinned and nodded, then trotted back to Tobias.

He tossed a wave her way as they headed for the dining hall.

Candace turned the conversation over in her head for a while, wondering what happened to upset Ella enough to walk away from Jackson. As much frustration as Candace had with him, it must have been something bad for Ella to ditch him after sleeping with him for months. Candace knew the kind of attachment that came along with the treatments, so that couldn't have been easy. But maybe there was no imprinting with those two. The thought of Jackson feeling that way about anyone was totally weird. Could someone as abrasive as him ever get close to another person?

The man himself strolled by not long after, dirt-caked up to his knees and a shovel slung over a shoulder. Her first thought was that he'd been off burying a body somewhere, but she focused firmly on her food to keep from saying anything to him about it. Even though she wasn't looking at him, she swore she felt his eyes on her. Couldn't he walk any faster?

He stopped about ten feet from her, and she looked up. Her frown deepened to a scowl when she took in his smug grin.

"What?"

Jackson chuckled and continued walking. He was barely past her when he spoke.

"I knew you liked it rough."

In a surge of anger, Candace dove in to her connection. She called to the underground aquifer, summoning a spray of water up through the dirt to blast him in the back of the head. He spun, steam rising from his hair and clothes. His jaw clenched, muscles twitching.

She glared back at him. "You have no idea what I like.

Keep guessing, Sunshine."

"Who said I was guessing?" He fired back. "I had a front row seat for weeks."

She flinched, pinching her eyes shut as the ghost of Adrian's touch shivered through her. That was low, even for Jackson. Not saying a word, she collected her trash and stood, dumping it in a nearby garbage can as she left him there.

She would not let him see her cry. Never again.

"A N D H O W are we doing today, Miss Bristol?" the tiny old man asked as Candace settled into the easy chair.

Every day of the last week was the same. "Meaning, what? Have I crawled back into bed and decided to give up today? No, I haven't."

"Excellent. And how did you sleep last night? You look better rested than yesterday."

She sighed and resigned herself to going over all of it again. "About the same. Tossed and turned. Had a nightmare or two. I don't think that's going to change any time soon."

"Tell me about them."

"What?"

"The nightmares. What did you see?"

She leaned forward on her knees and pressed the heels of her hands against her eyes. "The same thing as yesterday. And the day before. And the day before that."

The dreams were always the same. Adrian was frozen before her, Candace pleading with him to give up the poisonous power he was draining away from his victims. But, unlike that night, she couldn't turn away from him as she sucked the life, the water, from his body. He transformed, shriveling into a desiccated, screaming corpse, reaching for her, accusing her. She awoke in a cold sweat every few hours, still feeling his electric fingers closing around her throat.

"Your mind has twisted those events into grotesque visions. You must learn to let go of the guilt."

"Oh, that's all?" she asked, eyes wide. "Well, you should have said so in the first place! I'll just wave my magic wand and… Oh, wait. That's right. This isn't a fairytale where I can snap my fingers and just get over it."

The shrink frowned at her. "Sarcasm will get you nowhere, Miss Bristol."

She flopped backwards in the chair, frustrated. "Neither will these sessions. You ask me the same questions every day. Nothing changes. The only thing that makes me feel any better is when I'm swimming or training, but no one will let me anywhere near the practice rooms. I'm all but living in the pool because I'm not allowed to do the only other damn thing that gives me any sense of purpose. So you'll pardon me if I'm a little irritable."

He pushed up his glasses and entered something into his tablet computer. "So you wish to continue training then?"

"What else could I possibly do with myself, Doc? Seriously? It's not like I can walk out of here and go back to a normal life now. This is it for me. There are no other options."

"And you believe you're ready to work with other ANGELs again?"

"I'm ready to not be sitting around twiddling my thumbs

anymore."

He was quiet then, studying her. Candace sighed. She shouldn't be so disrespectful, really. "I'm sorry. I don't want to be rude or anything, but I'm bored out of my mind. All I'm doing is sitting around stewing in my own head. I need something else. I need a reason to keep going, and, right now, I'm running on empty."

Tapping a finger to his lips, he continued to weigh her words. Finally, he set the tablet aside and leaned towards her. "You truly believe you're ready?"

"I won't truly believe anything until I've been given the chance to try."

"A valid point," he said. "All right, Miss Bristol. I'm willing to give you your chance, but on one condition."

To her surprise, a small spark of hope flared to life. She didn't know she had any of those left. "Which is?"

"We will continue to meet twice a week so I can monitor your recovery. No one wakes up one day and is miraculously recovered from a traumatic experience. I want to make sure you continue down the path to good mental health."

It was about the best she could ask for given the situation. Candace thanked him and was allowed to leave. As she left the office, her hands shook. Was she ready? Could she actually do it? What if something else happened and she totally lost it?

Swallowing, she took a deep breath and pushed the fear aside. Fear got her into that mess in the first place. Doubt drove her to make mistakes she couldn't fix. If she was going to do it, she couldn't let those things derail her again.

Tomorrow she would be back on track. Maybe there was a superhero in her yet.

CHAPTER 3

I T W A S not what she planned for her first day back in training.

Candace stared at the open floor of the Showcase, more than a little nervous. It had to be a joke. Surely there was more than a single glass of water for her to use, right?

"Ready to begin?" She knew that voice. It was Dr. Poznanski speaking over the PA system.

"Ready for what?" she asked, looking down at the glass, skeptical.

"It's accuracy day."

That was all the warning she got. Something whizzed past her, disturbing her hair. Candace ducked, hearing another headed her way. Adrenaline pumping, she finally got a grip on herself and searched for the targets. Clay disks spun and whirled through the air, at least twenty of them, and all gunning for her head.

Shit.

As she dodged another one, she tapped into her connection, finding the water glass instantly. She focused, trying to tumble away from another target, but it clipped her shoulder. Pain flared to life, and she glanced down to see blood staining the sleeve of her gray t-shirt. Holy crap. Blades of some kind armored the disks. They weren't messing around.

Another target came whirring toward her and something inside her snapped. Candace sliced upwards, pulling the water into a thin blade, her strike powerful enough to shatter the clay disk as it rocketed forward. It blew into a million tiny pieces, but she didn't stop. Again, she spun, destroying another enemy.

Twirling and attacking, she decimated one after another, fueled by the pain in her arm. She never stopped moving. She never stopped her assault. She was alive, every inch of her singing with purpose. It was a dance with death.

She loved every moment.

One last strike, and silence fell. Shards of clay and bits of metal rained down around her in a final, syncopated finish.

Candace remained crouched, catching her breath, sweat dripping from every pore and strand of hair.

Damn, that felt really good.

"Excellent work, Miss Bristol. Please follow your escort to the observation deck."

Observation deck? That was new.

Candace stood and left through the bay doors on the bottom level. Jackson waited on the other side, looking impatient.

"Did I miss the wet t-shirt contest?" he asked, raising an eyebrow.

Not about to play his game after what he said to her a few days ago, she grabbed three bottles of water from the cart in the hall and kept walking. His words still stung, and she hadn't healed enough to play visceral sarcasm tennis with him yet. A camouflaged solider stepped away from the wall and led her to a small staircase. They climbed four flights before emerging into another hallway. Seven doors down, he keyed in a passcode and admitted her.

Someone handed her a towel.

"Nicely done, *mami*," Hector said.

When she finished wiping her face, she looked at him. He leaned against the glass wall, wearing an impressed grin.

"You guys were watching?" she asked, glancing around. Most of her training group was present: the Pryor twins, Ryan and Bradley, and Ella, Dina, Hector, and Andrew. The only ones missing were Jackson and Chloe, but Jackson was up next in the Showcase. She couldn't imagine that Chloe would be very effective there anyway, but more likely she was still keeping her distance from Candace.

"Today's demonstration is to show your fellow ANGELs what you're capable of," Dr. Poznanski said, coming in behind her. "Your cohort is here, but the veterans are scattered around the observation deck as well. Since your training involves them too, they want to see what they're getting into."

Candace stared at him, suddenly glad she went first that morning. If she had known all of that, she would've been a nervous wreck.

She wandered over to the window and looked down. A small whirlwind swept across the Showcase floor, cleaning up the debris from her demonstration. That had to be True's doing. She'd know that cyclone anywhere, having been in close quarters with it on multiple occasions. As she watched, someone lifted the sleeve of her t-shirt. Dr. Poznanski scrutinized the damage she took on that first and only hit before murmuring something to himself and wandering off. He returned a moment later with a small first aid kit and patched her up with liquid skin that seared like fire when it hit the wound.

Candace closed her eyes and connected, directing the water in her body to surround the area, soothing it instantly. When she opened them again, he gave her a curious look.

"You stopped the bleeding. Interesting," he said. "Make sure you have that properly seen to in the clinic after this business is concluded or you'll have a scar."

"I will."

Dr. Poznanski nodded once then saw himself out.

Ella leaned up beside her, a goofy grin on her face.

Candace frowned. "What?"

Her grin widened, and she all but burst with excitement. "You were so amazing down there! I mean, wow!"

"It was pretty cool to watch," Bradley Pryor, said, adjusting his glasses. "Your accuracy is astounding."

Andrew chuckled. "I hope you saved some targets for the rest of us."

Ella continued to rave. "You destroyed everything like you were a ninja or something! And with just a glass of water! Oh my God, Candy, I'm seriously jealous!"

Candace started to smile at the gushing praise, but she

faltered and looked away. "Don't be."

"But—"

"No. Don't be jealous." She rested her forehead against the glass and closed her eyes, letting the coolness seep into her skin. A month ago, she would've been overjoyed at being so impressive. As it was, she could only wish she was a lot less awesome. "I would trade you if I could."

Her words were enough to dampen the mood and no one spoke again until Jackson took the floor. Candace let go of her worries, focusing instead on watching him.

Rather than a glass of water, his source was a single oil lantern. Knowing what she'd done with limited resources, she imagined he wouldn't have any trouble either. Sure enough, when the targets came flying out, he was immediately on them, obliterating each one with a burst of white hot flame. It was captivating. He moved like a cat, effortless and graceful. The way he twisted and turned to dodge was magnificent. The muscles in his arms and chest rippled with each movement, and she couldn't tear her gaze away. Jackson was incredible. Compared to his finesse on the floor, Candace probably looked like a beached whale flopping around.

But he got cocky. Candace could tell by the smirk on his face.

His focus was on a disk flying in from the left, and he never saw the one barreling at him from behind him to the right. She winced as it grazed his face, leaving a bloody gash along his cheek. Enraged, he sent a massive fireball at the offending target, exploding it on impact.

As a result, he used up all his remaining resources in that one attack. Four disks dropped to the ground, completely untouched.

Visibly pissed off, Jackson kicked the useless lantern, sending it flying. It shattered against a lower window.

"Shit," Hector muttered. "*El cabrón* needs to get that temper in check."

Candace grimaced. She couldn't argue with that. Although, aside from his shoddy finish, she silently admitted that Jackson was pretty damned extraordinary.

Andrew vacated the room, as he was up next. She wondered if Jackson would follow procedure and return to the group, or if he'd continue pouting and storm out of the Showcase without watching the other demonstrations. If he was smart, which was still up for debate, he'd suck it up and learn what he could about everyone else.

It wasn't a shock to her when the door burst open, slamming against the wall, but everyone else jumped and backed away when Jackson entered. Candace turned slowly, mustering her best bored expression. Blood dripped down his face, but he didn't make a move to wipe it away. He stomped toward the window. Ella and Dina skittered away, giving him plenty of space. No one said anything, not wanting to incur the wrath of a riled pit viper.

Candace returned to watching the Showcase, the cleanup in full swing, including a power wash to get rid of most of the scorch marks on the walls. Was Dr. Poznanski not coming to see Jackson, even to patch him up? She supposed he was only there to let her know what was going on, but still, Jackson was bleeding and probably needed more medical care than she had.

When it was apparent neither Jackson, Dr. Poznanski, or anyone else in the room was going to do a damned thing,

Candace took matters into her own hands with a disgusted sigh. Even if he was an asshole, he didn't deserve to bleed to death on account of his own stupid pride.

Cracking open her last bottle of water, she poured some out on one end of her towel and snagged the first aid kit. She reached up with the wet cloth to wipe his face, but he jerked away and grabbed her wrist.

"What do you think you're doing?"

She scowled, fighting the urge to yank away from him. "Keeping you from bleeding all over the floor. It's a biohazard."

"I don't need your help."

She rolled her eyes. "Right. Because there are plenty of mirrors in here for you to do it yourself."

"Why should I bother? You worried about me, Sugar Plum?"

Candace stood her ground, not about to cow to his bull. "I worry about the *team*, Sunshine. Don't flatter yourself. Now shut the hell up and let me do what I can to fix the damage. Though there's nothing I can do about the rest of your face."

She smashed the towel against his cheek, her ability pressurizing his wound the way she had her own to stop the bleeding. That done, she dabbed at the rest of the mess, cleaning him up a little so she could apply the liquid bandage. She tried not to smile as he winced at the chemical contact. Served him right. Her work complete, she tossed the towel at him, not about to hang on to the bloody thing herself.

"You're welcome," she said, returning to her place at the window.

No one said a word. Ella caught Candace's eye, her red eyebrows raised, and an amused smirk lifted the corner of her mouth. Candace frowned and turned away, her attention focusing on the Showcase floor as Andrew stepped inside.

THE OTHER demonstrations were as impressive, albeit a little less explosive than Jackson's was. Andrew was given a few dozen nails, which he levitated and directed with enough force to destroy over half of the clay disks. Hector, whose ability Candace knew nothing about, surprised her with a handful of pebbles. He had the ability to send pressure waves through inorganic materials, and launched the rocks into the disks with as much success as Andrew. Ella's mimicry wasn't useful against flying targets, but she accurately duplicated the appearance of ten different soldiers, one after another.

Dina's resource consisted of one small rock covered in lichen. When the barrage began, her first act was to construct a temporary shelter, growing the structure from the plant material provided. The lichen sprouted vines, weaving itself into a tight mesh that curved above her like a dome. From there, she used smaller, loose tendrils to bat away the disks, and they cracked against the windows, rendered useless.

The Pryor twins were completely fascinating. They could only use their abilities in conjunction with other Supers. Along with the Pryors, True took the floor with another ANGEL: Kina Cross. She was about as nondescript as they came; average height, average build, mousy brown hair. Candace scoured her memory, but came up empty for information on the girl. She'd seen her around, of course, but hadn't made her acquaintance as yet.

The demonstration began, the twins splitting and standing behind either woman on opposite ends of the Showcase. True's whirlwind kicked up, but Candace focused on the other ANGEL. Kina's body didn't move, but her hair shot out in front of her, growing with alarming speed. Within seconds it was halfway across the floor, encroaching on True's whirlwind. Candace glanced at the Pryors. Eyes closed, they each had a glow to them, one blue, the other reddish. The light expanded outward, enclosing the women, altering their powers. True's whirlwind shrank to little more than a dust devil, though it was clear she fought hard against Bradley's red aura. Kina, on the other hand, experienced the opposite. The writhing tresses grew and grew, sweeping across the floor like a flash flood. A few clay targets were released, but all four were instantly shattered against windows when whips of hair lashed out simultaneously. Before long, True was surrounded, tied up, and completely incapacitated. The twins lowered their fields, and Kina's hair retreated. True's whirlwind returned to full power, but dissipated as the demonstration ended.

Candace's brain took over, extrapolating the uses for their additive and subtractive abilities. That could be incredibly useful in the field, pending it could be directed properly. If one of the twins missed the mark, he could end up weakening an ally or boosting the enemy. They'd need lots of practice to ensure accuracy.

The others filed out of the observation room, and Candace followed at a distance, still lost in thought.

"And what did you think, Miss Bristol?" Dr. Poznanski

asked as he caught up to her.

"They were all very impressive," she said.

"But?"

She frowned and stopped walking, the others disappearing down the stairwell. "But they need more practice. Hector and Andrew could do with a lot more, actually. Dina seems to be doing well on her own, probably because of her work with Jamarcus, like mine with True."

He nodded appreciatively. "Yes, I agree the most effective method of training is mentorship. It helps to have an experienced ANGEL building up confidence and sharing their tips with trainees. Three of your team are without the benefit of this right now."

Her train of thought halted abruptly. "My team? But I'm not —"

He interrupted her with a wave. "Come, Miss Bristol, let's not play the humility card today. You know as well as I do that you are by far the best suited to lead them."

She wasn't at all sure what to do with that information. "I don't think I'm quite up to that yet. Last I checked I was still a borderline basket case according to you guys."

"You asked for a purpose," he said. "I'm presenting you with one."

That wasn't at all what she meant by that. Candace was barely capable of taking care of herself at that point, never mind eight other people. "What, exactly, do you want me to do?"

He smiled and guided her on down the hall. "As I was saying, three of your team haven't had the benefit of mentorship. I would suggest you begin there, assisting them with their training on a personal level."

"Three?" She frowned, thinking. "Hector and Andrew I know, but who else? Ella?"

"No. Her skills would be ill-matched to yours. I was referring to Mr. Lawrence."

Candace stopped dead in her tracks. "Jackson? You can't be serious. Wouldn't he be better off with a more seasoned ANGEL? There's no way he'll listen to anything I have to say."

Dr. Poznanski continued walking, shooting a last bit of advice over his shoulder before he disappeared into the stairwell. "Then perhaps you should look for a different method of communication in his case."

Candace stared after him, bewildered. Mentor Jackson? Was that even possible? A saint wouldn't have the kind of patience required for that monumental task. Dr. Poznanski may as well have told her to turn the Sahara Desert into a rainforest.

She sighed and continued out of the observation deck. That would teach her to ask for more work.

FINGERS RESTING on the handle, Candace considered her plan of attack. Hector and Andrew she could deal with easily enough. They seemed receptive to her, if nothing else. That was pending that Hector laid off the sexual innuendos, of course. Perhaps she should start with them and work her way up to approaching Jackson.

Satisfied with her decision, she opened the door to the dining hall and collected her lunch. Most of her group sat at one table, the exceptions being Ella, who was probably off with Tobias and, of course, Jackson, who was at his usual two-seater table at the back of the room. She slid in next to Dina and mostly listened to the conversation as she ate, waiting for a moment to catch Hector and Andrew. Jamarcus showed up as the meal ended and collected Dina. Setting her fork down, Candace decided it was time.

"Could I talk to you guys for a minute?" she said, looking at Hector and Andrew.

Hector leaned forward and grinned. "Sure thing, *mami*. What you need?"

She fought back a grimace and looked at Andrew.

He shrugged and stood. "I guess. I told Chloe I'd meet her at one though, so…"

Candace picked up her tray. "It'll only take a minute."

After dumping their dishes, they took the conversation to a table in the Quad, closer than she would have liked to the tree she used to sit under with Adrian. Swallowing hard, she turned her back to it and sat facing away. *Focus*. She had a job to do.

"So I was wondering if you guys might be interested in training with me," she said, getting right to the point. "You know, since we're all going to be working together anyway."

"Training how?" Andrew asked.

She shrugged. "Well, I don't know if you guys have much practice using your abilities in sparring matches. I did a lot of that with True, but I think I've gotten about as much as I can from it now. We know each other's moves too well."

Hector chuckled and waggled his eyebrows at her. "Oh, so you're looking for fresh meat, eh, *mami*?"

Candace sighed and ignored the overtones. "I figure it'll

be mutually beneficial for all of us. It's in everyone's best interest if you learn to combat a wide range of abilities. I wouldn't say I've mastered defense against air attacks, but variety is the spice of life. You get bored, you get sloppy. Plus, I'd like to see how you guys do against each other and against me. True gave me some great tips, and I'm all about paying it forward if you're interested."

Andrew looked dubious, and his question was hesitant. "I dunno, Candy. No offense or anything, but, are you, y'know, okay?"

She closed her eyes for a moment, took a deep breath, then nodded. "I don't think 'okay' is the right word for it, but I'm not going to freak out and try to kill you or anything." Neither of them seemed very convinced. "Look, how about this. We can start off with me playing referee while you guys face off. I can watch for your weaknesses and help you improve if you don't want to go one on one with me yet. If nothing else, I'll be better prepared to work with you out in the field, and you still get the benefit of what True taught me that way."

They were quiet, considering it.

"Well?"

Andrew rubbed his chin, then nodded. "Yeah, I think that could work. You in, Hector?"

"Sure, why not," he said. "Better that than going a few rounds with Amir or something. When you wanna start?"

"We could go later this afternoon," she said. "Or after dinner if you're up for it. Since tomorrow's a full schedule, it could be our only opportunity before Thursday."

"Three o'clock?" Andrew asked.

Hector shrugged. "Yeah, sure."

"Sounds great. Meet me here at three?" She tried not to be smug, but she was pretty damned proud of herself for talking them into it.

That settled, the boys took off. Candace lingered at the table, thinking over what sort of things she might have them do. Maybe starting them from zero, as she had, was a good plan, then adjusting from there.

The sudden quiet left her uneasy. The last time she was there, she had a chilling conversation with Adrian that would haunt her forever. She sucked in a ragged breath. There'd be no avoiding his ghost. Everywhere she went, there would be a reminder of him, no matter how small.

She eased off of the bench, unable to look at their reading tree. Maybe someday she could without wanting to vomit, or crawl into bed and cry.

But today was not that day.

CHAPTER 4

"C O M E   O N, boys," Candace said, standing over them. "It wasn't that bad."

Hector muttered a Spanish curse into the ground where he lay on his stomach, panting. Andrew wasn't much better off, managing an angry thump of his fist against the dirt. They looked like hell, covered in dirt and dozens of tiny cuts and bruises.

Candace put them through their paces, for sure, but it wasn't anything she hadn't done to herself and worse. Their little spar was nothing compared to the all-out battles she had with True. They were doing pretty well though, considering they'd only been at it for a week.

She hopped up on a large boulder and grinned. "I warned you against sparring already. Neither one of you knows when to hold back and when to go all in yet. So, yeah.

You might want to rethink this and spar with me next time. I can play to your level." She giggled.

"Man," Andrew moaned as he sat up. "What the hell, Hector? That boulder to my ribs could have killed me."

Hector coughed and spat dirt out of his mouth. "Then ease up on the branches, bro. I think I have splinters in my ear."

"Anyway," she interrupted. "I have a few things that might help you out if you want to hear them. Some stuff I noticed." When she had their attention, as much as she could in their battered states, she continued. "First off, you both need to learn how to split your concentration. You need to be watching at all times, not tuning the world out and focusing inward. Have you practiced following that cord, rather than just pulling on it? The more you practice that, the quicker it will come and the less time you'll spend getting things to happen." She flicked her wrist upward and a spray of water shot into the air. The display did the trick, causing both Hector and Andrew to sit up, newly interested. "Eventually, you'll be tapped in constantly and it becomes second nature. Like breathing. When you stop to think about it is when you run into problems."

They settled into a pattern of try-fail-lecture, try-progress-lecture since beginning the sessions. It was getting easier. Every time they were a little more attentive to what she told them. As a result, they were finally showing improvement. When they insisted on sparring that day, she did her best to warn them, but, naturally, they wouldn't take her word for it. As a result of their impatience, both ANGELs were going to have to visit the clinic for patching up. Dumb boys. They would get it sooner or later.

They knocked off for the evening and hiked the mile back to the compound. Along the way, she noticed freshly dug trenches. Hector and Andrew continued on while she stopped to look, the two of them completely engaged in verbally reliving each blow they scored against the other.

She cocked her head to the side, following the lines in the dirt. It turned a corner, and she continued tracking it until it turned again about a quarter mile away. When she finished her survey, she discovered it was a square patch of land someone sectioned off. How odd. What was the purpose of it?

Jumping over the two-foot wide ditch, she explored the interior, but stopped when she saw the scorched vegetation.

Jackson.

Was that his own private training ground? That could explain the ditches. Those would act as firebreaks if a blaze got out of his control. She turned slowly, assessing the field. Had he dug all of it by hand? Thinking back, she remembered seeing him covered in dirt and carrying a shovel. It must have taken him weeks to carve out the space. Candace didn't think he had that kind of dedication in him.

The most burned out area was in the middle. A swirling pattern of plant carnage spread out from a center point, creating beautifully macabre whorls of blackened earth. Lumpy piles of ash were scattered in other spots at various distances. The remnants of targets, maybe? That couldn't be very challenging. Still, if he were desperate to practice, what else could he do?

Her shoulders slumped. It wasn't like he had a sparring partner.

In the fading daylight, Candace made her decision. It

was time to help him.

"GOOD MORNIN'," Dr. Eliot MacClellan said, smiling as he paced the floor of the classroom, the barest hint of a Scottish brogue in his words. "First of all, congratulations on completin' your treatment cycles. I'm familiar with your names and abilities already, though I've only met a few of ye personally." He cast a meaningful glance at Candace, causing her to shrink into her seat a little. "As ye know, today we'll be introducin' ye to the ANGEL Project's preferred mode of transportation. It takes some gettin' used to, so we'll do this in baby steps. Even if you're not prone to motion sickness, you'll likely be tossin' your cookies before the lunch break. Let's hope for all our sakes' you folks ate a light breakfast this mornin'."

He strode over to the desk and activated the flat panel screen on the front wall. "We're goin' to give ye a little tour first, just a video to start. It's goin' to go over the basics of the shuttle and what your expectations should be goin' in." He tapped another button and the lights dimmed.

Candace leaned forward as the movie began, and nearly fell over the front of her desk by the time it ended. The interior of the shuttles were stunning — plush leather seats, all black and chrome with multi-colored lights everywhere. There was a button for everything: emergency ejection, personal heat or air conditioning, and water stations with retractable straws that self-sanitized at every use. The tech specs were even cooler than all the bells and whistles. At its max speed, an ANGEL shuttle could travel more than twenty-six hundred miles an hour, over twice as fast as what the officially released information stated. It was no wonder Supers could get from there to Vegas in under twenty minutes. It was mind-bending to think something that fast was even possible.

The shuttles were piloted remotely from the compound, but, in an emergency, could be operated from the cockpit. Every ANGEL was given basic training for such an eventuality, but only a handful ever achieved proficiency with it. Candace's fingers itched. What she wouldn't give for a shot behind those controls. She could almost feel the yoke in her grasp, responding to her touch. She shivered. Oh yes. She had waited for that moment for months.

After the film concluded, they were escorted into the next room and divided into two groups. A pair of simulators took up most of the space. They didn't look like much — only two black pods. Strangely, they didn't appear to be attached to anything or wired to the floor in any way. Candace looked up and did a double take. Was it her imagination, or was there a distinct line — a breakaway point— in the center of the ceiling? Not allowed any more time to think about it, Candace was ushered into the pod on the right with the Pryor twins and Jackson, while Ella, Dina, Hector, and Andrew went to the one on the left. Far too excited to be bothered by Jackson's presence, she strapped herself into a seat after taking a peek at the front controls.

Dr. MacClellan came through, made sure everyone was secure, and briefed them on safety measures. Just like an airplane, there were lifejackets under their seats, but there were also emergency eject buttons. Those would only activate if any anomalies or problems were detected in the shuttle during flight, in order to keep twitchy newbies from falling out of the sky.

"Now," Dr. MacClellan said as he paced the open center area. "If ye'll reach above and behind your heads, ye'll find facemasks in that compartment. While the g-forces are somewhat controlled within the shuttles, these are still necessary. They're also your emergency airsick bags, as they funnel away any unpleasantness in flight. Until ye're all used to this, these are mandatory."

Candace reached back and removed the headgear, tightening the straps behind her ears. At least with that thing on, the big black front piece that covered her mouth and nose would hide her blissed-out grin and she could drop the pretense.

"Think you can handle all this excitement, Sugar Plum?" Jackson's smug voice came through the headphones.

"You are so not ruining this for me, Sunshine," she said, shooting him her best withering glance through the visor of her headgear. He *would* sit across from her, probably only to spoil her view.

"Betcha you puke first," Bradley said to his brother from across the aisle.

Ryan snorted, shifting in the seat beside her. "As if. Loser has to clean the winner's bathroom."

"You are so on."

"What do you say, Sugar Plum?" Jackson chuckled. "I wouldn't mind a bit of maid service."

She rolled her eyes. "You'll have to make do with self-service, Jackson. You're probably used to that, though, huh?"

"Wouldn't you like to know."

"Jesus. That thought alone is enough to make me puke. Please, don't elaborate. I got enough of that when you were with Ella."

That shut him up. Asshole.

They were so busy talking that she almost missed the first rumbling motions of the takeoff. She held her breath and closed her eyes, committing each sound to memory. It was incredibly realistic. It really felt like they were moving.

Her eyes popped open. Hang on a second.

They *were* moving. Up.

Her head tilted back, as though she could see through the roof.

The split in the ceiling. Holy shit, were they actually going to fly? They couldn't possibly. Their ship wasn't equipped for that. There were no engines or wings or anything on it. Something loud clanged against the top of the pod. Maybe it was a track of some sort meant to shoot them around a room, like the giant centrifuges astronauts used to train in. That had to be it.

Didn't it?

There was movement in her peripheral vision and she turned her head to the cockpit. A front panel lowered to reveal a window to the world outside.

They were moving up through the hangar.

Maybe that was a screen.

An incredibly high-definition screen.

Her grin widened as she saw Trevor Ching stroll into the control room, tossing a wave at the recruits on his way.

Oh my God. Oh my God. Oh my God.

They were actually going to fly.

Candace clutched at the arm rests, trying to contain elated laughter. The others would think she lost her mind if she started giggling. Had they noticed? She glanced around and took in three stunned expressions.

She let one little giggle loose. "Hope you boys aren't afraid of heights."

A quiet hum was all the warning they got. The hangar dropped away and *boom!* The pod shot forward, pushing her sideways in her seat. The power. The speed. Dear Lord, it was incredible. Eventually, her body adjusted to the momentum enough that she could turn her head to see out the window again. The world rushed by in a blur, and she focused on the furthest point she could. Towns and cities flew past, one by one, until the skyline of Las Vegas became visible. It was there and gone in seconds, and the pod banked, twisting through the air. At the first turn, she had to block out the sound of retching in the headphones. She giggled. Both of the Pryor twins were totally puking. She glanced at Jackson, grinning. He looked a little green himself. Two more turns and he was done. Unable to control it, Candace busted out laughing.

It was a good thirty minute flight round trip, and she deflated a little as they jerked to a stop. When the back bay door opened, she unstrapped and jumped out of her seat to greet Dr. MacClellan.

He stared at her as she bounded out of the pod.

"Miss Bristol?" he said. "Everythin' all right?"

She couldn't help herself. She hugged the man. "Oh my God, that was awesome! When do we get to do it again?"

Choking on laughter, he extricated himself and pushed her to arms' length. "Well, I do believe this is a first. You certain ye're all right? No unpleasantness at all?"

She shook her head, grinning. "Nope. I'm fine. Those guys, however..." She looked over her shoulder and giggled as Jackson and the Pryor twins stumbled out of the pod. "They might need to lie down for a while."

"Interestin'," he mused. "Make sure you mention this at your next checkup. I imagine Dr. Poznanski will be verra keen on your inner ear. It must be due to your ability, though I canna say for sure what exactly. That's not my area of expertise."

When the second pod came back, it was a similar sight. All four ANGELs tumbled out of the back and immediately bent over the large plastic trashcans scattered around the room.

Dr. MacClellan sighed. "Ye may as well cut out for the day, Miss Bristol. This lot likely won't recover for a while."

She hesitated.

"Was there somethin' else you needed?"

Candace bit her lip, considering the wisdom in her request, but she couldn't let the opportunity pass her by. "The video mentioned piloting training. Is there a chance I could... Well, how soon are we allowed to start that?"

He chuckled. "One thing at a time, Miss Bristol. Although, usually once an ANGEL can fly without gettin' sick we give the green light."

"So, since I'm fine, does that mean—"

"Hold on to that, lass," Dr. MacClellan said. "It's possible this was a fluke. That'll be up to Poznanski."

She frowned, but shrugged it off. "Well, I guess I've waited this long. What's a few more weeks?"

"You have a good day, Miss Bristol," he said and grinned

at her, striding off in the direction of her pod, tablet in hand.

Satisfied she did well, Candace left the simulator room, starving and ready for lunch.

NEITHER HECTOR NOR Andrew were up for training that afternoon, so Candace took to the pool instead. As she swam, her thoughts drifted back to Jackson and his training grounds. She still hadn't figured out how to approach him about the issue. Any help she gave him was always done under the radar. Asking him outright seemed pointless. Of course he'd say no and would probably find some way to berate her for even daring to broach the topic.

The problem continued to plague her through dinner. She sat by herself, as her cohort was still recovering from the morning flight. Finally, a distraction in the form of the Pavo Team came through the door.

Candace hadn't spent much time with True or Amir the last few weeks, as she was still a little embarrassed by her behavior after the Adrian incident. Allen was with them, but Gabe was absent. There was no trace of him since he visited her room. Was he still laid up in the clinic?

She waited until they were seated, but was hesitant to go over. She wasn't certain she'd be welcome anymore. True caught her staring and Candace blushed. True waved her over, saving Candace from having to ask. Maybe they would have some insight on how to handle the Jackson problem.

Picking up her tray, she reseated herself beside Allen.

"Hey, sugar," True said, smiling. "How you feeling today?"

"Better than the rest of my training group." Candace grinned. "I think they're all airsick from the flight this morning."

Amir swallowed a bite of food. "Did you not go with them?"

"I did," she replied. "I just handled it better."

Allen gaped at her. "Wait, are you telling me you didn't get sick? *Everybody* gets sick the first time in the air."

She shook her head and grinned. "Nope. I was fine. It was so awesome! I can't wait to get another shot at it."

True chuckled. "Well, it's good to see you excited about something again."

Amir leaned forward, considering her. "So Candy, have you given any thought to team placement?"

"Team placement?" she asked. "Not really, no. I figured they'd assign me somewhere and that would be it."

Allen snickered. "Yeah, after all the wheeling and dealing maybe. After the Showcase the other day, people are already trying to cash in favors to get you on their teams."

She blinked. "What?"

"You know how they do the draft for the NFL?" Amir said, waving around a breadstick.

"Um, sort of."

"Well, it's kind of like that," he said. "We scout the new ANGELs and divvy them up amongst ourselves. The Project admins have some say, but we're pretty good at balancing out the talent on our own. Anymore, their approval is a formality."

Candace tapped her lip, thinking. "So, you want to give me a hint on where you think I'll end up?"

True shrugged. "It's early yet, but Volans is a front

runner. They're still down two after losing Kelly and Angelo last year. Others have been filling in when they can, but they're stretched pretty thin."

Candace winced. That was a painful loss for the ANGEL Project and the whole country. Kelly Arno and Angelo Bains were fatally wounded during a rescue attempt the previous fall. New Orleans was hit hard by a hurricane, and buildings were collapsing left and right. The pair died, buried when a warehouse collapsed on them. She shuddered. Reports said they'd been skewered by ceiling support beams.

Something else occurred to her. "Wait, the Volans Team isn't West Coast. I thought the Eastern teams only drew from the trainees at the Virginia compound?"

Amir sighed. "Normally, that's correct, but they haven't had any viable replacements in their recruits. They're looking for power players, and the last few batches haven't resulted in anyone even close to what the Physicals in your group can do. So, heads up on that one."

"Well..." she said, frowning. "That might make all my efforts pointless then."

"What efforts, Candy Cane?" True asked.

She rubbed her chin, thinking. "Dr. Poznanski asked me to work with three of the guys in my cohort that didn't have mentors. I've started working with Andrew and Hector to help them improve their abilities." She looked at True. "Sort of what you did with me, only more subtle. They don't know I was asked to. They think it was my idea and that I want to improve with them. Not that I don't, but they aren't even up to what you and I ended with yet."

Allen choked on a drink of water. "Poznanski told you to mentor them?"

She nodded. "It feels weird, since we're from the same training group and all, but I didn't get the impression it was optional for me to not try."

"Hmm," Amir mused. "I don't think you have to worry about getting shipped out then."

"Why's that?"

"Poznanski did the same thing with me back in the day. He's grooming you for a Team Leader position. The East Coast doesn't need any more of those. They've got more Alphas than they know what to do with."

True turned and looked at him. "He did? You never told me that."

He slipped an arm around her waist and winked at her. "You never asked."

As Candace watched them, her heart ached. Not too long ago, she had someone like that. But now she didn't. She never would again. She would never put another person at risk that way.

"Didn't you say three?" Allen asked.

"Huh?" she said, not following his train of thought.

"You said Dr. P told you to work with three of the guys, but you only mentioned Hector and Andrew."

Candace sighed and rubbed her temples. "Yeah, about that. That other one is a problem. I was actually hoping you guys might have some advice for me."

"Ah. So it's Jackson then, eh?"

She nodded. "It's been two weeks and I still haven't figured out how to approach that mess. I mean, I know for a fact he's looking for more ways to improve, but it's like trying to offer a porcupine a hug or something. Where do I even start? I'm just dreading the whole thing."

Allen let out a low whistle. "That's rough. I can't say that I have any advice from my end, but after seeing you two in hand-to-hand combat, make sure you give me fair warning if you figure it out. I don't want to be anywhere close if you go at it with your abilities. I might have to find a fallout shelter or something. Or maybe sell tickets."

She rolled her eyes. "I'm glad you find my suffering so entertaining." She took a bite of salad and chewed thoughtfully. "So where's Gabe hiding? I thought maybe I should talk to him again, now that I'm, y'know, not catatonic anymore."

True grimaced. "He's still in the rehab unit. He's... having trouble getting back up to speed."

Closing her eyes, Candace took a deep breath. Endless ripples of destruction.

"It's not your fault, sugar," True said. "Adrian was one of his closest friends. He's trying to work through what happened. Are you sure you can handle diving into that again?"

"You say diving in as though I'm out of it," Candace said. "I'm not." Her appetite gone, she stood, picking up her tray. "I'll see you guys later."

As she dumped her dishes, there was a tap on her shoulder. She turned and met Amir's warm smile. "Sneak up on him. Knock him on his ass."

She balked. "Gabe? I don't think—"

"No, not Gabe," he said, whispering. "Jackson. Get him into a fight. Don't ask, just attack him."

Candace stared at him, flabbergasted. "Are you sure that's smart?"

A knowing grin spread across his face. "Let's call it

speaking from experience." He cast a glance over his shoulder. "He's not the only ANGEL with trust issues."

Hold on a minute. Was he saying that's what he'd done with True? She considered it. Candace knew firsthand what happened when True got angry. If she could survive that, Jackson couldn't be all that bad.

"The rehab unit is the second door on the right past the clinic desk. You shouldn't have a problem getting in to see him since you're family," he said, switching gears.

"Thanks," she said. "And thanks for the advice. I'll do what I can to get him back to you guys, okay?"

"Good luck, Candy Cane. If he'll listen to anybody, I'm sure it's you."

She watched him as he headed back to the table. Even after seeing her at her lowest, Amir had faith in her. If nothing else, she owed him for that.

CHAPTER 5

CANDACE KNOCKED on the door and waited. No answer. She knocked again, but that time opened it enough to stick her head in.

"Gabe?"

He was propped up in bed, right leg elevated in a weird contraption. The brace around his torso was gone, replaced by compression bandages. He stared blankly at a small TV on the wall in front of him, the light from the screen the only illumination in the room.

He looked half dead.

Swallowing her guilt, she flipped the light switch and walked in, not waiting for an invitation. His eyes never strayed from the television, however, to which she responded by unplugging it from the wall.

"I was watching that," he said, glaring at her.

Candace ducked under his leg and sat at the foot of his bed. "And I was correcting your rude behavior. Deal with it."

"Well, someone's feeling better."

She shrugged. "Amazing what a bath will do for a person. What about you? Why are you still in here?"

Gabe flicked the TV remote at his leg. "They're waiting for the fake bones to take."

"Fake bones?"

"They had to replace what Adrian crushed."

Hearing his name was a punch to the gut. She sucked in a slow breath, easing herself through the pain.

"You didn't know?"

She exhaled. "I guessed it was him."

By invoking that name, he shook her confidence in the whole visit. She had no idea what to say next.

He tossed the remote to the side and lifted an arm, motioning for her to squeeze in beside him. Candace crawled over, easing onto the sliver of bed and trying not to hurt him. She rested her head on his shoulder and sighed as he pulled her against him. The last time they'd done that, she was ten years old and escaping from a nightmare brought on by a contraband horror movie she insisted they watch. In so many ways, Gabe was a big brother to her every time she needed him.

"I'm sorry," she sniffled, trying not to cry.

Gabe kissed the top of her head. "It's okay, Candy Cane. What happened wasn't your fault. He was unstable."

"But I could have *kept* him stable," she whispered. "He lost it because he didn't have me any more. I abandoned him, and I didn't know how much he needed me. I said horrible things to him that I didn't mean, that I didn't even want to say, but I thought…" She choked. "I thought…"

When she didn't continue, he squeezed her gently. "You thought what, Candy Cane?"

She took a shaky breath and pushed through. "I thought I could protect him from me."

"From you?"

"From what I saw in the Mirror."

He went quiet.

"But it ended up being right anyway, even though I tried to prevent it."

"That's what the Mirror showed you?"

She nodded, shuddering at the memory. "It was horrible."

"Yeah," he said, very softly. "I know."

They laid there, enjoying the closeness between them, the comfortable silence where words weren't necessary. She didn't know which of them needed it more. After a few minutes, she could breathe normally again and the tears dropped back below the surface, but never as far away as she wanted them to go.

"You should tell me what happened," she whispered, breaking the silence.

He stilled beneath her, hesitant. "Are you sure you want to know?"

"No, but I think you need to tell me."

Several heartbeats passed before he spoke again. "All right." He took a deep breath. "Well, I couldn't find him until dinner the day after we talked, but I tracked him down when he tried to get into the Showcase. By then, he already killed one of the guards."

She closed her eyes and forced herself to stay there. In

no way did she want to hear any of it, but Gabe needed to say it and needed her to listen.

"He wanted to show everybody how powerful he was. He started ripping equipment out of the floor and throwing it across the room. They let me through to try talking him down. I thought I could. For a second, I thought I did. But I messed up. I told him he was going to hurt you if he kept going like that, and he snapped. Candy, I've seen a lot of fucked up people in the last year, but Adrian... Adrian was worse than all of them combined. When he ran out of things to throw, he threw *me* instead. Tossed me around like I was nothing. Whatever it was he did after shattering my leg and breaking five of my ribs, I couldn't tell you. The next thing I knew, I was waking up in the clinic and it was three days later."

It was her fault. Guilt flooded her, pushing silent tears down her cheeks. "I'm so sorry, Gabe."

"Candy, please stop apologizing," he said, placing another kiss on the crown of her head. "By the time I found him, the Adrian we knew was long gone. There was no turning back for him. What you did..." He hugged her tightly. "What you showed him was mercy. I know it hurts like hell, but if it was that easy for him to go over the edge, nothing you could've done would've prevented that, even *if* you stayed with him. All it would have done was made it harder for you to end it."

"But what am I supposed to do now?" she sobbed into his shoulder. "Part of me died with him, and I don't know how I'm still breathing. I'm terrified of myself, Gabe. I don't... I can't..." She broke down into hiccupping whimpers.

He smoothed her hair and let her cry it out. "We all are,

Candy Cane." he whispered. "Every one of us fears the monsters we're hiding. You just came face to face with yours a little sooner than most."

CANDACE WANDERED back to her room around midnight. She stayed with Gabe to watch mindless shows about normal people with normal lives doing normal things to moderately humorous ends. She couldn't remember the last time she watched anything on TV. It hadn't even occurred to her to look for one since she arrived at the compound. With their heavy conversation and the late hour. she was wiped by the time she crawled into bed.

As a result, she was grouchier than usual in the morning. Hector and Andrew were taking the morning to practice their techniques individually, so there wasn't much for her to do. Candace considered taking Dina up on the offer of seeing her garden. but she had her monthly checkup scheduled for that day and was unavailable.

The idea of being outside was appealing, so Candace went for a run instead. As she jogged along a faded trail, she searched for other places for Hector and Andrew to spar. Introducing new terrain would keep them on their toes.

A small explosion jarred her. She stopped and looked around, taking the opportunity to drain one of her water bottles. The noise came from the left. close to the place she'd been using for Hector and Andrew's practice sessions.

Jackson. It had to be.

Amir's advice was to initiate a fight with him, to catch

him off guard. It was a perfect opportunity.

Still questioning the wisdom of being there, she stayed low and out of sight as she crept closer to his training grounds. Candace needed to get the lay of the land and his position in it if she was going to have any chance of success. A collection of trees and shrubs provided enough cover for her to scout it out.

Jackson was surrounded by smoldering piles of charred wood, with others in varying states of blackened ruin. Even in the sunlight, he was glowing, flames dancing through his wavy hair and around his fingers. His back was to her, his focus on a row of crudely built stick men.

It was now or never.

Ropes of water shot up through the ground, tangling around his ankles and calves. Jackson flailed, startled by the cold contact, and he tried to jump away. She held fast and emerged from cover, the ropes continuing their ascent upward, surrounding him.

"What are you doing out here?" she asked. "Trying to start a wildfire?"

He muttered an unintelligible curse.

Grinning, she dragged him around to face her. "What was that, Sunshine?"

"You'd better start running, Sugar Plum," he growled.

Something stirred inside her, a sudden, urgent need for confrontation. "And why would I do that? I'm not afraid of you."

His face hardened. "Maybe you should be."

She lifted an eyebrow. "Yeah, right. Give me one reason why."

Jackson burst into flame, her liquid bindings evaporating

into thin air. His arms shot out, fire spilling towards her. She leaned away, easily avoiding it. Candace sent up her own spray to cool and counteract the blaze, putting it out instantly.

"Nice try, Sunshine," she said, smirking. "But I'm not impressed. Got any new tricks up your sleeve?"

The muscles in his jaw twitched. She successfully pissed him off, if nothing else.

A circle of fire shot up around her, and she whirled, dousing the flames as she spun, and leapt away at the first break.

She giggled. "Aw, that was kinda cute. What else you got?"

"Still hanging on to that death wish, Candy Cane?" He crouched low, palms against the scorched earth.

Candace snorted. "If I did, I've got far more effective means of accomplishing that goal." Just to goad him that much more, she hit him in the face with a cold blast from the aquifer.

Jackson wiped a hand across his mouth, and she caught the flicker of a smile. It threw her off, leaving her slow to react to his next move. Jackson surged forward, an arc of heat and light preceding him. She barely got a water shield up in time to block it. He pressed in on it, steam erupting where the barrier met a blazing blade. She held her ground, allowing him to creep forward until his face was inches from her own, letting him believe he was gaining ground. His eyes burned as brightly as his weapon, locking onto hers with an unnerving intensity even through the shimmering blockade, but she would not falter. She had him.

At the last second, he knew something was up, but it was too late. Candace wrapped him in a liquid cocoon and sent him flying. The water mostly broke his fall as he landed.

Mostly.

He coughed and spluttered as he rolled to his side.

"You're sloppy," she said, hands on her hips. "You let your temper get the best of you. You're far too focused on me, and not worried nearly enough about watching your own back."

She turned and walked away, keeping alert for any sign of movement or another attack.

A wall of fire sprang up in front of her, singeing the ends of her hair as she jerked to a halt.

"Where do you think you're going, Sugar Plum?" he whispered in her ear.

God damn it, how did he get behind her so fast?

Candace didn't move, not about to let him see her flinch. "I got bored."

His breath was hot against her skin. "Looking for a little excitement, were you?"

"I was looking for a challenge." She didn't dare turn to meet his gaze, focusing instead on the conflagration raging before her. "Guess I should look elsewhere."

"You seem pretty challenged at the moment."

He was too close. Good grief. Those goddamn hormones. She thought she was past that.

Candace doused the flames and stepped through the wall of steam left in its wake. With a little distance between them, it was easier to think. "Not really."

"You're gonna get burned if you play with me, Sugar Plum."

She rolled her eyes. "Really, Jackson? I'm not sure you could be any more cliché if you tried."

He snorted. "I've been called worse."

"I can do better, if you like, but I see no reason to add insult to injury."

"Injury? I think you overestimate your wit," he said, crossing his arms.

"I always pull my punches when my opponent is outmatched."

He had the strangest look on his face.

"Don't hurt yourself overthinking that one."

"Don't."

She frowned. "Don't? Don't what?"

Jackson dropped back into a fighting stance. "Don't pull your punches."

She considered him. "You don't believe in mercy?"

"Mercy is subjective."

Of course he was right, though his words struck deeper than he probably realized, and for a different reason entirely. But pulling her punches wasn't going to help him, and the only reason she was *there* was to help him.

Wasn't it?

"Fine," she said, shifting to a defensive posture. "I won't hold back then, but remember that when you're laid up in the clinic."

He launched himself at her, guns blazing. She slipped into a rhythm — blast, duck, dodge, roll, extinguish — letting him show his moves. After several cycles of avoiding fireballs, she found his weakness. For a split second, he would lower his guard to power up. If she could time it exactly right…

Blast.

Dodge.

Roll…

The column of water slammed into his gut, knocking him off his feet. She struck again, the hit propelling him into a mid-air spin. Jackson tumbled, but took another shot at her. She countered with her own, blowing it back in his face. He shot, she blocked, moving so fast it was impossible to tell who was attacking and who was defending. The distance closed between them, the short-range blasts exploding until it was one long stream of fire and water twisting together.

She had one more move to play.

Candace eased off the forward pressure only enough to redirect some of the current. She lost some ground, but it boosted his confidence, and he poured it on thicker. It was either act, or lose her eyebrows. When the water slammed into his back, he was completely unprepared.

There was one flaw in her plan. She hadn't stopped to take his momentum into the equation.

Jackson flew forward, directly into her, knocking her onto her back. Her skull slammed into the ground and the wind rushed out of her lungs.

"Shit," she groaned, cringing. It was tougher to breathe than it should have been.

"Kinda backfired on ya, huh, Sugar Plum?""

Her eyes flew open.

Jackson's face hovered over her.

So close. His lips were right there, soft and full. If the rest of him was that warm, how would they feel?

"Does this mean I win?"

Was he closer? Oh God. No way. No way was she going to let that happen.

Panic surged through her and she flooded her system,

arms thrusting full force as she pushed him off. Jackson landed ten feet away, curling his shoulders inward, cursing through gritted teeth.

She jumped to her feet and stomped away, splashing mud everywhere as she went. "Tell the boys in the clinic I said hi," she shot over her shoulder.

Fuck, she messed up big time with that last attack. Getting pinned like that… what was she thinking? Scowling and caked in wet dirt, she fumed the whole way back to the compound. That wasn't a mistake she could afford to make again.

THE SECOND flight was better than the first. They started off with a tour of the hangar, learning about the control room, and the mechanisms for takeoff and landing. The whole system worked with electromagnets, similar to a railgun. It was completely fascinating, and she was pretty sure most of her cohort hated her a little for all the questions she asked.

Her enthusiasm for the shuttle was only dampened by the constant awareness of eyes on her. She could never quite catch him at it, but she knew, without a doubt, that Jackson was staring at her the whole damn time. It was a conscious effort not to mentally relive their sparring match the day before. Every time she stopped focusing on the shuttle training, she would see his face, a breath away from hers, and wonder for a split second what would have happened if she hadn't stopped him.

Don't think about it.

Do. Not. Think. About. It.

For fuck's sake, it was Jackson. He was rude, arrogant, derisive, insulting, smug, and completely infuriating.

And he didn't care about her. He didn't care about anyone.

God damned hormones.

Candace finally got a break from his relentless gaze when it was time to go up again. They dropped the pretense of the pods entirely, although Candace suspected they were typically used to transport more people than could fit in a single shuttle. Calling them "simulators" had been someone's idea of a joke, and she suspected it was Dr. MacClellan's.

They split into halves again, and she was seated with Dina, Andrew, and Bradley Pryor.

"Is it true you didn't get sick at all last time?" Dina asked as she strapped in next to Candace.

She nodded. "Yep, but it's possible that was a fluke."

Bradley snorted and pushed up his glasses. "Fluke, my ass. You were laughing, Candy. That's not right."

Candace reached back and pulled out her headgear. "I wasn't laughing at you guys. Well, I mostly wasn't. After all the bluster beforehand it was a little funny to watch you all barfing your brains out. I did genuinely enjoy the ride, though."

Andrew sighed. "You enjoyed it?" He shuddered. "I just want to get it over with. I'll be happy if my stomach settles by dinner tonight."

Dr. MacClellan came in to check on their harnesses, left them with a few tips on how to reduce the effects of motion sickness, and they were off. The same rush of excitement came over her like the previous trip, heightened by knowing it was the real deal. She let her body relax, rather than bracing for the blast off. Bracing would cause muscle strain. You could only fight gravity so much before you hurt yourself. Dina didn't make it two minutes before she was sick. That triggered Andrew, apparently a sympathetic puker, and Bradley wasn't far behind. Like before, Candace stared out the cockpit window, captivated by the speed as the Earth flew by. The route was different that time, taking them north, over mountains and forests. Somewhere over Oregon, they banked, went through a few corkscrew maneuvers, and headed home.

Admittedly, Candace felt a little guilty. The spinning moves were probably done to try and shake her up. It didn't work. She'd confer with Ella later and see if their flight was any rougher than the first one. If her suspicions were correct, she might see about training separately to spare anyone who would have to ride with her in the future.

Once again, she was excused while her cohort bent over trashcans. At least she restrained herself from hugging Dr. MacClellan when she exited. She headed for the dining hall, and then spent the rest of the afternoon in the pool. About four o'clock, she decided to visit Gabe before dinner, to see how he was holding up.

"Anyone alive in here?" she said as she poked her head through the door.

"Ha ha," he said. "Yeah, they haven't killed me yet."

There was marked improvement in his color, and he actually smiled back at her.

"So what's the status, cuz?" Candace asked.

He lifted his t-shirt, flashing his bare torso. "Ribs are all healed. The leg is still a work in progress."

She climbed onto the cot with him and snagged some of

the popcorn from the side table. "Good. They couldn't do anything about your face, though?"

"You steal my popcorn and then insult me?" he said, feigning shock even as he shifted to let her in beside him. "That's harsh."

She snuggled into his side and looked at the TV. "What's on today? Anything good?"

Gabe snorted. "Nada. Nothing good comes on until after dinner. You smell like chlorine. Did you even bother showering before you decided to get all cozy with me?"

"Nah, I know it's your favorite perfume so I figured it'd be a treat." She shoved a handful of popcorn into her mouth before snatching the remote.

"Seriously?"

"C'mon," she said. "It's been months since I've vegged out. Let me flip channels for a bit."

"Anyone ever tell you that you might be a little overbearing?"

"Only you." She grinned. "Oh! Crappy monster movie! It'll be awful. We have to watch it."

Gabe groaned. "I think my condition just took a turn for the worse."

"Eh, you'll live," she said, settling onto his shoulder.

They zoned out to the tune of a genetically modified zoo gone awry. It was blissfully horrid. Before long, they were both laughing loudly at the ridiculous dialogue and overacting, to say nothing of the half-assed special effects. A corpsman was kind enough to bring her dinner in with Gabe's and she enjoyed her food maybe more than any meal since she first arrived at the compound.

She sighed wistfully. "You know, I think I'm going to

miss this when they finally kick you out of the clinic. Try not to heal too fast, okay?"

Gabe picked at his pot roast. "I'll see what I can do."

His tone was strange, and she chewed thoughtfully, wondering if there was something new bothering him. She swallowed. "Wanna talk about it?"

"Hmm?" He glanced up at her, then back to his food. "Nah, not really."

Candace set her fork down and stared at him. "Well, that answer there reeks of bullshit."

He sighed, resigned. "Do you think... never mind."

"Not gonna happen. Do I think what?" With a reaction like that, no way was she going to let him slide. If talking to her the other night helped him improve so drastically compared to how he was before her visit, she was prepared to pry every last dark secret from his head if it meant him getting better.

"Do you think you'll ever... you know, find someone else?"

The bottom dropped out of her stomach and she closed her eyes. She wasn't prepared for that one.

It wasn't something she wanted to think about. That wound was still bleeding. But Gabe needed something, and she was the only one that could give it to him.

Hope.

"I..." she started, then faltered. Gabe searched her face, and she strengthened her resolve. "I don't know yet. I think it's too soon for me to explore that idea much. I guess I'd like to think so, but it'll be a while."

He didn't respond, returning to absently stabbing the pot roast.

She pushed the table off to the side and took his fork,

crawling back into his arms again. She laid there for a good long time, letting him adjust to her closeness before she broached the next question.

"Who was he?"

She would swear his heart stopped beating.

"What?" he said, barely audible.

"The person you lost, who was he?"

"How…" Gabe didn't move. "How could you…? How long have you…?"

She giggled a little. "I've known you since we were in diapers, Gabe. Nothing about you shocks me. I figured you'd tell me eventually, but I thought I may as well drop the act at this point."

He didn't say a word.

Candace propped herself up and looked at him. "You know I don't care, right? You are who you are."

"Does anyone else… you know, back home. Do they know?" His face was all scrunched up, knotted in anxiety.

"I'm pretty sure your parents know, and I think my mom suspects, but I haven't really discussed it with them or anything. Hey." She set a hand on his cheek, forcing him to meet her gaze. "You didn't answer my question. You know I don't care, right?"

His eyes were watery, as though he might start crying. Candace decided to spare him, instead settling back into place.

Gabe wrapped his arms around her and hugged her tightly. "I love you, Candy Cane," he whispered as she felt the first tears drop into her hair.

Maybe he'd tell her about the guy, maybe he wouldn't. It seemed like enough to know she relieved at least that much of his burden. "I love you, too."

CHAPTER 6

F R O M   H E R position on the rock, Candace drummed her
fingers. They'd been at it for weeks — her, Hector, and
Andrew — and they still wouldn't agree to spar with her.
They'd laugh it off, say she was out of their league, but their
eyes told a different story.

They were afraid of her.

The guys took her advice and listened when she spoke.
That part was easy. They'd made more than enough progress
to face off with her and hold their own, but they still brushed
away her suggestions whenever she brought up the idea of
one or both of them squaring off with her. Every day it got
harder and harder to tolerate being sidelined. She needed to
test herself. How in control was she?

Candace turned her focus back to their fight. She saw
the impending result before they did. Andrew launched a

boulder at Hector, aiming for his chest. She cringed. With a single strike, Hector broke it apart and sent it shooting back at him. Andrew wasn't fast enough to defend against it.

To spare him injury, she sent up a deflective spray, knocking the broken rock to one side where it lodged itself in the dirt.

"Game, set, match," she said, standing. "Well done, Hector. Andrew, what the hell? That was a dumb move. You know better."

He stretched then rubbed his eyes. "I know, I know. I'm beat, though. I got greedy and thought he was worn down enough I might have a shot. Poor decision on my part. Thanks for the assist, Candy. Those rocks would've had me in the clinic for days."

The sun retreated under the horizon. "Well," she said, standing and zipping up her coat against the early December breeze. "It's about that time anyway. We're losing light and I nearly broke my ankle last time we stayed out here after dark. Let's call it a night."

She didn't bother bringing up her sparring with them again. There wasn't any point.

Her foul mood followed her all the way back to the compound, but it was alleviated a little when she saw Gabe in the dining hall. He was grinning at his teammates at their usual table, a pair of crutches leaning up against the end.

"So they finally let you out of your cage, huh?" she said as she sat down next to him. "You couldn't at least hold out until I finished watching that miniseries? So inconsiderate of you."

Gabe chuckled. "They got tired of listening to me whine and kicked me out. Sorry, Candy Cane. You'll have to find another invalid to leech off of."

Amir caught her eye and smiled, giving her the barest hint of a nod. She looked away, pretending not to notice the silent approval.

"So where were you all afternoon?" Gabe said shoveling food in his mouth. "I went looking for you earlier."

The dark cloud returned. "Mentoring."

"Oh yeah?" Allen said. "That pair, or…"

She glowered at him, not about to talk about the disaster that was the Jackson situation. "Yes, that pair." She ignored Amir's raised eyebrows.

"You're mentoring already? Jesus, Candy. Ease up on the overachiever thing, would you?" Gabe nudged her.

"It wasn't really my choice." She gave him a bland look. "It was strongly suggested I do so."

He snorted. "Ah, voluntold, huh? Fun times."

"Not really."

"You having problems, sugar?" True asked. "Andrew and Hector's latest Showcase demonstrations showed a lot of improvement. I figured it was going well."

Candace sighed and chewed while she considered what to say. "It's not going badly, I guess, it's just… well, they insist on only sparring with each other. Any time I bring up going against me, they find every excuse to avoid it." She skewered a piece of chicken on her fork and frowned at it. "I'm pretty sure I understand why, but it's still annoying. It'd be nice to have something other than lane markers and life preservers for target practice."

"No luck with the other one?" Amir said, his gaze piercing.

And then there was that. Candace hadn't been able to bring herself to go after Jackson in the entire week since their last match. Memories of their almost-kiss haunted her and kept her away.

"Not really, no."

Allen snorted. "That's bullshit. He's been staring at you relentlessly since last Wednesday, Candy Cane. What did you do?"

She sat up, alarmed. "He's been what?" Was he still doing that seven days later? She successfully tuned him out after two.

True flicked Allen's ear. "Way to be subtle, idiot." She sighed and turned to Candace. "He's right, though. I've been meaning to ask you about it. Anything you want to share?"

"No," Candace said, taking a bite. "He's stubborn and thinks he can do everything on his own."

True grinned at her. "Sounds a little like someone else I know."

Candace grimaced. "Not funny."

"Forgive the invalid," Gabe interrupted. "But who are we talking about here?"

"Jackson," Amir, True, and Allen chirped in unison.

He slowly turned his head. "Oh really," Gabe drawled. "You neglected to mention that little detail, cuz."

Candace took a few deep breaths and relaxed her white knuckle grip on her fork. "There's nothing to tell. He's as big an ass as he ever was. Can we please drop it?"

Allen snickered. "Okay, Candy Cane. You can play it cool for now, but you can't hold out forever. Those hormones'll get ya. You know you'll cave."

You know you'll cave.

Something inside her snapped. She had to get out of there. She rose from the table and walked away, dumping most of her food as she left the dining hall. All but running, she hurried down the corridors, desperate to get to her room before the tears took over. Why would they think it was anywhere in the realm of okay to joke with her about something like that?

Not when Adrian was still so close.

Not when she still saw him in her nightmares every night.

No. Definitely not okay.

She closed her door and leaned against it, sliding to the floor. Her shoulders shook with silent sobs as she hugged her knees. Why did it have to hurt so much? If that part of her heart would just curl up and die everything would be so much simpler. Instead, it festered inside her, hiding away until a single word, or a smell, or a room, or a fucking tree would show up and trigger the pain all over again.

"God damn it!" she yelled as she pounded her fists into the floor. She was trying so hard to get past it, to get some semblance of a life back, only to fall on her face at the slightest trace of him. It wasn't fair. It never let up.

Pushing to her feet, she decided she couldn't stay there, either.

Swimsuit and towel in hand, she headed for the pool.

IT TOOK her thirty minutes of swimming laps, but her head finally started to cool. Candace leaned back and floated in the center of the pool, eyes closed, focused on the sound of her own breathing. She let her connection fill her, easing the tension out of her muscles. It was a brief moment of peace.

Her eyes popped open when she felt the temperature rise.

Son. Of. A. Bitch. What was he doing there?

Righting herself, she found him immediately. Jackson stood, arms crossed and scowling, staring at her.

"What do you want, Sunshine?"

"A rematch."

Was he nuts? He wanted to challenge her? There? In the pool?

"I'm busy," she said, turning and swimming to the end furthest from him.

"You're about to not be."

She turned, ready to ask him what could possibly make her abandon her evening swim, when the temperature changed again.

But it wasn't by a degree or two.

The boiling began at the center, slowly spreading outward, steam billowing up to the ceiling. Too hot, she launched herself out of the water, barely avoiding the dangerous heat.

"What the hell are you doing?" she yelled at him.

"Leveling the playing field," he called back. She couldn't see him through the fog.

Fuck it. She was already irritable, and he had to take away her one refuge from her shitty day?

Gathering up what little water was left in the pool, Candace sent it all streaming towards his last position, and then some. He gave himself away when a shield of flames lit him up through the steam. As quickly as she dared, she

darted around the edge of the almost empty pool. Without a
ready supply of water, she was going to have to do it in close
quarters.

As the fire faded, she met him with a hard right hook.
Jackson reeled, but managed to block her next one.

"Not so tough without a source to pull from, are you,
Sugar Plum?" He leaned into her, smirking.

She glared at him. "Who said I didn't have a source?"

The condensation from the walls and ceiling rained
down on him from all sides, pricking him like needles, a few
drawing blood before he flamed out. They hissed and fizzled
as they struck his armor. New tactic. She changed course,
collecting it on the ceiling, and drew it into puddles along the
wall. The fire went out and she sent one sphere after another
sailing at his head, his torso, finally taking him out at the
knees. He didn't stay down long.

Controlled bursts of fire shot at her, never touching
anything they weren't meant to. Admittedly, he had quite a
bit of restraint when he wanted to.

And that's when she realized her next move.

She giggled as she ducked another fireball. "I had no
idea our little tussle the other day rattled you so much,
Sunshine. You shouldn't bottle up your feelings that way."
Another sphere smacked him in the shoulder. Bingo. Bring
on the distractions. His temper was his weakness.

"Should the Queen of Letting Everyone Know How She
Feels really be handing out advice?" Fireball. It went wild
and she doused it, sending a second and third sphere his way.

"Maybe if you listened to it you wouldn't suck at this so
much," she said, laughing again. Sphere. Sphere.

There was so much steam in the room she could barely

breathe, let alone see him when he wasn't shooting at her.

Which would be why she didn't expect his hands closing over her upper arms.

"I wasn't the one flat on my back last week, Sugar Plum." His lips brushed against her ear as he whispered.

At the contact, her eyes fluttered and she sucked in a gasp. With nothing but a damp swimsuit covering her, she felt every inch of his body pressing into her.

Good. God. His chest was rock solid, warmer than a down comforter in the dead of winter.

"Let me go, Jackson," she said, her voice threatening to betray her.

"Why should I? Didn't you tell me I liked the helpless type? You're not so bad when you're helpless."

Her anger bubbled up, raw and jagged. She swallowed and pinched her eyes closed, searching, reaching, calling. "You picked the wrong day to piss me off."

"I'm not afraid of you."

She let out one last breath and opened her eyes. "Maybe you should be."

His chuckles were cut off by the screeching of pipes. It rattled the walls and shook the floor. Confused, Jackson dropped his hold on her and she stepped away, turning to face him.

"And here's your reason."

The wall burst open, and a torrent of water slammed into him. The force of the spray shattered a window and he washed out into the night, steam rushing into the cool night air behind him.

Candace was absolutely positive she would be in serious trouble later. For the moment, however, she didn't give a shit. He didn't have permission to touch her like that, to make her feel that way. Only one person was allowed to do that.

And he was dead.

She stepped over busted concrete, rebar, and pipes. The women's locker room door banged closed behind her as she left.

STEPPING OUT of the shower, the pounding on the door startled her. Candace swallowed past the knot in her throat. She'd been expecting it since last night. Throwing her robe around her, she rushed out of the bathroom to answer the summons.

The soldier in the hallway did not look happy.

"Someone would like to speak with you, Miss Bristol," he said. "Please dress and come with me."

Crap. They were going to skewer her for that business at the pool with Jackson. She nodded silently and closed the door, changing as quickly as she could and throwing her wet hair into a bun. The soldier escorted her down the hall and through the compound, taking her to an office past the clinic.

Jackson was already seated inside, across the desk from Dr. Poznanski. Another man in an Army uniform stood at the back, arms crossed and looking generally unpleasant. His name tag brought her to a dead stop.

General Michael Jacobs: military overseer for the entire ANGEL Project.

The wrinkles of his dark skin were chiseled into his face,

deepened by his displeasure with the current situation, likely. How many of his gray hairs was she responsible for?

She didn't give Jackson so much as a passing glance or glower as she sat in the chair beside him, not even checking him over for signs of injury.

"I assume you know why you're here?" Dr. Poznanski asked.

She nodded, trying to remain calm.

General Jacobs straightened and stepped forward to lean on the desk. "The two of you decimated the pool last night, to say nothing about the damage to the grounds with the flooding. Half of the compound was without water until midnight thanks to your little spat. Do you have any idea —"

Dr. Poznanski lifted a hand, cutting off his tirade. "I think they get the gist, General. Care to comment on the incident, Miss Bristol? Mr. Lawrence claims he was the one to instigate the fight, is this correct?"

Her jaw sagged a little in surprise. Jackson threw himself under the bus on that one? Well, it was the truth, but she didn't think he'd confess to it. "I was swimming when he walked in. I wasn't expecting him."

"And he attacked you?"

"He provoked the fight, but my temper got the better of me." Candace glared at him out of the corner of her eye. "It won't happen again."

Was it her imagination, or was Dr. Poznanski trying not to laugh? "You'll forgive me if I don't fully believe that. The two of you have a history of escalating confrontations."

She winced, unable to argue. Every time she was in close proximity with Jackson, things always got out of hand.

General Jacobs did not look amused. "Having second

thoughts about your recommendation? We expected more from you based on your assurance you were willing to work with him."

The blood drained away from her face. They had to bring that up? With Jackson sitting right there? Jesus. He was going to be completely pissed off. She closed her eyes and gritted her teeth. "No second thoughts, sir. No."

"Then I believe I have a solution to our problem," Dr. Poznanski said. "In light of this event, a little extra training might do both of you some good. You two will now have regularly scheduled sparring sessions in a room we'll designate for you, one set up to tolerate the extremes of your abilities. You'll face off two times a week beginning on Monday."

God damn it. She couldn't even cope with once a week at that point.

He wasn't finished. "In the interim, you're both assigned to cleanup duty. You'll begin with the landscaping you damaged, and, once the pool repairs are complete, there will be repainting and refinishing to do as well. Since you seem to need more practice working together, I think it will be a good exercise in team building."

Curiously, Jackson didn't so much as whisper a protest.

"Twice a week?" she said. "Are you sure that's—"

"Enough?" Dr. Poznanski cut her off with a smile. "You're right. Let's make it three. Monday, Wednesday, and Friday."

She snapped her mouth closed. Anything else she said might make things worse.

"That will be all," he said. "Mr. Lawrence knows where the groundskeeping equipment is stored. Get started right after breakfast. You're dismissed."

Jackson rose and headed for the door. She wondered if there was anything she could do to get out of it, but with a warning look from General Jacobs, she scrambled out into the hall.

She didn't speak to Jackson as they headed away from the office. At some point, he fell into step beside her. Why couldn't he leave her alone? Hadn't he done enough damage for one twenty-four hour period?

"What recommendation?" he asked as they passed the clinic.

Stupid General Jacobs. Why did he say anything about that?

"You shouldn't ask questions you don't want the answers to."

"If I ask, I want to know."

She sighed. He wasn't going to drop it. "When Dr. Curtis went over my final test results, she asked me if I thought you were suited to being an ANGEL, to working with a team."

Jackson stopped walking. She didn't.

"You said yes?"

"They let you in, didn't they?" Candace said. *Just keep going. Don't turn around.* She chanted it over and over in her head.

She got all the way to the dining hall before he blocked her path, his hand pushing the door closed.

"Why?"

Deep breaths. She met his gaze, unflinching under the heated scrutiny.

"Because I believe in second chances, Jackson. Everyone deserves an opportunity to be better. Even you."

He didn't move. Was he trying to make her regret speaking for him?

"Get out of the way. I want to eat breakfast. We have a lot of work ahead of us."

Jackson dropped his arm, and Candace wrenched open the door, not waiting for him to follow.

Everyone stared at her as she took a small table in the back corner. Screw them. If they wanted to know something, let them ask. She didn't have time for gossip, or the patience to deal with it that morning.

"You know," Gabe said as he eased into the seat across from her, leaning his crutches against the wall. "Next time you get an appetite for destruction, there's a few rooms I wouldn't mind you getting rid of for me."

She continued eating. "So not in the mood, Gabe."

"I can see that," he said. "Can I ask what happened, at least? I mean, I get why you left us last night. I'm sorry about that. It was over the line. None of us realized how far until it was too late, though." He paused. "Wait, that wasn't why you —"

"No," she said. "Although it probably set the tone for the rest of the night. I went for a swim. Jackson showed up."

When she didn't offer anything else, he reached across and tilted her chin up. "And?"

Her shoulders sagged and she grimaced. "He wanted a rematch and wouldn't take no for an answer."

"A rematch?" Gabe asked. "But the hand-to-hand combat was months ago."

"He was referring to last week," she muttered. "I took Amir's advice and started a fight with him. He lost."

That was actually debatable, but she wasn't about to go

there.

Gabe chuckled. "So you did do something. I knew you were lying. Why didn't you just say that in the first place?"

"Because I was trying to forget about it," she said softly, then sighed. "I don't want to talk about it. It's bad enough I have to clean up the mess I made last night, now I have to spar with him three times a week on orders. I may actually kill him, Gabe. I don't know if I have the patience for that much of his bullshit."

When she looked up, he was trying not to smile, but doing a really poor job of it. "Candy?"

She narrowed her eyes. "What?"

"I don't think you're worried about killing him, so much as kissing him."

Her mouth dropped open. "I am not!"

He shook his head, with a sad smile. "You haven't been able to shake that guy since day one, Candy Cane. I know how much you cared about…" He stopped shy of saying his name. "Honestly, seeing now how Jackson's been fixated on you from the moment I sat down here, I don't believe for one second there isn't more going on with you two than pure animosity. Sometimes the line between hate and love is so blurry you can't tell which is which."

He was wrong.

He *had* to be wrong.

She wouldn't let him be right. Not again. Not that time.

He chuckled. "You never could resist a challenge. It doesn't get much more challenging than Action Jackson, so I probably shouldn't be surprised."

Candace closed her eyes and focused on breathing. "Please stop."

"Candy—"

"Please," she repeated. "I can't, Gabe. The thought of it… I can't. So, please, for me. Leave it alone, okay?"

His hand closed over hers. "Candy?"

Slowly, she lifted her eyes to his.

"One more thing and I'll drop it."

She didn't stop him.

"If you do, it's all right. It's not a betrayal, so don't think that. It's important that you keep moving forward. He would want that for you."

Clamping down on the tears, she looked away. "He would want to be alive."

A long sigh eased from his lungs. "Okay, I promised to let it be and I will." He squeezed her hand and picked up his crutches. "Come find me later, Candy Cane. My breakfast is waiting over yonder."

She nodded and tried to smile as he hobbled away from the table. But then, as she watched Gabe go, she finally caught him.

Jackson barely blinked, apparently not at all bothered she had him dead to rights. She held his gaze for a moment, making sure her expression left no question she was irritated. He looked more curious than anything. Did she confuse him? Good. Let him keep guessing. Maybe while his brain was occupied he'd keep his mouth shut and she wouldn't have to talk to him all day.

She turned back to her breakfast.

Yeah, right. Like anything that day would be that easy.

CHAPTER 7

WHAT A MESS.

Debris from the pool wall, including pipes and concrete, littered the ground, shards of glass twinkling in the morning sunlight. At least someone was nice enough to put a giant dumpster nearby for them.

Candace hopscotched through the minefield of trash to start from the area closest to the receptacle. She bent and picked up a broken cinder block, tossing it in to land with a loud, hollow thunk. One down, a bazillion to go.

Ten minutes into cleanup duty, Jackson finally showed, his arms laden with a dozen water bottles. As she continued picking up trash, he took his time, setting each bottle in a neat row beside the dumpster. He took one look around, turned, and left.

She stared after him, gaping. Where the hell was he going?

When he rounded the corner, disappearing from view, she was so angry she couldn't form words. With no better plan, she continued cleaning. She imagined each chunk of concrete she threw landing on his head.

Another fifteen minutes passed, and she cleared a good ten-foot square of all the detritus she could find. A trashcan landed beside her as she leaned down to pick up a metal shard. As she straightened up, Jackson met her blank stare with an agitated one of his own. He handed her a pair of thick work gloves.

"Get everything but the glass," he said. "We'll burn out the grass later so we don't miss any of it. There's strips of new sod and some seed we can use to fix it after."

She stared at him, waiting for the insult or sarcastic comment she was sure was coming. He was being far too helpful and straightforward. What was he setting her up for?

He bent and picked up a chunk of concrete, launching it into the dumpster. "I worked the grounds until they approved me for training," he said.

"What?" she asked. Was he actually making conversation?

He gave her a derisive look. "Did you think I sat around all day or something? I worked. Same as everyone else here."

Honestly, she hadn't given it any thought, but it made sense. Adrian had been a librarian, after all. That was a job. It never occurred to her that Jackson did anything but make a nuisance of himself.

"I see," she said, resuming cleanup.

The silence stretched out for a minute or two before he spoke again. "What about you?"

Candace tossed a broken pipe. "What about me what?"

"Did you have a job back home, or did you sit around

living off your parents' good graces until your ship came in?"

And there was the sarcasm. It was only a matter of time.

"I worked. My mom insisted. So did I."

"Where?"

God. Couldn't he shut up for once and let her get through her punishment in peace and quiet?

"At a gas station. Nothing special."

More silence.

"So, was it just you and your mom then?"

She set her hands on her hips. "What, now you give a shit about me? Why are you so damn curious all of a sudden?"

Jackson hefted a full block and heaved it over the side of the dumpster. "I'm not allowed to make conversation?"

"It's a little out of character for you."

He stopped and looked at her. "And what do you know about my character? Or anything else about me, for that matter."

She balked. Damn. He kind of had her there. "You never seemed very inclined to engage in conversation before." She flashed him a sardonic smile. "You weren't interested, remember?"

Fumbling, he missed the junk he reached for. "Yeah, well, fine."

As he passed her going back to the dumpster, she barely heard him mumble something about second chances.

Damn it. He *was* actually trying. Either that, or it was his most elaborate setup yet. Maybe he was mining her for information he could use against her in the future, looking for a weakness.

Candace took a deep breath and let it go, collecting an armload of trash. "Yes," she said as she trashed them. "Just me and my mom. My dad left about ten years ago. You?"

He paused again, shaking his head. "No."

"No? No what?"

"No parents."

Ouch. Yeah, he probably didn't want to talk about that, and she decided not to ask.

It effectively shut down the conversation.

They worked up to lunch, and she made sure to take numerous water breaks to avoid having to refill the tank in front of him. Seeing her like that would definitely be too much temptation for him, and she'd be dealing with a whole new level of teasing. Or worse. She didn't want to think about the alternative.

When they decided to break at noon, Jackson bent to pick up a water bottle and stopped. He cocked his head at her. "Jesus, Sugar Plum, how much water do you need in a day? There's only one unopened one left."

It was the first time all day he called her that. The nickname settled over her like a comfortable blanket.

"That's about half of what I drink before dinner, Sunshine." She knocked back the last of her own bottle. "At least I saved you one."

She left him with a smirk and walked away, starving and ready for lunch.

BY THE end of the day, they successfully cleaned up most of the trash and torched the grass. The next day they removed all the glass and covered up the burned area with new sod after Candace soaked the ground. She spoke with Dina about fixing the damage on three of the trees, but when the time came, Candace noticed something very odd about one of them.

It was faded, but it was definitely there.

There was a handprint burned into the bark of one of the trees.

How weird. She placed her hand on the mark, comparing it for size.

"What's that about?" Dina asked, looking over her shoulder.

Candace shook her head. "I dunno. I don't think it's from a few nights ago, though."

Dina stepped in closer and squinted at it. "Yeah, you're right. This is months old. Bizarre." She straightened and stretched. "I'm going to run back to the shed and get a new seedling to replace that bush there. I'll be right back."

"Yeah, sure," Candace murmured, continuing to study the mark.

"Where's she running off to?" Jackson asked as he strolled up, handing her a bottle of water.

As she reached for it, she stopped. It couldn't be.

She grabbed his wrist with one hand, taking the bottle with the other, and pulled his palm against the tree.

A perfect fit.

Jackson jerked away. "What the hell are you doing?"

The pieces started to click into place. She didn't answer him, instead propping herself up against the tree and looking into the pool area. The window was back in place, and the far wall was nearly patched up. If she stood just so...

Oh hell no.

She whirled on him. "You were watching me?"

Jackson retreated a step, his body already slipping into a defensive posture. "I have no idea —"

"The fuck you don't, Sunshine," she said. "That day you pulled me out of the pool. I felt the water getting hotter. I didn't know what was causing it and was trying to figure it out. And suddenly there you were, saving my life? That's incredibly convenient. But this?" She set her hand against the burn. "That's evidence, Jackson. And all signs point to creepy."

He bristled and stepped forward. "Creepy? I was out here reading. You think pretty highly of yourself, don't you?"

"So you're saying you weren't watching me?" She crossed her arms and stared him down. "You're saying that you just happened to be standing in a place where I wouldn't see you, getting all hot and bothered over a book? Do you think I'm stupid?"

She blinked and he was in front of her. How the hell did he move so fast?

Jackson set his hand in the print and leaned in closer. "You're not stupid, Candace, but, let's be honest. Would it really bother you so much to know I was looking?"

Her heart raced as she spat out a lie. "Would it bother me to know some arrogant ass was using me for his own private entertainment? You're goddamn right it does."

With his arm propped against the tree, above her left shoulder, and his body blocking the largest escape route, she slid right, trying to get away.

His hand slid over her hip, pushing her back into place. "Nice try, Sugar Plum, but I'm calling your bluff. You're lying. I think you like that idea a hell of a lot more than you're willing to admit."

"Don't, Jackson." The alarms in her brain clanged loudly. It was going to end badly if he tried to get any closer. Her resolve was crumbling, but she refused to give in.

He chuckled and leaned in, whispering in her ear. "All you have to do is say the word, Candace."

When his lips brushed her ear, she shivered, closing her eyes. "Last warning," she said, barely able to speak.

"I'm not afraid of you." His words danced across the exposed skin of her neck, so warm it gave her goosebumps.

And then the panic hit, rising up through her like a tidal wave.

A quick knee to the groin was all it took. Jackson dropped like a limp rag.

She jumped away as he fell, her breathing almost as ragged as his.

"What are you two doing?" Dina asked as she came around the corner and took in the scene.

Candace smoothed her ruffled feathers and glared at Jackson. "Teambuilding."

"Huh?"

She shrugged it off and pointed to the plant in Dina's hands. "Is that all you need?"

Dina nodded, still staring at the prone, cursing Jackson.

"Great," Candace said, smiling. "Let's get that planted and we'll be all done here."

At some point, Jackson wandered off, probably to find an ice pack, and she finished up with Dina, watching on as she sped up the seedling's growth until it matched the undamaged shrubbery. Candace surveyed their work. "This looks pretty good now," she said. "Thanks, Dina. I appreciate the assist."

"No problem." Dina smiled and brushed off her hands.

"I prefer this over offensive training any day. If you ever want to do more remodeling out here, I'm happy to help."

Candace laughed. "Oh, I'm in no rush to repeat this, but thanks for the offer."

"Hey, Candy?"

"Hmm?"

"Are you and Jackson…" Dina hesitated, thinking, then decided against saying whatever it was.

"Are we what?" Her shoulders tensed. There was nothing between her and Jackson. Nothing.

Dina shook her head and sighed. "Never mind."

Candace relaxed, glad to drop the subject. "Uh, okay."

"C'mon." She jerked her head back toward the nearest door. "Let's get cleaned up before dinner."

CANDACE CAME prepared the next morning. It was painting day. The walls were back up and the pool was ready to be finished off. She rounded up coveralls and everything. A new sense of determination filled her after the test of her willpower the day before; she would not be cornered like that again.

She might not be able to say no next time.

But when she pushed through the locker room door, she screeched to a halt.

It was all done. Painting, cleanup, even the grouting on the damaged tiles on the floor was finished.

A piece of paper was taped to the wall. She grabbed it, and read.

See you tomorrow, Sugar Plum.

What?

Jackson did all of it by himself? Overnight? She stared at the wall, the floor, not believing her eyes. Maybe it was his way of apologizing, or maybe he'd done it to make her feel bad for crippling him yesterday.

Candace had no idea how to take it.

As there was nothing left for her to do, she headed back to her room to change. It left her with the problem of having no plans for the rest of the day. Maybe she could round up Hector and Andrew for a practice session, but she disregarded the idea as soon as it came to her. It would only irritate her. Wandering over to her bookshelf, she perused the titles of the few favorites she brought with her from home. She got to the end of the row and choked.

The Morania Chronicles: Book 4, Warrior's Curse.

They hadn't finished book three. There was one chapter still to go.

But she couldn't do it. Those books belonged to him, and he was gone. She might be able to read them someday, but not yet. Not any time soon.

Candace needed something new to read. Once the idea of getting lost in a story occurred to her, it was the only thing she wanted to do. And that meant the library: the place she avoided for weeks, unable to face the ghosts she was sure to find there.

It was either endure them for a short time, or hear his voice in her head, unavoidable and ever-present, as she read the *Morania Chronicles*.

The closer she got to the library, the slower she walked. By the time she got there, her heart pounded and her breath came in heavy gasps. She stood there, staring at the door, unable to touch it.

It opened and Deborah appeared. Smiling warmly, she extended a hand. "The first steps are always the most difficult," she said. "Need some help?"

As their fingers touched, the tension eased out of her. She nodded. "Thank you."

Her smile widened as she pulled her inside. "I'm glad you came to visit today. You're doing so much better. I've missed talking with you."

Deborah didn't let go of her hand, and Candace didn't complain. She was so relaxed she thought she might melt into a puddle on the floor. Somehow her legs kept moving, though, following along through the rows of books until they reached an aisle near the back.

"I have a book for you," Deborah said, reaching up to the shelf second from the top.

It looked vaguely familiar, but Candace couldn't place it. Her brain was fuzzy, like the time she had her wisdom teeth removed and they put her on codeine for the pain.

Deborah giggled. "Sorry. I'll ease up some. I figured this would be hard for you, so I'm blocking you a little. I hope you don't mind."

Candace shook her head as some of the fog dissipated. "No, I don't mind, I guess. I'm sorry, you're doing what?"

"Well, really I'm boosting the endorphin production in your brain. It's a form of therapy I've used in the past when helping others with post-traumatic stress." She stopped. "Oh goodness. I should have asked you first. I'm so sorry."

Candace chuckled. "This is one thing you will never have to apologize to me for," she said. "Thank you. I didn't know how I was going to get through this."

She pulled her closer and leaned in to whisper. "Can I tell you a secret then?"

"Sure." Candace said.

"He never told anyone, but there was a reason he read these books," she whispered.

Candace frowned at the paperback in her hand. She knew why she recognized it. It was the one she caught Adrian with when she snuck up on him before their treatments started. "It wasn't just a guilty pleasure?"

Deborah shook her head, her black hair waving softly. "For him, they were educational. I only figured it out because…" She stopped, hesitating. "Because we…"

Candace looked up, suddenly understanding the pause. "Because you were together for a while, right?"

She blushed and nodded. "He told you?"

"Accidentally, yes. He thought I'd be upset if I knew."

Her face pinched together. "Were you?"

"I was more upset he didn't tell, me, but no, I wasn't upset about the history itself." Candace considered her expression. "Can I ask you about it? He never really said much. If it's too personal, you can ignore me, but, I was wondering, why did you break it off?"

Deborah sighed and touched the bookshelves, wistfully looking at the titles. "It was because they were going to approve him for treatments."

"Wait, what?" Candace asked. "Adrian always seemed so bitter about no one wanting him because he wasn't fully in the program. You broke up with him because he was going to be? Why?"

Deborah sighed again. "Remember how I told you ANGELs are so much louder to me than normal people?"

"Oh," Candace said, but it took her a moment to fully process it. "Oh! Oh, I get it. It would have overloaded you to be with a Super, um, like that." Wow. Awkward.

"Yeah. Like that." Her cheeks were redder than apples. "Anyway, you should read that book. I think you might get a little laugh out of it, if nothing else."

Candace nodded. "Are there any others? I'm a pretty fast reader and, well, I think for now I'd like to keep my library visits to a minimum, in case you aren't here."

Deborah smiled, understanding, and chose three more from the shelf, all in another series. "I always preferred these. Paranormal romances about angels." She giggled. "Not the superhero kind, sorry."

Candace laughed. "That's totally okay. I think I get enough of the superhero thing now to fill my quota."

Deborah walked her out of the library, not once letting go of her hand. Even with the empath's interference, though, there was a dull, melancholic ache in her chest as she passed the information desk. She couldn't imagine getting through the trip without Deborah.

"You're welcome," she said, squeezing her hand. She opened the library door and released Candace. "Let me know what you think of those, okay? No one ever wants to talk books with me these days. I'd love to compare notes with you if you're up for it."

Candace noticed a definite change in her mood without Deborah's touch. The sadness was returning, but slowly. "I'd like that. Sure."

"You'll come down gradually," she said. "You might have a little headache later, but it won't be too bad. An ibuprofen or two should take care of it. The clinic will give you a small bottle if you ask for it."

Candace turned to go, but added one last thing. "Thanks for everything, Deborah. Really."

"You're welcome. I'll see you later."

She tossed her a wave as she headed back to her room, curious to find out what about those books had been so educational for Adrian.

CHAPTER 8

IT WAS baffling. He never said a word the entire time. From the moment Candace walked into the specialized room, Jackson was silent and all business.

One side of the one-hundred-foot room was designated for her with two waterfalls pouring from the wall. His side held two massive stone braziers, each at least three feet in diameter and blazing. Aside from that, there was nothing visibly unusual about the room; only white, fire-retardant padding from floor to ceiling.

She took her place between the waterfalls and they began. Their shots were tentative at first, but before long they were fully engaged in battle, turning the room into a sauna faster than the ventilation could keep up with them. For the most part they were even, but inevitably Candace took a final shot that finished the fight. By the end of the first week, their sparring matches went from a thirty-minute affair to an hour and a half long. He was getting better every time.

But Jackson never spoke. Not a word.

After their second Monday session, his silence was irritating, but she thought perhaps it was for the best. Without his constant teasing and that stupid nickname to provoke her temper, it was easier to control her attacks, develop new ones, and find his weaknesses. In that, she was always successful. Jackson had a habit of hesitating every time he was going to try something new. It gave her the opening she needed to knock him down. Every time, his failure pissed him off and he'd come back swinging. The day he figured out how to stop thinking about it so much would be the day he might have a shot at beating her. Even so, the burns and tears in their black skinsuits were testament to the punishment they both endured.

Between those exercises, Candace was busy with other things. She still checked in on Hector and Andrew, but they were far enough along that there was little need for her presence anymore. She also helped Dina with a new water feature in her garden.

Mostly, though, she passed her hours either reading, or in flight training.

After her checkup that Thursday, they determined that her control over the fluids in her body stabilized her inner ear to perfection. It resulted in a weekend of grueling balance tests. At one point, they tasked her with cartwheeling down a balance beam ten times, and she even danced across the catwalk high above the Gauntlet, dodging all manner of things that they threw at her. It was ridiculous, really. If she didn't know better, she'd have thought they were trying to kill her.

Her final test came in the form of a solo flight on the shuttle. Whoever drove must have had a blast. She lost count of the number of barrel rolls, sharp turns, and dives they took. They gave up after an hour. Candace never flinched, but her neck was incredibly sore from the jarring g-forces afterwards.

When the shuttle landed, she took her time unstrapping herself, wistfully wondering when she'd next sit in one of those seats. She rolled her shoulders, trying to work out some of the pain as she disembarked from the shuttle.

"Verra impressive, Miss Bristol," Dr. MacClellan said. "I canna say there's an ANGEL here that could have lasted that long."

Dr. Poznanski nodded. "I agree. I think we can safely say you're ready for the next phase of training."

"Piloting?" she asked, hopeful.

He chuckled. "Yes, well, that too, but I was thinking in terms of normal ANGEL progression. Typically, once a trainee can handle flight, they're sent out on a series of ride-alongs with existing teams. But, if you'd rather focus on piloting—"

"No!" she interrupted, then coughed to cover her outburst. "No, the ride-alongs will be fine. When do I get to go?"

Dr. MacClellan erupted in laughter. "Get to go? Ach, you are a strange one. Most new ANGELs are terrified of their first glimpse of the field."

She blushed. "Well, it's what I signed up for, so I'd think anyone would be itching to get started after all this."

"We'll send you out with the Orion Team first," Dr.

Poznanski said. "Their enemy difficulty level is typically not as high as what teams like Pavo and Corvus face. I'll let them know to expect you the next time they're called. Make sure you're listening for the summons."

Candace kept her face absolutely calm, intent on suppressing the scream of triumph that was fighting to get out. "I will, Dr. Poznanski. Thank you for giving me the opportunity."

"You're quite welcome, Miss Bristol. Enjoy the rest of your evening."

That was Sunday.

By Tuesday, she was twitchy, jumping every time there was a loud noise, expecting to hear the PA blare to life at any moment, calling out for the Orion Team. But, no. Pavo was called twice, Corvus once, and even Lacerta had an incident on Monday.

She sat with Gabe, Ella, and Tobias at dinner on Tuesday, picking at her food and not saying much.

"The Orion Team has worked hard to eliminate most of the dirty genetic evolution labs in the Northwest. Not being called is a good thing, Candy Cane." Gabe said. "Incidents are bad. We want *less* of them."

"I know, I know," she said, sighing. "But I know it's coming and I want to get it over with. I hate waiting."

"Our area's gotten pretty quiet the last year. It could be another week or more before we get called," Tobias said.

Candace grumbled to herself.

"You're crazy, Candy." Ella pointed her fork. "I won't be doing ride-alongs for a while, but I'm scared stiff of it."

Tobias snaked an arm around her and gave her a squeeze, kissing the top of her head. "It's not that bad, sweetie. Besides, your ability isn't team-applicable. You're a case-by-case send-in. At most, they'll send you on one or two missions and then mostly use you for recon after that."

"So I'll be working alone. That's reassuring." She rolled her eyes.

He chuckled and squeezed her again.

That old hurt flared up, but Candace tried not to show it. Ella seemed so happy, and she wasn't about to ruin that for her.

The alarms blared to life. "ANGEL Team Orion, assemble for duty! Shuttle departure in T-minus five minutes!"

Candace jumped to her feet, unable to contain herself. She was so excited, she nearly forgot her tray and had to run back for it. She sprinted for the female changing room outside the hangar and had her clothes off and unblemished skinsuit on in record time.

Kina Cross was already waiting in the launch bay, along with Trevor Ching. Tobias wasn't far behind and he laughed a little when he saw Candace ready to go ahead of him. The last member of their party, Gilbert Rodriguez, strode out of the male changing room and ushered them into the shuttle.

"Okay folks," he said as they strapped in. "We've got a mystery tonight. Tobias, we'll need to send you ahead to scout it out."

"Where are we headed, Gil?" Kina said as the shuttle hummed to life.

"The Moda Center in Portland," he said, grimacing. "And it's a bad one."

"Y O U   S T A Y at the back, rookie," Gilbert said as he hit the button to open the bay doors. "I don't care how awesome you are. Until you know how we work, you shut up and stay out of sight. Got it?"

Candace nodded, humming with anticipation. The moment had come: her first real test. What would be waiting for them?

They heard the screams as soon as the doors opened. People were crying, terrified, scrambling to get out of the events center. Ambulances were on scene, as were firefighters and policemen. The wounded were everywhere, save for the patch of parking lot asphalt cordoned off for the ANGEL shuttle. The team hustled down the ramp, Gilbert in the lead. He stopped to confer with a man in a dark suit, and then they gathered around to get the details when he was done.

"NSA says it's a Sparkler," he said. "A big one."

"Sparkler?" Candace asked. They froze and stared at her. "What? Is that bad?"

"Candy." Trevor said, his voice vibrating her body down to her boots. "You may want to stay behind for this one."

"What? No. Why would I?"

"A Sparkler is the code word for an electrical ability," Gilbert explained.

He might as well have punched her in the stomach. The air rushed out of her lungs and she closed her eyes. She had to get past it. No matter what, it was her job, and she was going to do it.

"I'm not staying behind."

Tobias lowered his voice. "Candy —"

"I'm not," she said, cutting him off. "I'm fine. We're losing time. Let's get on with it."

Gil studied her closely for a moment, and she met his gaze with defiance.

"Fine," he said. "Okay, we're going around through the loading docks. It's ground level and closer to the action. Tobias, you go ahead per usual and get a look around. We'll be right behind."

They broke and ran for the rear of the massive building, using hockey team buses as visual markers for the entrance. Once inside, Tobias ran ahead and they followed at a distance.

They waited in a corridor outside the lower level doors. A cool breeze came from the arena interior, and with it, the scent of burning things; plastic, fabric... flesh. Good God. What a horrible smell. The scene inside would undoubtedly be worse. Her stomach knotted, the stench coupling with her tension, causing a surge of bile to rise in her throat.

Tobias returned. "He's on the ice. Multiple fatalities. Looks like most of the players and some of the audience too." He shuddered. "Bad doesn't begin to cover it."

Gilbert thought for a minute. "What's the status on the ice?"

"Still frozen."

Another pause. "Kina, do you think you can shut down the refrigeration system?"

She made a face. "Can I flip a switch? Yeah, I think I can manage."

"Good. Take Tobias with you. If you can't turn it off, break it."

They ran off in search of the sub levels.

"You two are with me. Candy, we'll need you. Are you sure you're up for this?"

Not about to give in to her doubts or fears, she swallowed. "I am."

"Then let's go."

Instead of heading in low, they sprinted up the stairs to the second spectator level, taking the high ground. They crouched down, easing along the wall, into the darkened arena. The overhead lights had exploded, leaving only the emergency lighting and the bursts of crackling illumination coming from the rink to see by.

As she crawled to the railing on her belly, Candace got her first look at the enemy. Relief rushed through her as she blew out a held breath. The man looked nothing like Adrian. If he had…

She pushed the thoughts aside and concentrated. From what she could make out, the hulking figure below was all muscle and mostly naked, save for some torn up jeans. He didn't even have shoes on his feet. Blasts of lightning flew from his outstretched arms, striking the empty seats below them on the opposite side. It was enough illumination to show her some of the carnage.

Dozens of bodies littered the ice and the stands. None of them moved, some were bleeding, but mostly not. Candace gagged as she realized the source of the smells outside. That man had fried the victims alive.

Gil tapped her shoulder, motioning for her to follow him to the right. Trevor was nowhere in sight. In her preoccupation, she missed his departure. They stopped at the next break in seating, and he pushed her back into the tunnel, a finger to his lips. He moved back out and Candace lost sight of him.

The sound of metal ripping away from concrete made her cringe. A similar sound echoed from further down; Trevor, most likely. The man in the center howled with rage, and the rink lit up. Bolts of electricity shot into the stands, and seats flew down to the ice. Did they hope to hit him with projectiles, maybe injure him enough that they could get close? A sinking feeling crept over her. Why wasn't Gilbert using her ability? The guy stood on frozen water for God's sake.

Frozen water. Ice. That's why he sent the others down to shut off the refrigeration: to melt it. They were buying time.

She blocked out the sounds of battle, searching for liquid. If they were trying to minimize damage, pulling from the pipes would be a bad idea. It would effectively ruin the building. There was some liquid pooling on the surface, and she gathered it as best she could. It wasn't much.

At a lull in the action, she risked a peek outside. Gil crossed to the other side of the tunnel, avoiding as many of the sparking arcs of energy as he could while he bent and twisted metal from the ceiling and stands with nothing but his mind, shooting it off to the rink below. They were heavy pieces and moved slowly. The Sparkler either avoided them or blasted them into molten shards. A quick glance told her Trevor was having about as much luck.

Her skin tingled as one of the bolts of lightning struck not twenty feet from her. She sucked in a breath. When the smoke cleared, Gil wasn't there anymore. Searching frantically, she spotted him on the level below, his limbs and back draped over a row of seats, every angle unnatural. Another explosion jarred her out of her paralysis.

The flying chairs stopped.

Holy shit. Trevor.

Disregarding all caution, Candace sprinted out of hiding and down the walkway to where she last saw the giant. Small bursts of electricity followed her as she went, but she didn't stop until she reached the tunnel nearest Trevor's last position. She slid to the floor, the impact of the concrete barely registering as she dodged a close strike. How much water did she have to use?

She paused for a split second and weighed it.

It would have to be enough. She only had one shot.

Candace ran out into the hall and back through at the next break. Trevor was lying face down on the concrete not five feet from her. She inched towards him and checked for a pulse.

He was still alive, but barely.

The entire left side of his body was burnt, some of it still smoking. The smell made her gag, but as she stared at someone who had been so protective, so encouraging, dying in front of her, something else bubbled to the surface…

Rage.

The man on the ice howled again, electricity shooting from his fingertips up to the ceiling.

Candace called to the water, poured her anger into it, forming it into pure strength.

And then she wrapped it around his neck.

Tighter.

Tighter.

With a violent jerk of her arm, the man's spine snapped. She felt the reverberations of the bones cracking through her connection.

He crumpled to the ground, leftover bursts of light passing out of him like ripples in a pond.

And it was silent.

IT TOOK both her and Kina to carry Trevor away from the Moda Center. Tobias collected Gil on his own, not showing any emotion as he walked out of the building. Once outside, medical personnel helped load Trevor into the shuttle, strapping him to the floor instead of a seat, tubes and life support machines hooked up to him everywhere. Tobias stayed behind, telling the girls to report back and get Trevor seen to while he wrapped up with the authorities. They would send a shuttle back for him and the fallen ANGEL later.

Kina cried the entire trip home. Candace was numb. She spent the flight watching Trevor, willing him to keep breathing, continuously checking that water circulated through his body.

"You're not allowed to die on me," she whispered to him. "Don't you dare."

When they landed at the compound, it was amidst a flurry of activity. Candace waited patiently, letting everyone do their jobs and attend to the crisis. Finally, someone sent her to her room to wait for a debrief.

That was not how it was supposed to happen.

Not on a ride-along.

Gil was dead. Trevor might not make it.

She killed a man.

Candace laid down in bed with the lights on, still dressed. They would come for her eventually, so there was no point in trying to sleep. Not that she could. Not that night.

Three hours later, she was still staring at the ceiling, reliving every second of the evening. Someone finally knocked. A soldier led her out, back to Dr. Poznanski's office again.

It was the second time in as many weeks that she came face to face with General Jacobs, not something she wanted to make a habit of.

"Miss Bristol," he said, his voice tight. "Trouble seems to follow you around like a shadow."

She gritted her teeth against a harsh reply as she sat down.

Dr. Poznanski pulled out a tablet and started typing. "We've gotten the report from Mr. Sokol, but his information was secondhand, for the most part. Miss Cross was of little help, due to her emotional state. Can you walk us through the events of tonight?"

Candace took a deep breath and closed her eyes. She told them everything she saw or heard from the moment the shuttle landed in Portland, to the moment she returned to the compound. It sounded cold, robotic, as though her voice was coming from the other end of a long tunnel.

"And you say this gen-evo was stable? There was no breakdown of his tissue?" Dr. Poznanski said, rubbing a hand across his chin.

"Aside from being extremely angry, yes. He was physically stable," she replied. "How is Trevor?"

"He'll live, fortunately," General Jacobs said. "But he'll be out of commission for the foreseeable future."

She lapsed back into silence.

"You did well tonight, Miss Bristol," Dr. Poznanski said. "Be proud of what you accomplished. If this is indicative of what we should expect of you in the future, be aware that you've set the bar very high for yourself."

A bar surrounded by dead bodies, she thought with a shiver. But maybe she would be wrong about that.

She *had* to be.

The General cleared his throat. "That will be all. You're dismissed."

She rose and started for the door, but turned back to them. "Do the others know... what should I tell people about Gilbert?"

Dr. Poznanski gave her a sad smile. "Word will be passed in the morning. Please refrain from speaking about this incident until then."

She took a deep breath and nodded, then let herself out.

CHAPTER 9

CANDACE TOOK Wednesday off. Having barely slept the night before, she was in no mood to deal with anyone or anything that day. She skipped breakfast. The thought of eating turned her stomach. Water was plenty for her anyway. The books from the library kept her mind on other things.

She made one exception to the Do Not Disturb sign that she stuck on her door, and that was to let Gabe in. When she answered, he dropped his crutches and pulled her into a tight embrace.

"I'm okay, cuz," she said gently. "Here." She propped him up on the doorframe and picked up his crutches. "Come inside."

He limped over to the bed and sat, looking haggard. Red-rimmed eyes watched her as she closed the door and sat beside him.

"You're awfully calm about this," he said.

She sighed and rubbed her face. "I know. That worries me a little, if you want to know the truth. I take it they told everyone then?"

"Word spread, yeah. Gil..." his shoulders sagged. "Gil was my mentor for a while."

Candace wrapped her arms around him and hugged him. "I'm so sorry, Gabe. I didn't know."

Granted, she was pretty rocked by his death, but she didn't really know him all that well. For her cousin, losing Gil must be like if she lost True. She held him while he cried, letting him overflow with sadness in her arms. She let him go when he started to settle and his breathing eased, then fetched a cool, wet washcloth from the bathroom and let him wipe his face. She didn't say a word until he did.

"What happened?" he asked.

She bit her lip. How much was she allowed to say? "What did they tell everyone?"

"That he died fighting. He died a hero."

"He did," she said. "The guy last night... he was bad, Gabe. Really bad. He killed a lot of people before we got there. Gil had me stay down while they tried to unfreeze the ice rink, so I didn't see all that happened clearly. They were buying me time. Right after Gil fell, he got Trevor too. They said he'll survive, but..." She closed her eyes, Trevor's bubbling, blackened skin burned into her memory. "He won't be the same after what happened."

Gabe stared at the floor, wringing the washcloth absentmindedly. "What ability?"

Candace swallowed hard. "Electricity."

At that, his head shot up, and he dropped the rag. "Candy... are you... did you...?"

"I did," she said, only answering one of his questions.

He set a hand against her cheek. "Then you did what you could."

The first tears slipped past her closed eyelids. "I should have done it sooner. If I had—"

"Don't," he cut her off and pulled her to his shoulder. "Don't think about that. You saved people. Focus on that."

"It's wrong that I don't feel bad I killed someone. I didn't even think twice about it," Candace sobbed. "I'm mad at myself for following Gil's instructions and not trying to take that son of a bitch out sooner. It was easy, Gabe. It took ten seconds and I snapped his neck like it was nothing. I shouldn't be okay with that part. I should be... I should be..."

"Shh..." He smoothed her hair. "You shouldn't be. Doing what you did saved lives. I know it's not easy to deal with, but you didn't have any other choice. It was him or you and who knows how many others. So don't. Don't tell yourself you should feel guilty. You do that, and you're sunk, Candy Cane. It'll eat you up. You're too good for that. The world needs you. *I* need you. So, for me, okay?"

"Dr. Poznanski told me to be proud of what I did," she said, sniffling. "That's the stupidest thing he's ever said to me. I will never be proud of killing anyone, Gabe. Ever."

He kissed her forehead. "And that's why the world needs you, Candace. That's exactly why."

CANDACE SPENT the afternoon by the pool, reading as she waited for it to finish filling.

She was halfway through Adrian's book when she caught it.

The heroine was injured, hospitalized when the bad aliens attacked the good aliens, as she got caught in the crossfire. The hero visited her, head hung in shame that he put her in the middle of it. The woman's hands had been burned and she couldn't hold on to anything.

The hero started reading to her.

Her jaw dropped when she realized that was what Deborah referred to when she said they were "educational" for him. Adrian read romance novels to learn how to get a girl?

She was torn about the discovery. On the one hand, it was manipulative, but on the other, she really enjoyed the things he put into practice from the books. It would be incredibly silly to get upset about it.

She smiled to herself. Sneaky bugger. He was too smart for his own good. She wondered at what point he had stopped relying on fiction and been himself. How long did it take her to put him at ease? Nothing stood out as a huge change in him, but gradually she became the most important person in the world to him.

The heaviness returned to her heart. She closed the book and set it aside. She became so important that losing her drove him over the edge of murderous insanity.

The pool wasn't quite full, but it was close enough for her. Candace stripped down to her bathing suit and dove into the water. It embraced her like a long lost friend and she let go.

An hour into her swim, there was an announcement over the PA system. "All ANGELs report to Auditorium A for a situation briefing beginning in thirty minutes."

An all-hands meeting? That couldn't be good.

Candace collected her things and hurried back to her room to clean up.

The room was mostly full when she arrived. Every ANGEL on the premises, all thirty of them, down two without Gil or Trevor, occupied the seats of the small auditorium. Some were still trying to process the news of the death, and others shifted nervously in their chairs. She sat down beside Gabe. He met her questioning look with a shrug.

Dr. Poznanski stepped onto the small stage. The screen behind him faded up to the ANGEL logo as the lights in the room dimmed.

"Good afternoon, ANGELs," he said, taking his place behind the black podium. "I'd like to tell you that this gathering is for positive reasons, but, given the events of last night, I think you've probably surmised this isn't the case."

A shot of the Moda Center, mid-crisis, displayed behind him and Candace flinched.

"Last night, the Orion Team encountered a hostile gen-evo unlike any we've seen in the western United States before. They arrived on scene, discovering over twenty-five civilian casualties, with others wounded and some still in critical condition at this moment. As you know, we lost one of our own, team leader Gilbert Rodriguez, and Trevor Ching remains under watch in our medical facilities. Thanks to the other ANGELs on site, the threat was neutralized, but another problem has come to our attention as a result."

While Candace was relieved Dr. Poznanski kept her name out of it directly, she didn't like the sound of the new problem.

The picture of the events center changed to that of a boardwalk. "Over Labor Day weekend, there was an incident in Myrtle Beach involving a gen-evo who took out several piers and caused as many casualties as this one in Portland." The screen changed to a beach. "South Beach in Miami faced a similar one in October. Both this one and the South Carolina attacks were perpetrated by a set of twins, at a one-month interval. They both bore this mark."

He showed two side by side pictures of a brand in human flesh. As Candace studied them, the letters H, E, and X emerged from the tangled scars.

"As these perpetrators were siblings, we saw no cause for alarm," Dr. Poznanski paused and a third photo appeared, "until last night. The hostile gen-evo in Portland also bore this brand, but had no familial ties to the other two, nor any other discernible relationship. Given this new information, we've come to a conclusion: we have a new enemy, and they have achieved physical stability in the treatment process."

The lights came up and the screen went dark. The room was deathly silent, as though everyone held their breath.

"This enemy is unprecedented," he continued. "Not only is this HEX organization a complete unknown, but these new Evolutions are strong, lacking anything in the way of compassion. They kill without prejudice, and are drawn to crowds. We believe this is intentional, purposely done to achieve the maximum possible damage to where these hostiles are unleashed. They are also considerably more powerful than any we have faced before. The Western Teams have already lost one at the hands of this organization, with another sidelined, and there have been three losses to date in the Eastern Teams. To this end, we may have a solution."

He stopped and looked around, taking in their faces. "We've developed a new formula: GEF-42. It builds off of the existing changes brought on by your first round of treatments, boosting your abilities, recovery times, reflexes, and mental processing even further. However, the extent of the effects is relatively unknown."

He let it sink in for a moment.

"Eventually, you'll all go through this new round of treatments, but I will ask for volunteers to go first, as there is some risk involved."

No one moved. No one spoke.

He cleared his throat. "This would be the time for you to come forward."

"I'll volunteer."

Candace nearly fell out of her chair. She swiveled around to visually confirm what her ears heard.

Jackson's hand was in the air.

"While I appreciate your enthusiasm for this, Mr. Lawrence, I think it would be best if the more seasoned ANGELs took on this challenge."

His hand lowered, but his level of insistence did not. "That's strategically stupid, to be blunt. It's ridiculous to even consider removing your strongest, most trained fighters from the field for an experiment."

"He's right," Candace said, surprised at the sound of her

own voice. She looked away from Jackson to Dr. Poznanski. "I saw what the one in Portland could do. If you get more like him, or worse, you're going to need your best weapons at the ready. I'll volunteer, too."

"Candy," Gabe whispered in her ear. "What are you doing? You can't—"

"I can," she interrupted. "And I am. It makes sense. You don't take out your best warriors and send in the second string when the other team ups their game. Don't tell me I can't. I can't *not* do this. It isn't about me."

"Ah, what the hell," Hector said. "I'm in too."

Andrew popped up. "Without me? I'm not gonna let you win that way, man. Count me in, Doc."

Jamarcus threw up his hand, causing Dina to pale visibly. "I can't let the newbies have all the fun. Dina's more than capable of filling in for me if necessary. Sign me up. You need at least one veteran, here."

Candace smiled, a surge of pride welling up inside her for her fellow ANGELs. She looked back to Dr. Poznanski, waiting for his answer.

He took his time considering it, and looked up at the back of the room. Candace followed his line of sight to see the permanent grimace on General Jacobs's face. His eyes darted from one volunteer to the next, finally stopping on Candace. After a long moment holding her gaze, he nodded once.

"Well then," Dr. Poznanski said. "It looks like we have our first team. Be in the clinic first thing tomorrow morning and we'll begin."

GABE REFUSED to talk to Candace the rest of the day. She was sure he'd get over it eventually, but he needed a little time. She knew he was only being protective of her. Soon enough he'd understand it was the best solution, whether or not he liked it.

She sat with Jamarcus, Dina, Hector, and Andrew at dinner, to discuss what might happen as a result of the new treatments. The one thing they could all agree on is that it was a game changer. Aside from that, however, they had nothing but uncertainty.

"What if something goes wrong?" Dina said, nibbling half-heartedly at a carrot. "I mean, how much testing could they possibly have done on this new formula?"

Jamarcus was doing his best to reassure her. "If they didn't think it was safe, they wouldn't take the risk, hun. They can't afford to lose anyone at this stage."

"I agree," Candace said. "If these attacks continue and they lose at least one ANGEL every time, putting five at risk in one go isn't an option."

And then it happened.

He plopped his tray down and sat down like it was the most normal thing in the world.

They stared at Jackson, none of them believing their eyes.

"What?" he said, digging into his meal. "I thought this was a team meeting."

Jamarcus was the first to recover. "We were discussing the extent of the testing they've done with the new formula," he said. "Thoughts?"

Jackson chewed and swallowed. "I imagine it's safe enough, but I guess we won't find out until tomorrow, huh?"

Leave it to him to ruin things. Poor Dina was going to be a mess all night and tomorrow.

"Are you feeling okay?" Candace asked. "You're not stroking out or anything, right? No fevers? Hallucinations?"

He rolled his eyes at her. "I'm fine, Sugar Plum, but it's nice you're so concerned."

Yep, there was his normal sarcasm. She frowned. Only, that wasn't the normal Jackson. What had gotten into him? Was it some sort of power thing? Was that what he wanted out of the new treatment: to be stronger than everybody else?

"So how do you think our abilities will change?" Andrew asked, changing the topic. "I mean, what do they call us now, Super Supers? Turbo-charged?"

Candace snorted. "Guinea pigs is probably a more fitting descriptor."

"Super two point oh," Hector said, chuckling.

Even Dina giggled at that one.

Candace tried her best not to stare at Jackson for the rest of the meal, but with him sitting across from her it was difficult. As much as she thought about it, she couldn't figure him out. He was almost pleasant company. He had to have an angle, but whatever it was, he hid it well.

"Well, it'll make our little practice sessions more interesting, that's for sure," he said, winking at her.

She balked. "Are we still going to have to do that? I mean, I would think with these new treatments going on they'd let up on that punishment."

Jackson frowned. "Punishment, huh? I thought we were training."

Candace paused. For a split second, he looked a little hurt. Funny, considering he never would've considered her help before she attacked him in his makeshift Showcase. He really did want someone to train with, didn't he? All that time, she thought he was only sparring with her on orders. It made her wonder what else she didn't know about him.

He stood and lifted his tray. "Well, my social quota is filled for the week. See you guinea pigs in the morning."

Candace stared after him as he walked away.

"Hey, Candy," Jamarcus said. "I know this sarcastic banter is kind of what you two do, but you might want to ease up."

She blinked at him. "What? Why? What did I say?"

Dina smiled. "I think Jackson was actually trying to get along with us. Could you not tell?"

Was he? She didn't know. It was all weird.

She sighed and picked up her tray. "Maybe you're right. If he's sincere, I shouldn't give him such a hard time about it. I'll keep it in mind." She shrugged it off. "Think I'll have a swim and turn in early. Good night, guys."

It bothered her the whole way to her room. The last few weeks with Jackson had been one bizarre thing after another. She never quite knew where she stood with him, or if she stood at all. Nothing about him made sense.

It was probably time she tried to figure some of it out.

CHAPTER 10

"BRISTOL," THE corpsman called her back into the patient room.

As before, they ran her through the full gamut of blood draws, screenings, and endurance tests. She didn't even feel the needles anymore, and the other stuff was about as interesting.

Dr. Nathalie Holtz was possibly bubblier today than she'd ever been. The new round of treatments was incredibly exciting for her, and Candace was a little concerned she might burst a blood vessel as wound up as she was.

"So," Dr. Holtz said. "It'll be like the last round, more or less, though we expect you to spend even longer in the recovery room after the radiation dose. We have Miss Nasik and Miss Delacroix on standby, but they'll be at a distance until we know how you're tolerating the changes."

Candace nodded.

"The injections will be painful, more so than the first round." For the first time all morning, her grin faded. "As a precaution, we're going to restrain you, and the shots will be administered via a machine instead."

A familiar flicker of fear passed through the woman's eyes, the same she saw in Hector, Andrew, and nearly everyone else she came into contact with. Candace didn't blame her one bit, and certainly couldn't ask anyone to put themselves at risk if the pain made her lose control.

"Then let's get started, Doc."

Dr. Holtz led her down the hall to another room. When they entered, Candace paused, taken aback by the contraption before her. It looked like a medieval torture device with slightly more padding.

But there was no going back. She kept her expression firm, not about to give in to fear or show signs of weakness. It was necessary, needed. She had to be strong.

She stood against the upright cot and placed her arms and legs into the open steel braces. Dr. Holtz closed them, the icy contact sending goosebumps across Candace's skin. The machine tilted backwards, laying her face up and staring into a tangle of hoses and cords connected to four mechanical arms, each bearing a syringe at the end. It was something out of a horror movie.

One last padded, steel band went across her forehead and Dr. Holtz cleaned the injection sites. "Remember," she said as she inserted an IV. "Breathe through it. It will help. The pain will fade."

"I'll give it my best." Candace closed her eyes. "See you on the other side, Doc."

Dr. Holtz squeezed her hand briefly, and the door closed and locked behind her as she left. A minute later, the hydraulics in the machine above hummed to life and it lowered.

"Just breathe, Candy Cane," she said, imagining Gabe's voice. "Just breathe."

A pause.

And then fire.

There was no gentle lead-up to the agony, no icy sensation to balance the blistering heat running through her veins. The laser-guided needles pumped pure pain into her body.

She screamed until she was hoarse.

It felt like an eternity, but eventually it ebbed away, leaving her weak and numb. The table tilted up and another arm descended, bearing the oral dose of the drug. Her mouth fell open and she gagged on the liquid the syringe squirted into the back of her throat. She almost didn't hear the IV drip click on.

Everything burned. Everything ached. Tears flowed down her cheeks as she sobbed through it, unable to scream anymore.

But she continued breathing. She got through it.

She was sure she would sleep for days.

DUST.

That's all she was.

She needed water. She would die in seconds if she didn't

get it immediately.

In the pitch black recovery room, it took her less than a thought to find the gallon jugs. The first one disappeared down her throat and she collapsed, writhing, moaning in pleasure.

Damn. It'd been so long since she let herself get dehydrated that she forgot about that part.

But she needed more... so much more.

After the second gallon, she laid there, panting and quivering with orgasmic aftershocks. There were no voices in her ears. There was no way Deborah could have coped with what Candace was going through at the moment.

There was some light in the room, but she didn't need much. Everything was crisp and clear, albeit far darker than usual. The third gallon went down slower and she finally started to feel human again. Well, superhuman, anyway. Odd that she considered it normal.

She lugged the fourth jug back to her cot and laid there for a while, mentally exploring her body. She was... shimmery. That was the only way to describe it. Right below the surface of her skin was something that felt the way water looked when light reflected off of it. She could see she wasn't glowing, but damned if it didn't feel that way.

"Hey, Candy Cane." That wasn't Deborah. "How have you been?"

She made at face at the infrared camera in the far corner of the room.

There was an audible sigh at the other end. "I know, dumb question. I'm new at this."

A pause.

"I'm sorry I haven't been to see you," Chloe said. "I

wanted to so badly. Candace. I did."

Candace waved it off. She understood. She was still amazed Deborah could stand to be around her.

"Thank you for that. I've been working on compartmentalizing, so I think I'm ready for you. Although, with this new round of treatments, it's going to be a challenge."

"How far away are you?" Candace whispered as softly as she could, but the noise still made her cringe.

"About three floors down. Pretty incredible, huh? It feels like you're in the next room."

Candace cracked open the water and took another pull. It helped ease the sensitivity.

"I wanted to tell you," she said. "What you've been doing, how much you've accomplished... It's amazing. Especially after what happened. Your turnaround is really inspiring. You're so strong, Candy. Everything about you."

She sighed. Chloe could say that until she was blue in the face, and Candace would never believe it. She drank some more. "I'm just surviving, Chloe. That's all."

"That's still an accomplishment. Don't undervalue that. How's the light level?"

"Tolerable," she whispered. "I'm getting there."

"Andrew talks about you a lot. It's kind of funny. I don't think he understands what you did for him or how you did it. I had no idea you were such a master manipulator." She giggled. "I could use some pointers there if you want to share sometime."

A master manipulator? Well, that was only a little yucky.

"Oh. I don't mean in a bad way. You only use your powers for good."

Candace huffed a laugh. "Trust me, Chloe, I'm not a

master anything. There are some people that are beyond me completely."

"Mmm. I think I know what you mean," she said. "Rather, who you mean. He's a tough one, but I think you're doing all right. You have more of an effect on him than you think."

She scowled. Jackson again.

"Still okay on sound?"

"Getting there." she grumbled.

"There's more to him than what he let's people see, Candy. Jackson has more walls put up than most. I haven't gotten close enough to really get through them, but he's not all bad. I promise."

She knew Chloe was right. Still, it irritated her that she knew so little. She wasn't even sure she wanted to know more. If she did, she might care about that jackass and that would be trouble for her. Letting someone like him get close to her...

She shivered and slammed the door closed on the possibility. No. Absolutely not.

Chloe sighed. "You'll get there, sweetie. Give it time."

"I don't need to get anywhere but out of this room and back into the pool," she said.

"That'll take time, too."

After another long drink from the jug, she laid back. The sooner she was hydrated again, the better. The desert was a terrible thing to have in her bones. As for the rest...

Well, she'd think about it later.

IT WAS after eleven before Candace got back to her room. It took her almost twelve hours to rehydrate. She yawned and stretched as she walked down the hall, but stopped when she saw Gabe sitting in front of her door.

When he saw her coming, he scrambled to his feet as quickly as he could manage and hugged her tightly.

"You might be worse than my mom." She giggled as she returned the embrace. "How long have you been sitting here?"

"About two hours," he said, not letting go. "I've been in knots all day, Candy. No one would tell me anything."

Candace finally extricated herself. "Well, you can come in for a minute and we can talk, but I'm exhausted, so not too long, okay?"

They went inside and she flopped down on the bed, stretching out on the mattress. Gabe perched beside her, still looking worried. He frowned and squinted at her face. "Your eyes are weird."

"So's your face." She smirked.

"You're hilarious," he said, rolling his eyes. "But, seriously. They're really freaky. Your irises keep shifting in the light."

"After all the fluids I drank and had pumped into me today, they're probably floating. I'm pretty sure I'm ninety percent water at this point."

He frowned and lapsed into silence, staring at his hands.

"Hey," she said.

Gabe looked up and she slid over, making room for him next to her. He hesitated when she patted the pillow beside her, but relented after a moment or two.

"You know," he said as she rested her head on his shoulder. "If you make a habit of this, people are going to think something's going on with us."

"We're cousins." She poked him in the side. "Don't make it weird or I won't let you be my teddy bear any more."

His laugh was genuine. "Your teddy bear? Jesus, Candy Cane. Don't ever call me that in public or I'll have to cut you off."

She wrapped her arm around his middle and squeezed. "I'm good with considering it emotional blackmail."

He snorted. "Right. We start playing that game and we'll both end up dying of embarrassment. Remember Brandon's graduation party?"

Instantly mortified, she couldn't control her blush at the memory of streaking through a cornfield at two in the morning. "Point taken."

"So…" he said. "Can I ask how it was?"

"You really want to know?"

"Yes. And not just because I want to know you're okay, though it's mostly that. They said we're all going to go through it eventually." He smoothed her hair and pushed it behind her ear. "So how bad was it?"

Candace sighed. "For real? It was probably the most painful thing I've ever gone through. Way worse than the first round. I'm dreading the next treatment."

"Great. Can't wait," he grumbled.

"I can't speak for anyone else, but my recovery time was ridiculous," she continued. "I lost track of how many gallons of water I drank after about six or seven. They had me plugged into an IV too, but it took two hours before they could get in the room to do that."

"You're really selling me on this whole thing, you know?"

"I thought you wanted to know? I could tell you that it was all glitter and rainbows and now I fart sunshine, but if you want to be prepared..." She shrugged.

"You have such an elegant way with words."

"Can I ask you a favor?" Candace said.

He kissed her head. "Absolutely."

She snuggled deeper into his arms, soaking up the closeness of him. "Will you stay until I fall asleep? I don't know how all this hormone stuff is gonna happen this time around, and I don't think I'll get to do this again for a while. If it's worse than last time, you should probably not touch me until I get a handle on it."

"Sure thing, Candy Cane," he said. "Anything else I can do?"

She sighed and closed her eyes. "I think that'll do it. I might need you to douse me in ice water randomly over the next few days, but that's it for now."

He laughed softly. "You got it, cuz. I'll do my best to put the fire out when I see him coming."

"That's not funny."

"Maybe a little?"

"No."

"You know you're going to have to consider it, Candy."

A yawn broke up her grimace. "Not tonight I don't," she said.

"Well, you know where to find me when you need to talk it out."

Candace gave him one last squeeze. "Thank you."

"You're welcome. Now get some sleep. I'll shut off the

lights on my way out."

She mumbled a good night and closed her eyes. She didn't hear him leave.

I T W A S almost ten before her thirst woke her. God, what she wouldn't give for a hose to drink from. She couldn't fill her glass fast enough to get as much water as she craved.

After about twenty minutes, she got into the shower and cleaned herself up. As she combed out her wet hair, her eyes caught her attention in the mirror, and she stared. Gabe was right. They were freaky. The color was a pale aquamarine, different from the bright blue they had been, and the variations in shadow and light constantly shifted.

Her hair was another matter entirely. As it dried, her frustration grew. What the hell? No matter how she brushed it, it drifted away from her head, like it was plagued by static electricity, only not. She frowned. What was that all about?

As she considered it, she took another drink of water. Her hair rippled outward as she swallowed.

Candace gaped at herself. God damn it. That wasn't what she meant when wished for wavy hair. Great. She couldn't even *pretend* to be normal anymore. Sighing, she threw the whole mess up in a clip.

All she had in her room was an apple, but it would have to do until lunch. She read for a while and snacked before heading to the dining hall.

True waved her over the moment she had her food.

"So how was it?" she asked and took a drink of water.

"Miserable." Candace looked at her, mesmerized. "Whoa."

"What?"

Candace couldn't get past it. She could feel the liquid as it flowed down her mentor's throat and seeped into her body. "Your beverage is talking to me. Weird."

True laughed. "Uh, sorry?"

Candace waved it off. "Not really anything to apologize for. I have no idea what to expect with all this, so there's bound to be surprises. Where's Amir?"

She shrugged. "Some team leader briefing. They're discussing how to divvy up the SAGEs."

"The what?"

"SecondAry Genetic Enhancement," True explained. "That's what they're calling you guys."

Candace giggled. "So now I'm a SAGE ANGEL? I feel like anything but. I don't even know my own hair anymore."

"Your hair?"

She glanced around to see if anyone was looking. It seemed clear, so she reached up and took out her clip. As she shook them free, her pale locks floated up, defying gravity. "See? Too weird."

True's eyes widened. "That's fantastic!"

She grimaced and pulled it back up. "Hardly. I don't even want to think about how badly it's going to tangle like this."

True took a bite of her lunch. "What about the other side effects?"

"Which ones?"

True gave her a look.

God. Again with that. "I don't know. So far so good, I guess." A tray landed next to her and Allen slid in beside her.

"Whats up, ladies?" he said, grinning at them.

His arm brushed hers. eliciting a yelp from Candace. Holy Jesus. Already? She scooted away from him, eight shades of red.

"The hell, Candy Cane?" He frowned at her. "What's your deal?"

She shivered. "Nothing. I'm fine. Sorry. Just... Don't touch me, okay?"

He looked confused. "Why? What did I... Oh." A devilish grin crept across his face. "Got an itch you need scratched, huh? Well, if you—"

"Allen," True growled a warning. "Don't."

He chuckled. "And Mama Bear rears her head. All right, True. I'll be nice." He winked at Candace. "I could be a lot nicer though."

She glared at him. "Not a chance."

Allen moved his tray and transplanted himself next to True. "It's probably more than you can handle anyway."

"I guess you'll never know."

True sighed. "Okay, kiddos. Be civil. So what are your plans for today, Candy?"

"Apparently avoiding people." she said, sighing. "I'll probably spend most of the day in the pool."

"You can't avoid everyone, sugar," True said. "Got a backup plan?"

"Drinking lots of water." Candace cracked a smile.

"Huh?"

She waved it off. "I'll tell you later."

The longer she sat there, the more uncomfortable she got. There were too many guys in the room, and each one that came in looked more tempting than the last. She had to get out of there. She finished her food and said goodbye to her friends.

The pool was an instant balm, and so much more than before. She wanted to lay there, floating, forever. Candace was so relaxed, she didn't even hear the locker room door close.

Someone was in the pool with her. She knew the minute he entered the water who it was.

Jackson was already swimming laps, apparently ignoring her. Candace sank down to the bottom, watching him move from one end to the other. Through no effort on her part, the feel of his body was instantly all over her, from toes to scalp. She stayed down as long as she could, about two of his laps, then emerged quietly in the farthest corner from him. With only her eyes and nose peeking above the surface, she tried to figure out how to get out of there without him noticing. God. If he said anything to her...

After four laps, he paused, catching his breath. He stretched his arms along the edge of the pool, frowning to himself as his legs idly kicked out. There was no way it was possible, but he looked even more toned than he did in his skinsuit. What a nightmare. Every particle of her body screamed at her to wrap herself around him like plastic wrap. Strangely, though, he hadn't seen her at all, even when his gaze roamed the room. His line of sight passed right over her as though she weren't there.

Her nose itched and she slowly lifted her arm, not wanting to call attention to herself, but desperately needing to scratch. When her hand got to her face, however, she froze, staring in amazement.

She could see right through it, as clear as the pool.

Candace gasped, then immediately squelched it and dipped below surface. Had he heard her? Shit. While she was submerged, she took the opportunity to look at the rest of herself, as much as she could. If she looked hard enough, she could see a faint outline. Even her suit was camouflaged. How was that possible? It hadn't been treated with drugs and radiation.

Focusing inward, she discovered what was going on. The thinnest layer of water covered every inch of her, reflecting and bending the light around her. The water was acting like a cloaking device.

She opened her eyes and grinned.

Time to have some fun.

After another quick trip up to get some air, she located Jackson. Surely it wouldn't hurt anything if she screwed with him a little. He couldn't really prove it was her since he couldn't see her. If she stayed silent, he'd never know and might chalk it up to his imagination.

Or his hormones.

Candace waited until he started swimming again. Pulling inside herself, she focused outward, instantly submerged in the consciousness of the liquid molecules around her. There he was, his muscles rippling as they propelled him through the water. Candace shivered, glad to be at a distance. She'd tried it before, but he'd known she was there doing it. It would be different.

When she touched him, she almost gasped. She couldn't imagine anyone being so fit. So strong. So warm. She grazed his shoulders, captivated by the feel of them. Then up along his neck, the cut of his jaw, back down to his chest, moving with each heaving breath he took. God. His abs. They might actually be made of steel.

He stopped moving.

Damn it. She'd gone too far, been too obvious. It was reckless.

"Where are you, Sugar Plum?" he growled, treading water. "I know you're here. Why don't you come out and play?"

Screw that. No way was she coming out. Not when he caught her again.

"Hide and seek, is it? Fine."

Candace plastered herself against the side of the pool, creeping into the corner. While he was under, she took another quick gulp of air, then sank down to watch his progress. She was still in the clear. Maybe she could sneak away while he searched.

She was almost to the corner nearest the locker rooms when he stopped. What was he doing? After a brief visit above the water, Jackson dropped down again, all the way to the bottom. His eyes were closed and he turned, slowly, rotating back and forth.

And then he froze, pointed precisely in her direction.

Crap! How did he find her? He wasn't even looking.

Time to go.

Candace shot up to the surface, moving as fast as she could. She got as far as pushing herself out to her waist when a hand closed around her ankle and yanked her back. Panicked, she barely got a breath before he pulled her under.

Gasping and choking, she broke through again.

"Nice trick, Sugar Plum," he said, an arm on either side of her. "But you can't hide from me forever."

Was she visible? A quick check showed her she was.

God damn it.

When she looked up again, she couldn't breathe. His eyes pinned her in place. Holy Moses, if she stared at him, she could see the barest flicker of a flame dancing in his pupils.

He grinned. "No witty reply for me this time, hmm?"

He was so close. Too close. Her pulse was racing, her head spinning. And the heat... it rolled off of him, pushing against her. Everything about him was full of need, of wanting. All for her.

Her body begged her to give in. It was only a few inches.

Fear paralyzed her, locking her limbs in place. Visions of Adrian danced before her and she shut her eyes, trying to block them out. Despite what Gabe said, everything about it screamed betrayal.

"Please, stop," she said, barely above a whisper.

The only sound was the gentle lapping of water against the sides of the pool.

Another moment passed and his warmth disappeared, replaced by small waves as he pushed away from her.

Candace spun and launched herself out of the pool, running for her towel and then the locker room. She sank down on one of the benches and tried to stop shaking. Terror rattled her from the inside out. Wiping at the tears that spilled down her cheeks, she wondered if it would ever go away.

She stilled when she realized what happened.

Jackson stopped. He backed away as soon as she asked him to. Even when everything she did to him told him not to, he had. Did he see how scared she was? Two words from her, and he held back. If he kept going, kept pushing her, it would've been easier. She could blame him. She could fight back. Anger kept her walls up.

But that?

His retreat was maybe the greatest kindness anyone could have shown her at that moment.

It only deepened the ache in her chest.

CHAPTER 11

SHE AWOKE with a gasp and a splash as she hit the floor.

Her bed and carpet were completely soaked through. What the hell?

Five-thirty. It was still dark outside. Candace pulled her knees up and rubbed her eyes. The nightmare was horrible. Adrian was working side by side with the HEX operative she killed in Portland: Adrian a shriveled husk, the other man with his head flopping around on his shoulders like a writhing snake. Their faces were burned into her retinas; their screams echoed in her ears.

She was still tired, but there was no way she'd get back to sleep after that. Candace got to her feet and shuffled off to the bathroom, pulling the water with her. With a wave, she sent it down the bathtub drain and went about refilling her tank. She needed to practice with her new and improved abilities, especially if they were going to make her spar with Jackson on Monday.

Craptastic. After last night's pool debacle, how was she going to face him again? It was simpler when he was a jerk and she could get mad at him. The new, softer side of Jackson changed everything. She'd have to bait him somehow, make him mad and crack back at her. Otherwise she wouldn't fight up to his level. She'd hold herself back because she cared about him.

Her toothbrush clattered into the sink as the thought registered.

What the hell? She cared about Jackson? When had that happened? How? Why?

No. Not Jackson. She couldn't afford that. There was very little likelihood he gave any consideration to her feelings ever. Opening herself up to that level of trust with him was on par with dancing through a minefield naked on the recklessness scale. It was inevitable she'd get hurt, and she couldn't take that. Maybe she could get out of the practices by using the new round of treatments as an excuse. If they didn't know the extent of what they could do yet, it was dangerous to spar with another person.

They couldn't really argue with that, could they? Caution was everyone's favorite word.

It was settled then. Today she would practice on her own. Tomorrow was the three-day checkpoint. It would be the perfect opportunity to argue against the scheduled sparring matches. She would buy herself some time to get a handle on her rebellious hormones.

First up, the pool.

She swam until eight, showered, and ate a quick breakfast, being careful to take a table at the rear of the room with her back to the wall so no one could sneak up on her. Since it was early, she had her pick of the training rooms. The control desk attendant handed over the keycard to the largest one with a direct supply of water and sent her down the hall.

It was the same setup as the room she sparred in with Jackson, minus the fire braziers. Candace sat in the middle of the room, centering herself, fully submerging herself in her connection. She called to the water and attempted to duplicate the camouflage technique she stumbled on in the pool. It worked, but it was less effective in the open. The surface of her body had a turgid, flowing appearance. It moved like water. If she could find a way to keep it still, it would be a handy skill to have.

Next up, she tried out her defenses. Her shields were three times as dense, and much larger. If she needed to, it would be possible to protect several people from an attack, whereas before she could only do so for herself and anyone directly behind or in front of her. Of course, she didn't have any sure way of testing how strong they were. Maybe if Jackson...

She pulled the brake on that train of thought. She could find any number of people to throw things at her if she asked them to, of that she was certain.

Her attacks were another matter entirely. It was best to start small. She didn't want to pull down any more walls her first time out as a SAGE. She snickered to herself. It felt silly to refer to herself that way, but maybe not any more so than calling herself an ANGEL, if she really thought about it.

Refocusing, she collected a handful of droplets and worked on speed and accuracy first.

Candace launched a single droplet into a dummy on the other side of the room.

Curious, she approached it to check for damage. What she found stunned her. A small hole in the left shoulder went clean through to the other side.

Fucking hell. A single drop of water could do that?

She giggled and jogged back to her starting position. Arm out, finger pointed like a gun, she sent off a full round of "bullets" into the dummy. She scanned it for damage and determined she needed to work on her aim. Two of them went wide and took out chunks of the padding on the walls. Candace repeated the exercise over and over again, improving a little each time, but still missing at least once per round. And her grouping sucked balls. Granted, she never shot a gun in her life, but if her hand was one, she should probably figure out how to do it properly. Making the water bullets less lethal was more her speed as well. If she knew how to set them to stun, she'd be way more likely to use that particular attack. To that end, she experimented with different things. Larger bullets did less damage, but after an hour she discovered that the gun was either on or off. There was no in between.

She moved on to other things after that. There was a spinning sprinkler technique that left nice needle scratches in the surfaces it struck, a curled wave that snuck up behind the enemy and curved over the top of the head to punch them in the gut, and, of course, her old standby ropes. That last one was much improved. They were thicker, stronger than before and required much less effort. She finished off with a surrounding bubble, an adaptation of her liquid cocoon with more wiggle room for the target, but no more chance of escape than the old version had.

Stealth, defense, and attack. The first could still use some work, but all in all, not bad for one morning's work. Stomach rumbling, she decided to call it and headed up to lunch. She'd need her strength for the run she was planning that afternoon.

FOUR SHRINKS.

Four.

They made her talk about her feelings to four separate people in four separate sessions that morning. She wondered if they thought they were going to catch her in some sort of lie by making her repeat herself that many times. The thirty-minute sessions were spaced out with the other medical screenings required for the check on how she was processing the treatments. Apparently her twice a week regular appointments weren't proof enough. And so, her morning went: blood draws, couch confessional, brain scan, couch confessional, endurance test, couch confessional, more blood draws, couch confessional, and finally the full body scan.

She was definitely going to have cancer by twenty-five. She had no doubts.

But then came the Showcase. About damn time. Was it going to be like the first trip there, where they kept her for hours, trying to wear her out? If they did that, they'd be there all week. Her energy levels were at an all-time high, and she had yet to exhaust herself in her own training. There was no way they could possibly be any harsher on her than she was on herself.

When she entered the Showcase floor, she smiled a little. They replaced the fountain she destroyed her first time. There were four test dummies, two on either side of the feature. She considered them, planning which attack method she would use on each one.

"Ready, Miss Bristol?" Dr. Poznanski's voice echoed through the Showcase.

She tilted her head up and scanned the windows. Who was watching today? Candace flashed a thumbs up and waited.

"Then let's begin."

All four dummies sprang into action, whizzing around the room almost faster than she could run. She grinned. Almost. Not that she needed to run.

Candace hopped up on the ledge of the fountain and chose her first target. It was too fast for her to use the gun with any accuracy, but not too fast for her ropes. She lassoed it and snapped the line taut. The dummy flew apart, the bottom half flying in one direction, the top half in another as she severed it in two. The second target she bubbled and launched into the air, sending it crashing back into the ground at a devastating speed. The third whizzed by, but a curled wave bent it in two.

She turned for the fourth and stopped. That one was different. It jerked to a halt fifty feet from her. That was when she heard it.

Tick. Tick. Tick. Tick. Pause. *Click.*

Candace barely had time to process what she heard.

BOMB.

She threw up a shield, encasing herself in a protective covering while flames and smoke rolled over her.

Jesus Christ. They actually tried to blow her up. Those people were insane.

Candace waited for the smoke to clear. In case they tried another sneak attack, she crouched behind the cascading curtain of the fountain and put on her camouflage. Assholes.

The ventilation kicked in and pulled the smoke up and out in a swirling cloud. True must be helping.

"Miss Bristol?" Dr. Poznanski said over the PA.

She bit back a giggle. Let them panic for a minute. Served them right.

The Showcase doors opened and four soldiers rushed in, scanning the floor for any traces of her. Floodlights lit up the ceiling. Were they looking for body parts?

"She's not here, sir," one of the soldiers called up. "Not a trace."

Eventually, Dr. Poznanski and General Jacobs both entered the arena, needing to see it with their own eyes, apparently. They all wandered around, scouring the ground, the windows, even the basin of the fountain and they still didn't see her. It was all she could do not to laugh.

Her knees ached after ten minutes of it, but she wasn't about to let them win.

"Everyone clear out," the General said. "We're not going to find her this way."

Every back was to her, headed for the door. Quietly, she crept out and sat down on the ledge.

"I swear to God and country, Poznanski, if that girl is gone—"

She whistled at them.

Fifteen heads swiveled around at the same time, all wearing the same stunned expression when they saw her.

Candace smiled pleasantly. "I haven't gone anywhere General. Nor do I intend to, well, pending no one successfully blows me up in the future."

Dr. Poznanski was fighting back a smile. "Care to explain, Miss Bristol?"

She toyed with the idea of keeping them guessing, but they'd find out sooner or later, and who knew what sort of tests they'd throw at her to get the information. "Camouflage," she said. Stretching out a hand to the spray behind her, she pulled the water into its thin coat over her body. "I haven't perfected it yet, so it only works well in moving water, but it has its uses." She shook it off. "Are we done then?"

General Perpetually Pissed looked like he had a few choice words for her little game, but Dr. Poznanski beat him to the punch. "I believe so, Miss Bristol. Thank you for an enlightening demonstration."

She was barely out the door when he spoke again.

"You may resume sparring with Mr. Lawrence tomorrow as per the schedule. You've both demonstrated enough control that we're fairly certain you won't kill each other."

Candace spun and began to protest. "But—"

"An inanimate object is no substitute for a live opponent, Miss Bristol," he said. "Tomorrow. One sharp."

She snapped her mouth closed and marched away. Son of a bitch. That's what she got for being competent. Part of her wished she let that stupid bomb go off in her face.

T R U E   P U T a hand on Candace's knee, stopping her from incessantly bouncing it for the fourth time.

"Is there a problem, Candy Cane?" she asked.

She stabbed at her roast beef and shook her head. "Nope. No problem. All good. Why?"

Her eyebrow arched suspiciously. "Because your knee has been bouncing faster than a jackrabbit on a sizzling blacktop since you sat down. You're shaking the bench."

Hell. She was a nervous wreck. Only thirty minutes remained until she had to face off with Jackson, and she could barely eat she was so wound up.

"Sorry," she said as she shoved a bite into her mouth. "Just antsy today, I guess."

Allen opened his mouth, likely about to say something inappropriate, but Amir stopped him. "Whatever it is, I'm sure you'll figure it out. But, if you need advice, just ask."

She nodded and sighed, but didn't offer any more information.

Fifteen minutes rushed by and she spent most of it conjuring up plausible excuses why she couldn't spar today. Everything from cramps to faking a mental breakdown occurred to her, but each one she thought of had a major flaw or drawback she wasn't willing to endure.

Ten minutes left.

True nudged her. "You'd better get going, honey. Don't you have a thing at one?"

She tried not to, but she winced.

Allen snickered behind his sandwich and she shot him a death glare. He looked up at the ceiling and off to the side, desperately trying to hold it in.

"I'm going," she muttered and picked up her tray.

True caught up to her as she dumped her dishes and pulled her into the hall.

"Candy Cane, I know what's got you in knots. You're being way too hard on yourself here."

Candace sighed. "It's not fair, True. I hate this."

"I know, sugar, but maybe it's better to get it over with. The first hit is always the worst, right?"

She couldn't meet her eyes. "This is different. This kind of hit… It's not a glancing blow. There's no defense for it."

True was silent.

Candace rubbed her face and exhaled slowly. "I gotta go."

As she strode past, the other woman caught her arm. "He might surprise you."

She rolled her eyes. "Oh, of that I have no doubt. If there's anything he excels at, that would be it."

True winked and let her go. "Good luck, Candy Cane. If you need me later, you come knock on my door, okay?"

Candace nodded and resumed walking. It felt like a death march.

S H E   G O T there first, skinsuit and all.

Candace stood with her back to the door, facing the water, letting it run over her fingers as she contemplated her first move.

The door opened.

Jackson walked across the floor and stopped in his normal position. He said nothing, as per usual.

God, her heart was racing.

It was stupid. She shouldn't be standing there, terrified to move. The more she thought about it, the more irritated she got. The whole situation was messed up, far beyond anything within her tolerance of bullshit.

Just fucking do it.

Do it!

She spun around, a spray of water following, streaming right for him. Jackson rolled to the side, countering her attack with a whirling tornado of flame. She doused it easily and sent another blast toward him. Still no effect. He launched a massive fireball her way. Tuck and roll.

Her mind settled back into sparring mode, finding his pattern again. She kept him at a distance, never allowing him any closer than ten feet in any direction.

But Jackson was better. Faster. Stronger. That small hesitation still persisted though, and she kept her upper hand. Their battle raged on, the room filling with steam until they could barely see one another. It added an extra level of difficulty, and Candace rose to the challenge. There was an exhilaration in their fights, a kind of violent animal that she could only let loose when she was with him that way. No one else could match her, especially not with the power-up.

A patch of fog cleared away and she caught a glimpse of his face.

He was grinning at her.

It broke her concentration. He took advantage, surging

forward for a close attack.

The wall shot up, barely in time to deflect his arc of fire. She held him to the perimeter, catching her breath.

"You can't keep me out forever, Sugar Plum," he said, a mere two feet from her, pressing in on her boundary.

"The hell I can't, Sunshine." She made a face at him.

Jackson laughed. "You're so damn cute when you're losing."

She gritted her teeth. "I am not losing."

"You will be when I stop going easy on you."

"Right," she said. "What are you going to do, sarcasm me to death? I know all your tricks, maybe better than you do."

She blinked.

He was gone.

"Do you now?" he whispered in her ear.

The wall came down and her last line of defense went up. Pure fear tripped the trigger and she stopped him.

Jackson couldn't move. Not unless she let him.

Dear God. She'd done it again.

Even when she'd sworn not to, to forget she could.

She hadn't even done it in Portland, when the threat of dying was very real and very immediate.

And yet, the moment his breath grazed her ear, it was an instant reaction.

The thing that scared her the most wasn't death.

It was Jackson.

Unforgivable.

It was beyond awful.

Candace took one step forward and turned. He was looking at her, watching her, but even with no control over so much as blinking, he wasn't afraid.

He wasn't afraid of her.

She sank to her knees and released him. Her shoulders shook with each ragged breath. "I'm so sorry," she whispered, eyes closed.

"You're sorry?" he said as he knelt in front of her. "I've been trying to get you to do that for weeks."

Her head jerked up. "You what?"

He shrugged. "I told you not pull your punches. Until you whipped out that last trick, I knew you were."

Candace stared at him, completely shocked. He provoked her to the point of hysteria to, what? Pit himself against her most horrific ability?

"You look surprised."

What the actual fuck? Was this really happening? "You... everything you've done or said to me from the moment I ambushed you, it was all to get me to... to..." Every emotion she could think of swirled around in her head.

"To what?"

The smug grin on his face broke something in her. Pure anger boiled and frothed in her stomach as she stood.

Her hand shot out, slapping him hard across the face.

"What the fuck is wrong with you?" She was shaking again, but for different reasons. "Do you have any idea what it does to me to do that to someone? Any clue? Or do you just not give a shit outside of whatever stupid personal test you wanted to try and pass? So long as it benefits you, fuck everyone else, is that about right, Jackson?"

He got to his feet and stared her down. "Feel better, Sugar Plum?"

"No, I don't fucking feel better! I feel sick. It's taking

every goddamn shred of self-control I have not to rip your black heart out of your chest right now and show you exactly how much not better I feel."

He took a calm step towards her. "You really hate me that much?"

"What the hell do you care?" She held her ground. "You've done nothing but been a miserable prick to me since day one, even when I've stuck my own damn neck out to help you against everyone's better judgment."

"Giving up on me then?"

There wasn't even an arms' length between them, but she refused to be forced back another inch.

"You've pretty much convinced me that's what you want. I'm done trying to rescue a princess who clearly doesn't want me to, no matter how badly he needs it."

"And what would you know about what I need?"

"Everyone needs something, Jackson," she said, less than a foot from him. "So you tell me. What is it you need? I'm done trying to guess."

"At the moment?" His fingertips brushed the line of her jaw. She refused to shiver. His hand settled on the side of her neck as he leaned in towards her.

She was going to call his bluff. Would he actually do it, or were they going to keep playing their game? "What, Jackson?"

His lips hovered over hers. "I need your permission."

"Why?"

"Because I'm not going to take what you don't want to give."

Speechless, Candace had no arguments left. Those tiny demonstrations of gentleness, of care, threw her into a spin.

EVOLUTION: SAGE

"All you have to do is say the word."

Frustrated, pissed off, and completely unable to fight it any more, she caved.

"Words are overrated."

With that, she closed the fraction of the inch between them, throwing herself at him, tearing at the zipper of his skinsuit. A bizarre mix of anger and untamed desire swept her up as she stripped the protective layer away. His hands were everywhere, clawing at her clothing, his need as insistent as her own.

God, his mouth. Something in her gut ignited and burned away any remaining sense she had when his lips met her throat. It was all skin and scent and sweat and not nearly enough of it. Finally free of their clothing, she pinned him to the floor, craving more of his kisses. He grabbed her, pushing himself inside her, unable to contain his passion.

Candace rose up, arching her back as the sweet sensation filled her. Her body sang in delight, her heady groans giving voice to the music in her veins. She had no idea how badly she needed it— needed him— and it overwhelmed her with total elation.

She ground her hips against him, relishing every moan she pulled from him. His eyes locked on to hers. "Say it," he growled through gritted teeth.

Say what? She couldn't think.

"Say the word, Candace. I need it." He stilled her hips. It was torture.

She grabbed his hands, begging for release. "Yes," she whispered.

Jackson sat up, one hand sliding behind her neck, into her hair. "Louder." He ran his tongue over her ear.

"Yes, Jackson," she cried, gripping his shoulders, her body demanding to be sated. "Yes!"

He pushed her back onto the floor, driving into her, stealing the air from her lungs as she exploded into euphoria. Her nails dug into his back as he continued thrusting, not ready to give in. He was hungry, desperate for every inch of her. She pulled at her connection, syncing her waves of pleasure with his, feeling it as he did. He was fighting, holding back against the climax.

"Let go," she breathed in his ear.

Her words were enough to push him over the edge. More than heat, but light itself released into her, revealing pieces of his secret self. Maybe for the first time, she saw him for who he was. The glimpse was fleeting.

Jackson lay in her arms for a while, his own still wrapped around her. There was so much vulnerability in seeing him that way. In that moment, something strange passed between them. He shared a part of himself that he'd never shared with anyone before. There was no way he would have let another person in like that on purpose. What she saw was something so sad, her heart still held the shadow of it.

What next?

What was she supposed to do?

What should she say?

He chuckled softly into the crook of her neck as his fingertips grazed her side. "This is going to make our little practice sessions a hell of a lot more fun, Sugar Plum."

Candace made a disgusted noise and shoved him off. "No, it's not Jackson." He would have to ruin the moment, wouldn't he? She grabbed her skinsuit and shoved her legs inside.

"Where are you going?" he asked, running his palm up her spine. "Not in the mood to cuddle?"

She stood and finished pulling it on, zipping it back up. "Cuddle? You're joking, right? You're about as cuddly as a cobra."

"You didn't seem to have a problem with that a minute ago."

Turning, she glared at him. "A momentary lapse in judgment. It won't happen again."

"You say that now, but you did give me permission." He smirked at her. "No takebacks."

Oh, for God's sake. She rolled her eyes and spun away, heading for the door. "No do-overs."

His laughter echoed off the walls. "And here I thought you wanted to learn all my tricks."

"In this case," she said, opening the door. "I'm content with ignorance." She slammed it behind her.

Her hand rested on the doorknob.

Fuck.

The guilt hit her then: absolute, total disgust with herself and her lack of self-control. She thought she might throw up right there in the hallway. She got through a shower and changed back into her polo and khakis, then left the training area.

The tears threatened to spill over.

She needed to talk to Gabe. She needed a reminder that someone truly cared about her, even if she didn't deserve it at the moment.

CHAPTER 12

"IT'S NOT that bad, Candy Cane," Gabe said, smoothing her hair as she sobbed into his shoulder.

"Yes, it is," she cried. "He's a total jerk and I... I..."

"Used him?" He chuckled. "There's nothing wrong with that."

"But it's *Jackson*," she sniffled. "Of all people, he's the worst choice I could have made."

"And why is that? The way I see it, he might've been your best choice."

Candace sat back and gaped at him. "What? How do you figure that?"

"Well." Gabe snagged a tissue and gently wiped her cheeks, handing her a few more to blow her nose with. "You're not looking to commit to anyone new, right?"

She nodded weakly.

He shrugged. "Then maybe Jackson is the perfect person here. Unless he's said otherwise to you, he doesn't strike me as the type to invest himself in someone like that. Take what you need, no strings attached."

She sighed. "You know that's never what ends up happening with these things. Someone always gets hurt."

He smiled at her. "So, if it's inevitable, maybe you should just roll with it. Don't waste your energy fighting."

She groaned and rubbed her face. "Are you being contradictory on purpose?"

"It's my natural state." Gabe leaned back on his elbows. "I dunno what to tell you, really. If you're both into it, why not go for it? Maybe you'll be more pleasant to be around. You're pretty cranky when you're not getting laid."

"It's entirely fucked up that this kind of discussion is normal for us."

Gabe laughed. "Why? Because we're cousins? Because I'm a dude?"

"Both." She wrinkled her nose at him.

"In case you didn't notice, Candy Cane, superheroes aren't normal people. You gotta hang on tight when you find someone to trust. With so few to pick from, I think we're pretty damn lucky to have each other."

"I know," she said, staring at her hands as she shredded one of the tissues. "I'm not sure I could've gotten through any of this without you."

He sat back up and hugged her. "You've had a rougher go of it than most. I wish there was more I could do for you."

Candace returned the embrace and pulled away. "It's enough that you put up with all of this from me. So, thank you."

"It's gonna be awkward for a while, but you'll figure it out. You're the smart one, remember?" He chuckled and grabbed his crutches as he stood. "You hungry? I thought we'd grab dinner if you think you're up for it."

She got to the door first to open it for him. "Yeah, I'm starved, but that's par for the course these days. You think you eat a lot now, just wait until they supercharge your superness. I keep expecting to weigh five hundred pounds every time I step on a scale."

The dining hall was as busy as it ever was, and no one even glanced her way when she entered. For some reason, she expected them to, like they'd already know what she did and who she did it with. She didn't relax until they sat down, joining Jamarcus, Dina, and Ella for the meal.

"So how'd your Showcase go?" she asked Jamarcus.

He shrugged. "Not bad. They'll probably be cleaning moss and leaves off of the ceiling for a week, though."

"It was pretty amazing," Dina gushed. "I got to watch the demonstration. Admittedly, I'm a little jealous. I hope they let me go for treatments next."

Jamarcus shuddered. "No, you don't. If I were you, I'd hold off until the last minute if you can."

Candace nodded. "I second that. It's hella painful, Dina. I hate that there are still four more rounds to go. Enjoy what you've got while you've got it."

"I, for one, am content with how I am," Ella said. "It's weird enough turning into other people. I can't imagine what the next level for me would be."

She didn't see him, so much as feel it when he passed behind her. Her spine went rigid and every hair on her arms stood up, as though Jackson's simple presence pulled at her.

Gabe coughed and nudged her, causing her to jump. Everyone at the table gave her a weird look.

"So, I can camouflage myself in water now," she said, hurriedly shoving food into her mouth and avoiding their eyes.

"You can what?" Gabe asked.

She choked down the mouthful. "Yup. Check it out." Candace extended her hand towards his drink and pulled a little of the liquid up, cloaking herself to the wrist. "Pretty cool, huh?"

Gabe rolled his eyes. "Please don't put that back in my glass when you're done with it."

Candace stuck her tongue out at him and wiped the droplets onto her napkin.

"I need to talk to you," Ella said, suddenly dead serious.

She looked up. "Huh? About what?"

Ella stood and walked around the table, motioning for Candace to follow. "Now."

What was that about? Had she done something?

Ella led her outside into the chilly December air and sat down at one of the picnic tables.

"Jackson," she said, her face scrunched up. "When?"

Candace winced. "It's not... We're not—"

"Don't bullshit me, Candy. I saw what happened just now. He was just as affected as you were."

Candace pressed her forehead into her palm and groaned. Everyone was going to know. "This afternoon. It's awful. The whole thing is so fucked up. I'm pretty sure we hate each other, but that doesn't seem to make a damned bit of difference to him. Honestly, I'm pretty sick about it."

When she was silent, Candace peeked at her. "I'm sorry,

Ella."

She snorted. "Don't be dumb. It's not about that. The jealousy train rolled through that station a long time ago."

Candace stared dumbly. "What?"

Ella blew out a breath. "Well, I suppose I may as well tell you. Maybe it'll change something for you, but maybe not. He doesn't hate you, Candace. Probably the opposite."

It didn't make any sense. How would she know? "What makes you think that?"

She leaned back and crossed her arms, rubbing warmth into her exposed skin. "Okay, well, here's the thing. You were right about me liking him. I did. A lot. More than I should have. He wasn't exactly a great boyfriend, not that he would ever let me call him that anyway. I thought, with my ability, maybe I could, you know, keep him interested in me. So when I was with him, I'd change." She took in Candace's stunned expression and misinterpreted it for lack of understanding. "When I say 'with him,' I mean in the biblical sense."

Candace winced. "Ella, that's awful. You deserve so much better than that. Is that why you broke it off with him? Because good for you, if so."

"Well," she said, grimacing. "Yes and no. I didn't mind that part so much. It was kind of fun pretending to be other people, but, yeah, it's a little fucked up. Anyway, none of them really seemed to have any effect on him aside from the usual. Well, except one."

She blinked, waiting for her to finish. When she didn't, Candace frowned. "Okay, I give. Who?"

Ella gave her a "duh" look. "You, Sugar Plum."

At the use of Jackson's nickname for her, Candace about

fell over. "You're joking."

"I'm not," Ella said. "Why do you think I was so mad at you that day? When I realized what his deal was, yeah, I was pissed. I really liked him, and he was basically using me because he couldn't have you. He'll never admit it, Candy, but I needed to tell you. Like I said, it wasn't even your fault. I was hurt and I needed someone to blame. Being angry at him didn't do me a shit bit of good. But you, you I thought I could do some damage to, and I wanted to spread the misery. I'm so sorry about that. Really."

Candace rubbed a hand across her mouth, at a total loss with what to do with the information.

"You okay?"

"Okay?" She snorted. "Definitely not. What the hell do I do with this, Ella? I have no idea how to feel right now, or if I should feel anything."

Ella wilted in her seat. "Are you mad at me?"

"What?" She took in her worried expression and gave her a reassuring smile. "No. Not at all. I guess... I'm sorry you got put in that situation. I hate that you went to those lengths when he was such a jerk to you."

"Well, I sort of did it to myself, really," she said. "It's not like I dumped him right then and there. I convinced myself for weeks that maybe I could still win him over. But when you broke up with Adrian..."

Candace swallowed. She didn't want to hear any more, but Ella needed to get it out.

Her voice dropped to a whisper. "That was why I was there that night, you know. I tracked Jackson down to the gym because I decided enough was enough. The Pryor twins were there by coincidence. When Adrian came in, gunning for Jackson, they tried to stop him." Her eyes closed and she bit her lip. "So did I. I thought I could talk him down if he thought I was you."

Candace went numb. Chilly tears spilled over, trailing down her cheeks. That's what Adrian meant when he asked her to prove she was herself.

"I shouldn't have brought that up, Candy. I'm sorry."

She shook her head slowly and looked away. "It's all right. I didn't know. It's probably better I do now."

"Is it?"

Shrugging, she wiped away the tears. "I try not to think about it too much, but, yeah, it's better to know the whole truth."

The wind kicked up, and she shivered.

Ella stood and started for the door, but paused beside Candace, considering. "You know, you might end up being the best thing that ever happened to him, Candy Cane. He needs someone that won't put up with his bullshit. I'm not strong enough for that kind of thing, but I think you are. For what it's worth, I hope it works out for the two of you."

Candace couldn't meet her eyes. "There is no two of us."

She chuckled. "And you're both so damned stubborn. Good luck anyway."

Ella returned to the dining hall, leaving Candace alone with her thoughts. Was it possible Jackson actually had feelings for her? Did that even matter? She didn't want that, didn't ask for it. She couldn't flip a switch and simply forget what she did the last time someone got that close to her. She was dangerous, and she was damaged, too. If something happened with the new round of treatments…

No. It didn't matter. Jackson wasn't asking for a

commitment, and she definitely wasn't giving him one. It was pointless to worry over. The only thing she knew for sure was that she couldn't give in to the hormones again. The longer they carried on, the more hurt there would be in the end. What happened today had to be a one-time thing.

No do-overs.

"WHAT ARE you waiting for, Sugar Plum?" he asked as another blast of flames ripped across the room. "You know you want to."

No matter what, she was determined to keep her head today. Candace wasn't going to let him get to her.

She decided to employ his tactic of total silence today. No one said she had to talk to him, after all. If she stayed away from conversation, she wouldn't get dragged into another heated argument, she wouldn't lose her temper, and she sure as hell wouldn't end up naked with him again.

"Not gonna play today, huh?" He chuckled as she countered another fireball. "That's a pity. If you hold back, you know you're gonna lose."

She spun and sent a round of needles directly at his face. One broke through, grazing his cheek and drawing blood. As badly as she wanted to, Candace refrained from making a smart remark. *Keep moving. Stay focused.*

"That kind of tickles," he said with a chuckle. "Last chance to get serious."

She bubbled him, but he burned it off immediately. He landed in a crouch and looked up at her, grinning.

"You were warned."

She blinked, and he was gone.

A sudden, sharp burning on her arm made her spin.

He was there and gone.

She turned again when the same pain hit the curve of her waist, barely catching a glimpse of him before he disappeared. What the hell was that? Burn tag?

Before she could check herself for marks, another of his touches ran along her backside.

Enough was enough.

She didn't need to see him to do it. Candace could feel him out. She grabbed hold and closed her grip around the water in his body. If that was what he was after, then screw it. Let him get a good, long, up close and personal look at how easy it would be for her to kill him.

Jackson's hand was extended, as though he'd been about to touch her face. She glared at him, then took her time examining the other places he put his hands, making sure she allowed him to breathe and have a pulse.

Jesus. He was running so hot he burned small holes in her skinsuit. Considering the things were made to withstand contact with fire already, he came at her with a temperature close to volcanic to cause that kind of damage. He stopped short of leaving more than small red marks on her skin, but they stung like a bitch. Not only that, but at the moment her ass was ready to pop right out of her clothing due to the small slit he cut across the material there.

After shooting him another dirty look, she crossed her arms and watched him for a moment.

"There's one of two things going on here," she said, pacing around him slowly. "Either you have a seriously suicidal streak, or you have an incredible amount of faith in me."

When she returned to the front of him, she stopped. "I don't have any explanations for either of those things, Sunshine, but I intend to find out which it is. I know which one I'm leaning towards."

She loosened her hold on him only enough for him to speak. "So tell me, self-destruction or trust, Jackson?"

"I'm pretty sure you won't kill me, Sugar Plum," he said, smirking.

Candace stepped forward, stopping inches from his face. "Why? You know I could. You've seen me do it."

He was fighting her hold, but she wasn't about to let him go. Wow. As hard as he was struggling, he really didn't want to have that conversation.

"Why do you trust me so much?"

She saw it in his eyes when he hit on a plausible lie. "Because you wouldn't hurt a teammate unless it was to the benefit of the entire team," he said.

"Hmm," she murmured and stepped back, continuing to circle him. "While that's not untrue, I think there's more to it than that." She paused next to him and leaned in to whisper in his ear. "Ella told me your dirty little secret, you know."

Even though he could speak, he said nothing, scowling at her instead.

As she walked, she ran her fingertips across his shoulder blades, slowly, then ducked under his outstretched arm. "Not going to tell me yet?"

"There's nothing to tell. Little Red liked to play games. I let her."

Candace reached up and brushed the hair away from his forehead. "I heard there was one game you had a particular affinity for. I wonder, was the real thing better than the imitation?"

The muscles in his jaws clenched so hard she thought he might break a tooth. Smiling, she inched closer to his face, stopping shy of making contact. "All you have to do is say the word."

He didn't flinch.

Candace pulled back a little to look at him. Tiny beads of sweat gathered on his forehead, testament to his internal battle. Honestly, she didn't think she could hold him like that too much longer, but she had no intention of being in the room when he could move again. Was it really easier for him to tolerate the paralysis than admit he cared about her?

She frowned. Whatever happened to him to toughen him like that must have been bad.

Laying her palm against the side of his face, she brushed a gentle kiss across his lips. She immediately wanted to do it again, but clamped down on her desire and hung on to her little remaining willpower. "Then that's how it'll stay, Sunshine. You keep your secrets. I don't need any more anyway."

Aware her hold was slipping, she decided to make as quick an exit as she could with her skinsuit ripped that way. Candace glanced over her shoulder one last time, then let herself out.

Pushing open the changing room door, she released him. Her words would have repercussions, but whatever they were going to be, she'd have to take them as they came. She struck a nerve with him, and Jackson had no tolerance for someone getting that close.

Why did she say anything at all? Revealing she knew about his infatuation with her would get her nowhere. Not that she wanted to be anywhere in particular. Jackson always brought out her extreme side. She simply couldn't stop herself when it came to their little games. What was she hoping to accomplish? Even if he admitted to having feelings for her, what would that change?

Nothing. It would change nothing. She didn't want a new relationship. She didn't want *any* relationship.

It was better for everyone that he keep his feelings to himself.

CHAPTER 13

" S O , " C H L O E said through the headphones. "What's new?"

She took a long pull from the water jug before replying. "Anything in particular you're asking about?" she whispered.

There was a long pause.

Candace sighed. Of course she should have expected that. "Did someone tell you, or am I just that obvious?"

"Ella mentioned it, but she didn't have to."

"Meaning what?" Candace asked.

"I can feel his traces." Chloe said. "Like fingerprints only…" She giggled. "Well, bigger than that."

Great. Exactly how permanent was that going to be? It wasn't like she could scrub it off of her aura or whatever. It was weird to think she was walking around with Jackson all over her energy signature. She took a long drink, half-wishing it was something a lot stronger than water.

"For what it's worth, it's the same for him."

That didn't make her feel any better.

"How was this round of the treatment?" she asked, switching gears. "Any easier than last time?"

Candace shrugged. "About the same. I think the recovery might be quicker this week. So far, so good."

"It looks that way from this end. You're tolerating the light and sound almost twice as fast."

"I'll take the small blessings where I can get them. How are you doing? Have they given you any idea if or when they're going to put you through this torture?"

Chloe groaned. "No. And, honestly, I kind of hope they don't. I'm barely getting a handle on this empath thing as it is. I can't fathom what it would be like with more on my plate. I kind of envy you Physicals. All you have to deal with is your own personal craziness. I get to deal with mine and everyone else's too."

"How…" Candace paused, thinking about her question. "How do you do that? It's gotta be really tough."

"Deborah's been showing me how to compartmentalize, like I mentioned before," she explained. "It's learning how to separate your emotions from the emotions of others. It can be really confusing when you're starting out. At first, I'd start crying or giggling or whatever because I was sure something was happening to me, and it would take me a really long time to realign my reality. Compartmentalizing doesn't let me shut it off, but it helps me differentiate between myself and everyone else. Does that make sense?"

"It does," Candace said. "Still, I don't know how you cope. For what it's worth, I'm sorry if I caused a lot of misery for you."

"Oh, honey," Chloe said, sadness laced in her words. "Don't be sorry. Please don't. What you went through... Don't apologize for your pain. Pain is part of life, and you had every reason in the world to feel the way you did. Taking a life is hard. I've seen the traces in a few others at the compound. I know what that does to a person. But doing that to someone you cared about so deeply, I don't know that I could come back from that. That's one thing I probably won't have to face as an Abstract. I don't have the ability to do that sort of thing directly."

Candace considered it. "I suppose there is that. You have to take the good with the bad. I don't suppose there's anything I can do to help there, huh?"

"Not really, no," she said, tired. "But thank you for thinking of me."

She managed to get out of recovery to make dinner. Exhausted, she sank down on the bench next to Gabe and tried to stay awake long enough to eat. Half way through the meal, the call went out for the Pavo Team to get to the hangar.

Gabe was still on the bench.

Candace looked at him. "When do they think you'll be healed enough to go out again?"

He grimaced and picked at his food. "They say it'll be at least another few weeks. It's really frustrating. I need to be out there with them, but my leg isn't cooperating."

"Do they know what the problem is?"

"It's just taking time to heal. Normal people would be out of commission for at least six months, maybe more given the extent of the damage I had. They said I'm lucky I kept it, actually."

"Does it hurt much?"

Gabe let out a long, slow exhale. "More or less all the time. That's another reason they won't let me out. They're worried the painkillers I'm on slow my reaction time. The light physical therapy and massages help some, but they can't really reach where it hurts the most."

She sighed, frustrated there wasn't more she could do for him.

Then she stopped. Maybe there was.

Candace drifted into her connection, searching for the water within his body. It only took a second and she had a clear map of the internal structure of her cousin. She traced from his right hip, down his thigh, sensing immediately where the problems began.

"Are you falling asleep on me?" Gabe snorted. "That's not rude or anything."

Her eyes popped open. "What? No, I wasn't. I was just..." she trailed off, continuing to think on it. "Would you let me try something?"

He raised an eyebrow at her. "Try what?"

"I think maybe I can help, but it's hard to explain. Are you about finished?"

"Depends on what you think you're going to do to me."

His words jolted her. "I... you... you trust me, right? You know I won't... that I wouldn't..." She bit her lip. She couldn't handle it if Gabe was afraid of her, too. Of all people, she'd crumble completely if she lost him.

His eyes went wide, and he grabbed her hand. "No. Not that at all, Candy Cane. It was just a joke. I'm sorry. Come on. Help me ditch this stuff. We'll take this elsewhere."

S H E   H O V E R E D inside the doorway to his room. His comment, even though it was meant in jest, rattled her. Especially with her boosted powers, very few people went out of their way to interact with her. Fewer still would risk touching her. It shook her confidence. Strange, as she never would have expected it to. The whole thing made her nervous.

Gabe leaned his crutches up against the wall and lowered himself onto the bed. He sat there for a moment, watching her pace.

"Candace," he said. "I'm sorry about what I said. I swear I didn't mean anything by it. I'm not scared of you or what you can do. If I was, you'd have known by now. Seriously. Come sit down."

She exhaled and flopped down beside him. "I don't want to hurt anyone, Gabe. I hate the way people look at me since…" She took a breath. "Since what happened with Adrian. Dr. Holtz, Hector, Andrew… even True stopped sparring with me, although there were a few other reasons for that. Still, no one wants to get anywhere near me. I hate it. I don't blame them, either."

His arm wrapped around her and pulled her into a hug. "Candy Cane, no matter what happens, I will always, always know that you're on my side. I trust you completely. I know you've got a handle on your ability and how drastic the situation would have to be before you'd even consider doing what they're afraid of. I'm not. I didn't mean to upset you, and I don't want you to think for a second that I wouldn't trust you with my life."

She held him tightly, overwhelmingly grateful to the universe for giving her the gift of his presence. "I won't do this if you don't want me to, okay? It's a total experiment on my part so don't feel obligated to subject yourself to it just to make me feel better."

He pulled back and studied her. "You think you can help, right? Is it going to make it hurt less?"

Candace chewed at a fingernail, thinking again. "Honestly? I'm not a doctor and don't know for sure. I can't say how much it will help with that part, but I think if nothing else it will help you heal faster."

"How so?"

"Lay down flat and let me check it out," she said. "I only took a quick peek so I want to make sure I'm right first, okay?"

He gave her a skeptical look, but complied anyway. Candace took a deep breath and closed her eyes, again letting her connection reach out to the water within his body. She traced the pathways of veins and arteries and muscles, searching for the problems. Her hand hovered over his leg, scanning and stopping wherever she sensed a disruption in the flow.

"It starts here," she said. "There are blockages where things are tangled or not laying correctly. There's a bit of what I think is clotting too." She opened her eyes and stopped. "What I might be able to do is break some of that up and straighten a few things out. I know how to control muscle movement, so I can be pretty precise."

She switched her focus to his face. "But only if you say

it's okay. I don't know if it's going to hurt when I do this or if you even want me to try. There's no reason to take any risks here."

"So, you're telling me you can rearrange the inside of my leg without cutting me open?"

She nodded. "I think so. It's a matter of pushing around the water inside your body is all."

"How do you know where it's all supposed to go? I mean, unless you spent the last year memorizing human anatomy and didn't tell me…"

"Like I said, it's kind of hard to explain." She bunched up her face and tried to think how to put it into words. "Okay, when you do your tricks with light, do you have to know exact formations of things in order to reflect them or make them look the way you want?"

"No."

"It sort of knows more than you do, right? It gets the gist of what you want it to do and fills in the blanks on its own?"

"Yeah." He nodded. "That's one way of putting it."

"Well, it's sort of like that with the water too, only, there's something like muscle memory going on as well. Your body remembers how it used to be, is supposed to be, and it wants to get back to that, but can't do that by itself. That's sort of filtered into the water, which I can use to push things back in place." Candace shrugged. "At least, that's what I think it's telling me. Potential energy without a means to start the process, but a desire for it. Make sense?"

"I think so. What about the clotting, though? That's pretty dangerous. I had no idea that was going on. Shouldn't we, you know, consult a doctor or something? They'd probably want to know about it."

Candace rubbed her chin. "Yeah, that might be better, but I don't know that they'll let me try this at all. They'll stick you on blood thinners or put you under the knife again before they let me anywhere near you, more than likely." She frowned at her hands. "I'm ninety-nine point nine nine nine nine nine nine percent sure what the problem is and that I can fix it. I just… I don't want to be wrong. Not for something like this."

Gabe sat up. "So, maybe we go tomorrow then? If nothing else, you can tell them where the problems are, right?"

She nodded.

He chuckled. "You should probably think twice about doing this. If they figure out you're useful in the clinic, you'll never get out of there."

The thought made her smile. "Oh, I don't know. That might be kind of nice. I won't be training forever, and it would give me something else to do. And I won't lie, being able to do something other than cause destruction, something that helps people like that, I'd really like to add that to my résumé."

"So how about this then," he said. "You go and get a good night's sleep. Tomorrow we meet for breakfast and then go to the clinic. If nothing else, I'm sure Dr. Poznanski will want to hear more about this."

Candace stood. "That sounds like a plan. I'm beat anyway, so doing anything now is probably a bad idea. Meet you at eight?"

"Done."

THEY WERE actually going to let her do it. Candace took a deep breath to steady herself. If she screwed it up, it was her cousin that would pay the price, not her.

Gabe was laid out on the table, plugged into an IV drip of saline with a backup of painkillers if it got to be too much. She didn't want him to hurt, but she was concerned that any drugs in his system would hamper what she wanted to do. If the tissue was unresponsive or sluggish, it wasn't going to work.

An emergency medical team was on hand to take care of him if anything went wrong, and others were gathered in an observation box above. So many people watching made her nervous. What if she couldn't do anything at all?

"So are we gonna start this show or what?" Gabe said. "No meds since last night makes for a very unhappy superhero."

Candace rolled her shoulders and tried to relax. "So stop talking and let me work already."

She took her place standing beside him and focused inward, fully submerging herself in her connection. When she was ready, she reached out, calling to the water in his body, following it as it circulated through his system. The first thing she came to was a small clot in his thigh. Candace studied it for a moment, taking in the shape and size of it, then used the surrounding liquid to pulverize it. It only took the slightest bit of pressure.

She glanced at his heart rate monitor, and then his face. He wore the strangest expression.

"That didn't hurt, did it?"

He blinked and his eyes focused on her. "What did you do?"

"Got rid of a clot. I want to make sure you're okay before I keep going."

He closed his eyes and relaxed. "You have no idea how much better that feels already."

She smiled. "I think there was a nerve close by, so it could have been causing you some discomfort."

"I don't even care," he said, sighing. "This is amazing, Candy Cane."

Candace decided she would take care of the rest of those first before rearranging his tissue. She didn't want to run the risk of knocking one of them loose and letting it fly off into his bloodstream. None of them were very large, but if allowed to grow they could potentially kill him. In all, it took about forty-five minutes before she was satisfied the leg was clear. On the off chance he had issues elsewhere, she did a quick check, but didn't find any others.

"How you doing, cuz?" she asked.

He grinned lazily. "Better than I've been in weeks. Are you done?"

She shook her head. "No, only with the clots. I started with that because I figured it wasn't going to hurt."

"I don't like the sound of that."

Candace grimaced. "Well, if I'm going to be moving around still-healing ligaments and crap, yeah, it's probably not going to feel good. Think you're ready for that, or do we quit now?"

"I'm in it for as long as you are, Candy Cane."

When he met her eyes, her breath caught at the total

trust she saw there. Leaning over him, she kissed his forehead. "Thank you," she whispered.

"Make it count," he said quietly.

Moving back into position, she went deeper, following the existing configuration of muscles and blood vessels and comparing it to where the water wanted it to be. She frowned. It wasn't going to be a single pass procedure. To avoid causing damage, she would have to do it in tiny shifts, making minuscule adjustments and softening up scar tissue. She started with pulsing waves of pressure that passed from his hip to the tip of his toes, loosening everything it passed through. She did that several times, blocking out the blissful groans from the patient. Deep tissue massage? Please. Those masseurs had nothing on her.

When the real work started, it was a different story. The first time she tweaked a ligament, Gabe sucked in a sharp breath. Candace pushed through, passing the alteration down the length of it, doing her best to ignore the quiet whimpers from the table. After allowing him a short break to catch his breath, she started on a nearby artery, one running down the length of his leg.

"Still with me?" she said, keeping her eyes closed, holding her focus.

"Yep," he said, straining. "All good."

"Hurts like a bitch, doesn't it?"

"I preferred the massage."

"The minute you say stop, I'm done. Got it? I won't do more than you can handle."

He made a derisive noise. "Are you kidding? I totally win at pain chicken."

Candace rolled her eyes. "You remember that when I'm

adjusting your calf muscles."

"Bring it."

What a clown. So long as he was still joking, though, she knew he was okay.

An hour later, he was no longer joking.

"Last one, Gabe," she said as she wiped the sweat from her brow. "You get through this and we're done for the day."

His breaths came out in forced exhalations. "Do it."

That one was going to be the worst. His calf muscle healed crookedly and was turned at the slightest angle. If left alone, it would be incredibly painful to walk, let alone run or anything else. Thanks to the IV drip, there was plenty of free water in his system, and she used that to cushion the nerves as she worked. Little by little, she turned the muscle back towards where it should be, although nowhere close to where it needed to go. Attempting to go that far would undoubtedly rip it, and Gabe would have much bigger problems. Candace eased her way down until she reached the base of his heel, and then let it go.

Gabe gasped as she finished, and attempted to bite back a cry. She laid a hand against his forehead and began a last soothing massage to disperse the pain more quickly.

"I'm done. That's it. You did it, cuz. You got through it."

"But I'm not all better yet, am I?" he said, eyes still pinched shut.

She sighed. "Afraid not. I can't fix it all at once. I can only go a little at a time so I don't tear anything. Think you can get through this a few more times?"

He cracked open an eye. "How many is a few?"

She looked at his leg, thoughtful. "Four, I think. It's hard to tell, but if everything I fixed stays fixed, then, yeah. Four sounds about right."

A throat cleared, and she turned away from Gabe.

"You've finished then?" Dr. Poznanski said.

She nodded. "For now. The changes need some time to set. He'll need to rest it for a while."

Another doctor and a nurse set in to examine Gabe and turn on the medication to ease his discomfort. As they wheeled him out of the room, she frowned.

"Where are they taking him?"

Dr. Poznanski guided her out of the room. "For imaging. While we were all watching on, it was difficult to know what you were doing and what changes, if any, you were successful in making. The doctors will also want to check him for any residual damage or blood clotting you may have missed. Which, by the way, was an excellent catch. They were so small we hadn't detected them when last we checked. When our imaging this morning confirmed your findings, I knew we had to let you try."

Candace let out a relieved breath. "Thank you for that. I'm glad to do something other than fighting for once."

Out in the hallway, he stopped and crossed his arms. "Tell me, would you have any interest in pursuing this type of work outside of helping your cousin?"

Her heart leapt. Hell yes, she did. If she could save lives instead of only using her ability as a weapon, she would like nothing better. "I would absolutely be interested, Dr. Poznanski."

"Then I have some recommended reading for you." he said.

"Reading?"

He nodded. "If you're going to be messing around inside

the human body, you'll need a good understanding of how it works."

Well, she couldn't argue with that. Feeling her way was all fine and good for that morning, but if she were in a critical situation, she'd definitely need more in-depth knowledge. "I agree."

Candace yawned, unable to cover it.

"You must be exhausted, Miss Bristol. The level of concentration you showed during the procedure must be very taxing."

She nodded. "Accuracy is always more difficult. It's been a while since I was that focused for that long."

He glanced down at his watch. "Well, since you've missed the beginning of your training session with Mr. Lawrence for the day, you may as well take the afternoon off. Get some rest and I'll have Miss Nasik round up a few books from the library that are a good jumping off point."

"Thank you. I'll get started on them right away." She yawned again. "Well, maybe after a nap."

Dr. Poznanski smiled and nodded. "We'll discuss this more later. I'm going to check up on your cousin and get started on some paperwork. Good day, Miss Bristol."

He strode off down the hallway, leaving her alone to drag herself back to her room. But even exhausted, she couldn't keep from smiling.

She could do more than wound and kill. Finally, she could use her ability for something truly good.

CHAPTER 14

S H E   W A S   asleep for all of thirty minutes before the pounding woke her. Panicked that something might be wrong with Gabe, Candace dashed across the room and pulled the door open.

Panicked turned into pissed off as she took in Jackson's irritated face.

"Forget something?" he asked.

"No, but you did. Like your manners. What do you want?"

"We spar at one. You didn't show."

"I was in the clinic. Dr. Poznanski gave me the day off."

His eyes moved up and down her body, taking in her pajamas. Damn it. She wished she was wearing more than a tank top and shorts. "Were you sleeping? What were you doing in the clinic?"

Candace crossed her arms over her chest. "Yes, I was. I was tired, not that it's any of your business. And why do you care what I was doing there?"

"I don't, until it affects my practice sessions."

"Right," she said, rolling her eyes. "So we're still playing that game, huh? Sure. Okay, Jackson. Everything's fine. Now go away."

She started to close the door, but he blocked it with an arm. "Not fine. You owe me a practice session."

"I don't owe you shit. Let go of the door."

"Not until you reschedule with me."

"I'm free Monday at one."

"Ha. Not what I meant."

"Look, I'm tired and I have no patience for this bullshit today. I was given the day off. Deal with it."

He smirked at her. "I am."

Exhausted and sick of dealing with him, she snapped her connection taut, paralyzing him. She stepped close, right in his face.

"Is this what you wanted, Sunshine?" she said, voice low and dangerous. "Need your daily brush with death to make it through your weekend? Fine. Let me give you the short version then. Here we are again. You can't move, you can't fight, you can't leave, and I'll ask you again why it is you're so intent on this, why you trust me so much. You give me a smartass answer that isn't anywhere near the truth, and then we both leave, pissed off and frustrated." She pushed his arm away, freeing the door. "I think that about covers it. See you Monday."

Candace slammed the door and released him.

He stayed for a minute or two. She felt him standing

outside, maybe thinking about knocking again. To what end? What was he hoping for? She sure as hell wasn't going to let him in her room. She didn't hear it when he left, but his presence faded. Bizarre. Was it a drop in temperature, or something else?

Candace rubbed her face, not understanding any of it. Instead of crawling back into bed right away, she went to the bathroom for a drink.

More knocking.

What the hell? Was her room Grand Central Station today? Everyone was suddenly so damned anxious to talk to her it couldn't wait until after she had a nap?

She jerked open the door, fully ready to tell Jackson to fuck off in clearer terms, but stopped abruptly when she took in Deborah's shocked face.

"Bad time?" she asked.

Taking a deep breath, Candace calmed herself. "No, sorry. I thought you were someone else."

"Ah, I'm guessing he was just here then."

She grimaced. "I thought he was coming back for round two of Piss Off Candace Day. Come on in."

Deborah walked in and set an armload of books on her desk. "I'm supposed to give these to you."

Candace wandered over to the pile and studied the titles. "I take it these are the books from Dr. Poznanski?"

"They are," she said, then paused. "Should I ask? This is pretty heavy stuff. Anatomy and physiology? What for?"

"A new experiment," she said as she picked up the top tome. "It looks like my ability has medical applications, so he suggested I educate myself."

"That's fabulous, Candy," Deborah said. "I can see

you're really happy about it, and I get why. It feels good to help people."

She nodded and set the book back down. "It does. It's a huge relief, actually."

Deborah smiled. "I bet. I'm glad for you."

"Thanks," she said. "Oh, before you go, can I give you some of these others back that I borrowed? I finished with two of them."

She walked to the bookshelf and pulled down the alien book and the first one in the angel series. "I see what you meant by them being educational for him."

She grinned. "It's a little funny to think about now, isn't it?"

Candace took a deep breath as she handed over the book. "It is. It made me realize how little I knew about him, though. He never really talked about himself much."

Deborah took her hand and led her to the bed to sit. "He didn't. It took me a long time to get him to trust me enough with some of it. You didn't know about his family?"

She shook her head and swallowed, letting Deborah's soothing ability seep into her.

"It was his father that was the problem. He didn't say specifically, but I'm pretty sure it was alcoholism. Judging by how withdrawn Adrian was, I can tell there was some abuse involved. All he ever told me for sure was that his mom and little brother disappeared when he was twelve. I don't know if they died or if she left, but I didn't push him. And then when I had to break it off with him, well…" Her eyebrows knitted together. "He wasn't about to let me back in after that. For what it's worth, we weren't ever serious the way you two were. We were friends more than anything.

Just, sometimes, a little more than that."

Candace squeezed her hand. "I'm sorry."

Deborah frowned. "For what?"

She sighed. "For being so wrapped up in myself. I didn't stop to think about other people in all of this. This is hard for anyone who knew him, not just me. I never even asked how you were feeling or if you were okay. You've been bombarded with everyone else's pain, mine probably more than most. It was very selfish of me."

Deborah's gaze settled on the floor. "Oh. It's okay, Candy. That's part of who I am. I'm an empath. Other people's emotions are what I do."

"But it's not okay, Deborah. You have feelings too." Candace stared at her. "Does no one ever ask you about yourself?"

She shrugged.

Stunned, the guilt crashed down on her and she grabbed Deborah, hugging her tightly. "That's not right. Everyone needs someone." Empathy flooded her, and she tried to wrap that care around her friend. It wasn't fair that someone so giving had no one to go to with her own problems, her own worries, her own sadness.

Deborah's fingers dug into Candace's back as the first sob shook free. How long had she been holding on to that? She smoothed her friend's hair and let her cry, determined to care for someone she neglected in her own egotistical misery.

It took a long time, but finally Deborah settled.

Candace pulled away and brushed the tears from her cheeks. "Better?"

She sniffed and nodded. "Yes, thank you."

"If you ever need to talk, about anything, you come find me, okay?"

Another nod.

"I mean it. You're the same as anyone else when it comes to this. You can't keep it all to yourself."

Deborah took a long, deep breath, then stood. "Thank you. I have to get back to work, though. I've already been away too long."

Candace walked her to the door and opened it. "Well, I'll be here when you need me."

Deborah paused in the doorway and turned, taking Candace's hand and squeezing gently. "Thank you, Candy. I mean it. You have no idea."

She squeezed back and grinned. "I have an inkling, but you're welcome."

When she was gone, Candace yawned, totally drained. Hopefully no one else would come knocking. It took all of two seconds for her to fall back to sleep.

THREE WEEKS.

Jackson didn't speak to her for three weeks.

Not so much as a "let's do this, Sugar Plum," or anything.

At first, it felt like a blessing. His silence made it easy for her to concentrate.

Then, it became an annoyance, a challenge to get him to say anything. Even so much as a curse when she'd blast him with a direct hit to the face would've been a success.

By the third week, she missed the sound of his voice. She

missed the stupid nickname he gave her. She missed the thrill of meeting his sarcastic barbs with ones of her own.

Worst of all, she was sorry she pushed him. If she hadn't pressed so hard for him to admit he cared about her...

How stupid. Why would she even want that? If he did give in, tell her how he felt, she would have to do the same. Candace didn't know if she could.

But she missed him. Terribly. More than she thought she ever might.

"Why don't you just tell him, Candy Cane?" Chloe said through the headphones. It was her final treatment.

She didn't respond, instead downing half a gallon of water.

Chloe sucked in a sharp breath as the repercussions echoed through her. "Don't try to change the subject, Candace," she said through gritted teeth. "I know that's why you did that."

"Why are you pushing this?" she whispered. "Telling him anything never does me any good. He won't care. He'll laugh at me, and then I'll never hear the end of it. It'll be one more way for him to make me miserable. So drop it, okay?"

"He might surprise you."

"Not this time he won't. Not with this."

"Would you prefer he find someone else?"

Candace choked, not wanting to think about it. "Nothing's stopping him. I'm sure he's —"

"No. He hasn't. Just you, Candace."

The jug stopped halfway to her mouth. "What?"

"He hasn't been with anyone else. I'd see it on him. He's two rooms away from you and I can feel him as clearly as I can you."

Jackson hadn't been with anyone else since they... what? Surely he could find another willing party. She knew why she hadn't, but him?

"That's ridiculous," she said. "He hasn't even talked to me in three weeks. He won't go anywhere near me. I hardly think he's —"

"He is. I don't know what else to tell you, Candace. He might be able to hide it from you, but he can't hide it from me."

She had no idea what to think about that. Should she think anything? It wasn't like she could force him to do something about it. If it was true, she had to wait for him to take the first step.

"I'm done helping him, Chloe. He doesn't want me to. I can't fight that battle forever. I'm tired of it."

She sighed through the headphones. "Okay, well, I'll let it go then. How's the sensitivity?"

Candace laid back on the cot and closed her eyes. "I'd say another thirty minutes and they can come hook me up."

"I'll let them know to prep, then."

She wandered out of the clinic two hours later, more tired than she was the week before. Grateful it was almost over, she came to a dead stop in the hallway.

Final testing. Would they put them through that again? Was it necessary? The Showcase and Gauntlet she didn't mind so much. But the last one...

Would she have to face the Mirror again?

She rubbed a hand across her face and kept on walking. Really, what could the Mirror show her that would be any worse than what she faced in her dreams on a nightly basis? What horror could it inflict on her that she hadn't already lived through or done to herself?

As she walked, she considered her last trip through. She thought about it endlessly during her weeks in bed, walking through that wasteland of ruined corpses over and over, wondering how much truth it actually showed.

Was it real? They called it the Mirror of Truth, but what was it, really? Was there a Super with the power to see the future? Certainly there were ones that could read her emotions, maybe some hiding somewhere that could read minds, but the future?

She stopped again when it struck her.

No. Not the future.

It showed her the greatest fear she harbored in her heart; one she hadn't told a single person about. Because of what they called it and how real the visions were, she took it as something certain; something she could do nothing about.

In believing it, and doing what she'd done, she made it a self-fulfilling prophecy.

What would it show her? What did she fear most?

The problem plagued her all the way to the dining hall and through the entire meal. The lighthearted conversation of the Pavo Team did nothing to alleviate her preoccupation. Even with Gabe off of crutches and well on his way back to one hundred percent thanks to her treatments, she couldn't shake the feeling she was missing something important.

It wasn't until he entered the dining hall that she realized what it was.

Even though the pull was the same, he never once looked at her. Not even a glance.

She knew exactly what the Mirror would show her.

But she had no idea how to fight it.

How do you keep something you don't have?

JACKSON WASN'T at their Monday practice. She waited for thirty minutes and he never showed. She didn't track him down after changing out of her skinsuit. There was little point.

Wednesday was the same. She spent her time in the pool, lingering longer than normal in hopes he'd turn up there instead. He didn't. She saw him briefly at meals, but aside from that, he completely avoided her.

Thursday was the last checkup. God, she was sick to death of needles and scanning machines. She waited in the exam room for the results, more than ready to be done with it.

"Everything looks as it should, Miss Bristol," Dr. Poznanski said when he sat. "I think your group is ready for final testing."

"Again?"

"It's a necessity, I'm afraid. We aren't going to place you in the field without total confidence in your physical, mental, and emotional stability."

"I understand."

"Then you know what comes next."

"When?"

"We'll begin tomorrow morning, foregoing the Showcase this time. I think we're all satisfied with your previous demonstrations in that aspect. Mr. Lawrence is excused from that as well, so you'll both report to the Gauntlet first thing."

Tomorrow morning. She repressed the shudder trying to wiggle free.

"Is there a problem, Miss Bristol?"

She let out a puff of air. "No. No problem."

He considered her for a moment. "You're concerned about the psychological aspect, I take it?"

Candace closed her eyes. "A little, yes."

Dr. Poznanski offered her a reassuring smile. "I think, given everything else you've come through in the past few months, you shouldn't have a problem."

"And if I do?"

The smile faded. "It's better to focus on success. Visualization is often a key factor for those who achieve their goals."

She tried very, very hard not to roll her eyes. His advice was right up there with "if you can dream it, you can be it" and "reach for the stars" on the cheesy scale.

His smile returned and he stood to go. "I think you'll be fine, Miss Bristol. Get a good night's sleep and have a hearty breakfast. I'll see you tomorrow."

There was nothing left to do but worry.

CHAPTER 15

SERGEANT WILCOX stood at the controls of the Gauntlet once again.

"Welcome back, you two," he said. "Can't say I expected to see you both again so soon, but, it is what it is. You're familiar with the drill so we won't waste time on that this morning. I'm sure you're both ready to get it over with."

Candace glanced at Jackson, but he said nothing.

"All right, Miss Bristol, you're up. Let's—"

The door to the staging area flew open. Amir entered, wearing his skinsuit and a serious expression. "You're both needed."

"Mr. Jones, maybe there's a better time to—"

"Now," he said, interrupting Sgt. Wilcox. "There's an incident, and we need both of them immediately."

Candace stared. Was he serious? "You mean in the

field?"

"Yes. Let's go. We need to hurry."

She didn't question it further and followed him out. They ran down the hall, heading for the hangar.

"Where are we going?" Jackson asked, and the sound of his voice nearly made her miss a step.

"The International Auto Show in San Jose. Reports say there's more than one, so we need all the help we can get."

She glanced at Jackson out of the corner of her eye. "Think you can hold your breakfast down for a little trip this morning, Sunshine?"

He didn't even look at her.

Her steps slowed, and she fell behind. Why? Why wouldn't he so much as acknowledge her presence? He might as well have slapped her.

"Candace!" Amir called from down the hall. "Let's move!"

She pushed it all away and focused. Just do the job. Nothing else matters.

Jackson didn't need the mask anymore. It seemed he was acclimated to traveling by shuttle. They were in the air less than four minutes. The scene was similar to the one in Portland, only the trail of bodies began outside. They were crushed under cars, crumpled on the sidewalk, everywhere. The law enforcement perimeter was half a mile away, leaving them to run the remaining distance after Amir got the latest on the situation from an NSA representative.

"There are two this time," he called back as they approached the outside of the convention center. "Both Physicals. Both telekinetic."

"Do we know where?" True asked.

"At last check, in the main hall." He grimaced as they

came to a stop and looked around. "We follow the carnage."

Candace fought back a gag as she took it all in. Half a dozen cars had been flung through the glass front of the building, plowing down people like bowling pins. At least a dozen corpses littered the grounds, some of them children.

They picked their way through silently, crouching behind overturned vehicles, and listening for any sound of activity. The loud crunching of metal screeched inside the building.

"We need to get them out here, in the open," Amir said. "We'll have a better shot at taking them down. There are fewer places to hide."

Candace frowned. "If these guys are HEX, they aren't concerned with hiding. If they know we're out here, it's likely they'll come to us. They're drawn to people, remember?"

True nodded in agreement. "She's right. We just need to announce our presence and we'll have them."

"So how do we get them out here then?" Allen asked.

"I can do it," Jackson said.

Her jaw fell open. "And how do you intend to do that?"

"I'm pretty fast when I want to be, Sugar Plum. Remember?"

She tried not to let the nickname affect her, but, damn, she missed it. "So, what, burn tag?"

"Burn tag?" He raised an eyebrow at her.

She gave him a look. "Think about that for a second, Sunshine."

A flicker of a smile turned up the corner of his mouth. "That sounds about right, yeah."

"You kids want to let us in on the game?" Amir asked, a little irritated.

She waved off the amusement. "You're better off showing them, Jackson. It's quicker."

She blinked, and he was gone, reappearing on the far side of the fountain.

"What the fuck?" Allen said.

"Yeah, that's about all the explanation I've gotten too," she grumbled and motioned him back.

Amir gave Jackson an appraising look when he returned. "You've been holding out on us."

She snorted. "Join the club."

Amir pinched the bridge of his nose and sighed. "Whatever. Okay. Jackson, go in, get their attention, get out. Lead them to us. Do. Not. Engage. Understand that? We want to take them alive if possible."

He gave a single nod and disappeared.

"Allen," Amir continued. "Get to cover. Stay to the concrete side of the building if you can. If we can get you in close, we'll try, but you're going to be more useful in recovery here. I'll stick with you until they're in the open. True, get topside. Take Candy Cane with you."

"No."

"What?"

Candace shook her head, reinforcing herself and pointing to the fountain in the center of the open entrance. "I need to be there. They won't see me. And if they get out this way and need motivation to come a little closer, I can give them that."

"You can't stand out in the open, honey," True said.

"I won't be." She flashed a smile and darted for the pond. Maybe it wasn't the most sanitary hiding place in the world, but it would do.

It was only a foot deep, but it was enough. The eight thin streams of water that arced across it kept the pool moving enough that her own shimmery camouflage wouldn't be detected. She stilled herself and waited.

The minutes dragged by and she was starting to wonder if something happened to Jackson.

Glass crashed as another car went sailing out of the convention center. Her mind raced ahead, calculating where it would land, if she was safe. She didn't move. The frame of some luxury sports car crumpled as it struck the pavement and cartwheeled out into the street.

"Where are youuuuuuu…" a male voice sang out into the open air, drawing closer. "I know you're not a ghost, speedy. Am I seeing ANGELs perhaps? Oh goody. New toys to break."

Another higher-pitched voice chuckled. "Don't be selfish, D. I want to play, too."

They stepped into view, right at the edge of the pool.

Don't move. Don't breathe. Wait for Amir and True.

Where was Jackson?

A fireball ripped through the air, knocking one of them to the ground, screaming. It came from behind her, out of her line of sight. *Keep moving, Jackson. Don't stop.*

The other man, still whirling around, searching for a target, doubled over as a solid mass of air struck his gut. The one called "D" flung himself into the water, still on fire. She pressed herself against the edge and concentrated. It was her chance.

Her ropes ensnared D, effectively trapping him. He screamed and thrashed, but she didn't let up. The second one pulled at him with his telekinesis, fighting her hold with the water while dodging attacks from the others. Enraged, he started flinging cars in all directions, smashing them back into the buildings and around the courtyard.

She saw Jackson the instant the enemy did.

He was on fire in every sense of the word: his hair, his clothes. He overheated while pouring on the speed, though how she knew, she couldn't say. The destroyed sports car lifted into the air.

Damn it, she was going to have to break cover.

Unable to maintain her camouflage and the ropes, she dropped her cloaking and blasted Jackson with a full bubble, instantly dousing him and throwing him out of the way of the oncoming projectile. The man whirled on her, screeching, and she dove away before one of the concrete spheres surrounding the fountains could connect with her head. It clipped her shoulder.

First hit.

No more hesitation. A single bullet was all it took and he went down.

A wild, tortured wail broke through her haze.

Her ropes. She dropped her ropes.

She flew through the air as someone shoved her out of the way. A car crashed down in the place she stood not seconds before. She scrambled to her feet when she heard the moan. Someone was under there. Someone who saved her.

She didn't think. She didn't have to.

The rope snapped taught.

Objects around her shuddered, fighting to fly into the air.

But she wouldn't let them. Even the man's brain was under her command.

Someone ran behind her. Jackson. He was all right. She saw another out of the corner of her eye. Amir. True flew by her in a gust of wind.

That left one person.

Candace closed in on the telekinetic, committing everything about him to memory. He was tall and thin, with wiry brown hair to his shoulders, parts of him singed and burnt from the fire. What was left of his black t-shirt and slacks dripped water, and it puddled around his combat boots. She etched his appearance into her brain.

He could join the other ghosts in her head.

His spine folded backwards, his legs wrapping around him, curling into a ball. She pressed the water together, condensing it, letting it crack his bones, tear his muscles, rip him apart and pull him back together.

She would not look away. Never again. She would keep it as a reminder of the monster inside, the one she let loose as yet another friend was torn from her.

When he finally stopped screaming, Candace sunk to the pavement.

Someone jerked her up by an arm.

"Don't wallow!" True yelled at her. "Allen needs you, so get your shit together and help him if you can."

Candace shook herself. "He's alive?"

"Barely."

They sprinted back to the wreckage. Allen lay beneath it, what had once been the front end of a silver electric car cutting across him at the stomach. She knelt beside him, unsure if there was anything she could even do.

"We need to get this off of him," True said, gathering wind around her.

"No, don't!" Candace said. "Don't touch anything. You move that car and it could kill him."

The breeze stilled.

She pushed the hair away from his face and looked at him. He met her gaze without any trouble. "So what's the other guy look like?" he said, straining.

"Don't talk," she said, gently. "Let me see what we're dealing with."

Trying to keep a grip on her panic, she pulled inward, focusing on the water within him. It didn't take long to see there was little she could do for him.

She laid a palm against his cheek and tried to smile. "Allen, I'm so sorry. It's my fault this happened. I didn't keep a hold on him. You saved my life." She took a shaky breath and tried to swallow the tears. "I wanted to return the favor, but…"

He sighed and closed his eyes. "It's okay, Candy Cane. It doesn't hurt. I'm guessing it went through, huh?"

She nodded.

True and Amir sat beside him, across from her.

"Suppose this is what I get for not following orders, eh, Boss?" Allen coughed a little. He wouldn't last much longer. She could at least slow the blood loss, give him time to say goodbye.

Candace tuned out their words, focusing on keeping Allen alive for as long as she could. A gentle touch on her shoulder stirred her, and she looked up at Jackson.

He nodded once.

Allen was pale, barely breathing.

"Let me go, Candy Cane," he whispered. His eyes fluttered open and rested on her face. "If it matters at all, it was worth the trouble."

The tears slipped free as she bent and laid a kiss on his forehead. "Thank you."

She released him, his last breath warm against her skin.

CANDACE DIDN'T speak again that morning. She stayed silent, watching Amir give statements, and arrange for transportation of both Allen and the gen-evos back to the compound.

Jackson sat beside her on the way back, allowing True and Amir to have their space and share their grief. Despite his warmth, everything still felt cold.

She would have to tell Gabe. She needed to do at least that much. He might hate her afterwards, but it was on her. Allen died to save her.

More blood on her hands. More reasons for everyone to steer clear of her.

When they disembarked, she left the hangar with a nod from Dr. Poznanski. She would hear about it later, for sure. Leaving her skinsuit back in the changing room, all she wanted was a long swim with no one else around.

When he touched her arm, she closed her eyes, afraid to move, not wanting to lose the moment.

"It wasn't your fault, Sugar Plum."

Everything in his touch pulled at her, but his words couldn't ease her ache. "He died because I wasn't fast enough, because I didn't kill the one when I had the chance."

"You were following orders."

"I followed orders last time and Gil died. I followed orders this time and Allen died. I try to save people and it ends up killing them, Jackson." She shrugged out of his grasp. "You have every reason in the world to be afraid of me. I don't blame you one bit."

He didn't follow her when she walked away.

The pool would have to wait. Gabe had to come first.

He answered her knock on his door with a broad smile. "Hey Candy Cane, what's —"

The look on her face was enough to render him silent.

How she got through the story, she couldn't say. She started from the beginning, from the disruption in the Gauntlet. She told him everything, not stopping until she was saved from the flying car.

"Allen," her voice dropped to a whisper. "He pushed me out of the way. But he…"

She couldn't look at him.

"What are you saying, Candace? What happened?"

The tears refused to stay back any longer. Candace covered her face with her hands. "I couldn't save him. There was too much damage. I couldn't… there wasn't anything I could have…" Her words died away, drowned in helpless sorrow.

Gabe said nothing.

She stood up and headed for the door. "I'm sorry. I'm leaving. I just… I had to be the one to tell you because it's my fault. It's my fault that everyone dies, and you should probably get as far away from me as you possibly —"

He yanked her back and surrounded her in his arms. "Please don't, Candy. Please don't go."

She choked on a sob as she clung to him. "You should

hate me. At least be angry with me. Something. Anything."

"It wasn't your fault. He was supposed to stay put. That's what he's supposed to do in situations like these. He knew, Candy. He took the risk."

"He should have let me die!"

Gabe pulled back and held her face. "Would you have let him if the situation were reversed?"

She shook her head.

"Then why would you think he could?"

Candace had no answer for that. At least, none she dared to say aloud. So many people were afraid of her anymore, she wouldn't doubt any one of them would have let her take the hit in that situation.

But Allen hadn't. Another ally gone.

"It didn't hurt when he went," she said as his arms closed around her again. "I made sure of that. He got to say goodbye."

At last, his tears fell. They dripped off his chin, into her hair. She absorbed them immediately, sharing his pain and loss.

"They haven't said yet, but I know these two were HEX," she said, not letting go of him. "I swear, Gabe, I will find who's responsible for this horror, and they will wish they'd never been born. For you, for me, for everyone that's died over this, I will show them what suffering is. There will be no second chances for them. Not when I find them."

CHAPTER 16

POZNANSKI WAITED two full days.

Sunday night, a note slipped under Candace's door informing her that her last finalization screening would be Monday at ten o'clock.

Because she hadn't been through enough already? Because she hadn't spoken with one of the staff psychologists for over two hours recounting the tragedy in San Jose? Because her chat with Deborah couldn't assuage her guilt? Because apparently they still needed to fuck with her some more?

The Mirror of Truth waited. They weren't going to give her a pass.

All of the SAGEs waited in the control room that morning, each of them looking as sick as she felt at having to go through it again. But Candace had a secret weapon. She knew their trick. It was going to be awful to endure, but her suspicions about what that thing really was prepared her.

"We'll draw for order," Dr. Poznanski said. "I know you're all anxious about this, and I don't want anyone to feel singled out." He borrowed a hat from one of the four guards and tore up five strips of paper, writing a number on each and tossing them around. His arm extended towards them. "Choose your fate."

When the others hesitated, Candace huffed and stepped forward, drawing a number. The others followed suit.

She unfolded the strip and glanced down.

"Two," she said.

Jackson drew the short straw.

"Oh well," he said with a smirk. "So much for saving the best for last." As he stepped up to the door, a dark cloud settled over Candace. She needed to say something to him. Anything. Her brain grasped for words, but none came.

It opened and closed behind him.

Too late. Her heart filled with dread.

There wasn't much room to pace, but she gave it her best shot. After fifteen minutes of waiting, she was ready to rip down the door. Her foreboding was borderline panic. Something was wrong.

"Dr. Poznanski," one of the control techs said, and her stomach dropped. "We have a problem."

"A problem?" He strode over to the panel in question, his face immediately registering alarm when he scanned the monitor. "That's not possible."

"It's off the charts, sir. If it continues, this level of heat…"

"Let me in that room," Candace said, no longer willing

to wait.

Dr. Poznanski turned towards her, frowning. "Miss Bristol, while I appreciate your concern here, I don't think—"

"No," she cut him off. "You *can't* think about this, because you don't know. I do. Something's wrong. He needs my help."

"You can't help him in this test, Miss Bristol."

Anger, raw and absolute surged up from inside her. "The hell I can't. If you don't open this goddamn door this minute and let me in there…"

"We have a means of controlling the situation. If Mr. Lawrence is unable to rein this in, he may have to be neutralized."

She knew what that meant.

She was going to lose him.

Permanently.

Candace squeezed her eyes shut, aware of the consequences that might come with what she was about to do. "Open. That. Door. I won't tell you again. He can't do this on his own. No one can. It's bullshit, and he doesn't know. The game is rigged so that no matter what you do, you lose."

She opened her eyes, fully connected. "You lose if you try to go it alone."

There was that flicker of fear. She'd seen it enough times to recognize it when she saw it.

For once, they had every reason to be terrified.

"I can't open the door. No one can survive the heat in there."

Wrong answer.

Candace snapped every single drop of water in the room to attention. Eight bodies froze at her command. She kept her eyes firmly fixed on Dr. Poznanski.

"I am getting in that room one way or another. You can let me in by choice, or I will take it by force. Listen to me very closely. I will *not* lose him this way. I. Won't. Turn on the water in there. I'll be fine. And if not, so much the better for everyone else if I go with him."

She dropped her hold, but not her piercing stare.

Dr. Poznanski didn't move for a moment, processing her words, perhaps.

"Mr. Cortez, turn on the water." He picked his way across to the door and punched in all but one number on the keypad, then turned to her. "Ten minutes. That's all you have. After that, we shut him down."

The door opened, emitting a blast of heat that made her flinch.

But she was *not* going to lose him.

The door immediately closed behind her and she called to the water, wrenching it free from warped pipes in the ceiling, and formed a protective bubble around her to block out the worst of the invisible blaze. Liquid hissed against the floor wherever it touched. The Mirror was the only light in the room, but orange, instead of her signature blue. She didn't see Jackson.

"Get away from me! Don't come any closer!"

It came from one of the dark corners.

He sounded on the verge of insanity.

"I'm not going anywhere."

"You shouldn't be here! You can't see me like this."

See him like that? Like what? "It's the Mirror, Jackson. It's not real."

"Get out of here, Sugar Plum. You'll regret it."

"I'd regret it more if I left. After what I did to get in here, you're going to shut up and listen to me. For once in your goddamn life, please, just listen."

Silence.

Taking a deep breath, she stepped into the edges of the light surrounding the mirror. The color shifted, the orange fading until it was a soft white. "It isn't what they tell us it is, you know. Want to hear my theory?" She shook her head. "Dumb question. Of course you don't. I'm going to tell you anyway." Candace inched closer. "See, I had a lot of time on my hands recently, and reliving my last trip in this room occupied a good chunk of it. Do you know what I saw then? I saw myself out of control, unable to stop taking from others, draining them dry. I saw what I could be capable of. I saw myself killing the people I loved the most. And I swore, then and there, that I would protect them. I would protect them by keeping them away from me. I thought they would be safe if I did that. Then, there would be no one for me to hurt, and they could stop me without hesitation if I couldn't stop myself." She paused, pushing past those horrible visions.

"By doing that, by taking what I saw as truth, I made it exactly that. I walked out of here believing that what I saw would happen. But now... Now I think I understand. The name is a lie. Mirrors can't show you anything but a reflection. It doesn't tell the future. It doesn't know the truth. It reflects what you *fear* to be true. When you accept that fear as reality, you're done."

He was closer. She could feel him behind her. How much time was left?

"But that's my theory, of course. Theories require evidence.

That means you have to experiment. I don't need a mirror to tell me what I fear most. I already know."

She paused briefly. "But there's a problem. I can't prove it wrong on my own. I need help."

As she took another step forward, the light shifted again, definitely blue.

"Do you want to see, Jackson?" Her words came out barely above a whisper. "Do you want to know the thing I'm most afraid of?"

She knew he was there, standing just beyond the reach of the light, but she didn't turn. Instead, she stepped forward again, arm out, ready to dive into another nightmare.

The surface of the Mirror rippled, distorting her reflection until it showed her what she knew it would.

Jackson backed away from her, that horrible flicker of fear in his eyes, the same as it was in everyone's. No matter what she did, how she begged, he ran. He would get as far from her as he could. He would never call her Sugar Plum again or frustrate her to the point of wanting to tear her hair out. He retreated. He was terrified of her and the monster within her.

"So, you see now," she said, silent tears slipping free. "Everyone is afraid of me, Sunshine. Everyone has been at one point or another. Even Gabe was afraid I was mad at him because he told me to keep away from Adrian that day. In all of this, everything that's happened, only one person has refused to be afraid of me. I've never once seen that hesitation in you. You know what kind of monster I am, you've seen it with your own eyes, and yet, still, I never saw your fear. Not once. If I ever did…" She choked and tried to recover, but her voice was no longer steady. "I know, without any doubt, that I'd be done. I can't live like that. I can't live a life where no one will so much as touch me anymore because they're scared of what I can do."

She took one more deep breath. "So the experiment begins. This is where you come in. I can't prove this one wrong. Only you can."

Silence.

"Are you afraid of me, Jackson?"

Her protective bubble, little more than a few inches from her skin, fell away.

But the temperature in the room had dropped. It was barely warmer than normal.

"You're wrong, Sugar Plum." The words he whispered in her ear bit into her like a million daggers. She closed her eyes against it, trying to pretend she hadn't heard him.

"But not why you think I might be."

Confused, she tried to turn, but he held her in place, his hands gripping her upper arms.

"I'm not afraid of what you can do. It's what you make me *feel* that terrifies me, Candace. I've spent most of my life keeping everyone out, and I was damned good at it. But you? I didn't stand a chance."

She couldn't speak. Her thoughts simply wouldn't settle into anything resembling coherent.

"I've hated you for a long time. I hated you for making me want someone. I hated you for being with Adrian. I hated you for what you dissolved into after he was gone. I couldn't stand it, Candace. No one thought I was worth helping, and I believed it. And then you helped me, for no other reason except that you could. You caught me in almost every lie I've ever told you. You challenge everything I say. You took everything I thought was true and turned it upside down."

Candace held her breath.

"Afraid doesn't come close to describing this, Sugar Plum. Nowhere near."

What came next? That wasn't at all helpful. If he actually was afraid of her, didn't that mean the Mirror was right? But, it still seemed wrong. She wasn't sure anymore.

"What did it show you?"

"It showed me that the monster I am inside is on the outside too."

She closed her eyes. "You're no more a monster than I am."

"If I'm not a monster, I don't know who I am."

They stood there a moment, debating the next move.

"Jackson, I'm going to turn around and prove you're not a monster."

"Don't."

"I have to. If we walk out of this room not knowing for sure, we'll both find ways to make these things true."

His hold on her arms loosened.

Eyes shut tight. Candace turned slowly. Her pulse was racing. What if she was wrong? What if all of it was for nothing, and when she looked he was gone? What if—

His lips, soft and warm, closed over hers, chasing away all the what-ifs. There was no room left for doubt with him surrounding her. His arms were so strong, so familiar, as though it was the most natural thing in the world. It was completion. It was wholeness. It was the match that lit up the darkness and grew into a conflagration so bright, any shadows that remained scattered and disappeared.

Gently, he pulled away and sighed against her mouth. "I

did my part. Your turn."

Her eyes fluttered open and she looked at him, scanning his face after catching his eyes for a moment. She forced a frown. "Well, that's… disappointing."

He tensed, slightly panicked. "What?"

Candace pushed the hair away from his forehead and trailed her fingertips down the side of his jaw. "Oh, nothing. I just thought you might've been kinda hot with a pair of horns or something."

He choked as she cracked a smile.

"You're fine, Sunshine. It's the same old jerkface you've always had."

At that, he grabbed her and crushed her against him, cutting off her giggles.

She didn't even pretend to care when the cavalry rushed in from either side of the room.

Neither did he.

THEY SAT through the exit interview together. No way in hell was she about to let him out of her sight after that. Dr. Poznanski wasn't as upset as she thought he would be, his expression far more curious than anything else.

They talked about what she did in the control room, and Jackson laughed at the full-on crazy she went when they wouldn't let her in initially.

"It's not funny," she nudged him in the ribs.

"Not funny?" He chuckled. "Maybe a little. But, why, Candy? How could you possibly know there was a problem before they did?"

She frowned and looked at the floor. "I don't know exactly. The same way I know when you're standing outside my door. The same way I feel it when you walk into a room. I can't explain it. Ever since…" Her face heated. "Ever since that first time, that's how it's been. Is it not the same for you?" She risked a glance at him. She wasn't sure what would happen since they'd admitted to their feelings.

He scrubbed his face with one hand while entwining the fingers of the other with hers. "Yeah, it's the same."

"Interesting," Dr. Poznanski said, leaning back in his chair. "I had no idea the new treatments would bring this level of imprinting with it. It's quite unprecedented."

Her spine straightened. "What? But I thought that was a one-time deal? Since I already…" She winced, realizing it was too late to take back the thought once it was out there. Jackson's grip on her hand loosened. Shit. They would have to talk about that later. For the moment, she squeezed his fingers and inched closer to him on the couch, hoping he'd understand.

"A new round of treatments brings new possibilities with it," Dr. Poznanski said. "Each one is a type of rebirth, so it stands to reason it's entirely possible. Everything about you is stronger now, emotions included. It hadn't occurred to me that imprinting could happen again, but it makes sense. Your protective instincts kicked into overdrive, Miss Bristol. Had I known, I would've been less hesitant to stop you."

She gulped and closed her eyes. "I'm only half sorry about what I did. I knew there would be consequences, but I did it anyway."

"Using your abilities against a staff member is a very

serious offense," he said.

"I know."

"But you did so knowing this? You weighed the outcome rationally?"

Candace nodded. "I did. I couldn't see any other alternative. I wasn't out of control. The opposite, actually. I knew exactly what I was doing. Whatever punishment you think is fair, I fully accept, but…" she took a deep breath and looked at Jackson. "I will never regret what I did."

Dr. Poznanski was silent for a long time. She had no idea what to expect.

"Well, there was no harm done, and given how the situation could have gone, I think we may owe you a debt of gratitude for what you did today. Without your interference, Mr. Lawrence would likely no longer be with us, and the ANGEL Project can't afford to lose anyone at the moment. As you both appear to be perfectly adjusted, even after viewing the Mirror a second time, I see no reason to withhold approval for field work."

Candace exhaled in relief at the same moment Jackson did.

"I also think we'll have to re-examine the testing process, specifically where SAGEs are concerned. Given your experiences this morning, I think we'll forego putting the others through it until we can devise a better method to test emotional stability in trainees. As the damage to the room makes it unusable for the time being anyway, this seems like a logical conclusion," he continued. "I may ask for your input regarding this later, if you have any to offer."

She was stunned. They were getting off with little more than a warning?

"Unless you have anything else to add, you may go."

They didn't linger, bolting for the door as soon as he said the word.

The walk down the hall was awkward. Neither of them were sure what to say. There was so much to talk about, it was impossible to decide where to begin.

Rather than initiate conversation, Jackson slipped his hand into hers. She ignored the surprised looks from those they passed in the corridors, letting him lead her where he would.

They stopped outside his room.

An old ghost whispered to her, pulling her attention to the next door down. As Jackson unlocked his, she glanced at Adrian's old room.

She needed to let go. There was nothing there for her besides hurt and regret.

He touched her face and she met his eyes.

Jackson stood in the doorway, watching her, waiting for her to make a decision. "Your choice, Sugar Plum. Take your time."

Candace smiled sadly and nodded. She stepped towards the room she spent so many nights in, curled up beside someone she cared for so much, but barely knew in hindsight. Her fingers brushed the handle, and when she looked up, she could almost see Adrian standing there, grinning at her the way he always did— not the horror that found her in nightmares, but the way he had been, kind and loving. Her arms dropped to her sides and she closed her eyes.

"Goodbye, Adrian," she whispered.

After one last moment, she turned away, leaving the specter alone to sink back into the corners of her memories.

INSIDE HIS room, Candace was suddenly nervous. She wasn't used to the gentle side of Jackson.

He sat down on the bed and waited for her. "Take a look around, Sugar Plum. You've reached the inner sanctum."

The joke elicited a smile from her, however small. Candace turned away from him and looked at her surroundings. She ran her fingers over the top of the desk as she passed it, noting the careful placement of every object on its surface. His bookshelf was filled with everything from science fiction to biographies to poetry, all categorized and alphabetized by author.

But there were no pictures. Even she kept a photo album in her nightstand, but he had nothing.

Then she remembered; he said he had no family.

"Find what you were looking for?" he asked, standing behind her.

"I don't think any of these things tell me much, Sunshine." Candace turned to face him. "But that's probably on purpose, right?"

He smirked a little and rested his palm against her cheek. "You think you're pretty smart, huh?"

She shrugged. "I do okay." When he leaned in to kiss her, she stopped him. "We are going to have to talk about all this. You understand that, right?"

"Do we have to do it this very second?"

She bit back a giggle. "Why? Did you have something else in mind?"

"Yes, and none of it involves talking, unless it's you screaming my name."

Candace raised an eyebrow. "That's mighty presumptive on your part, Sunshine."

"I prefer to think of it as realistic. Now are you about done, or should I just invoke the no-takebacks rule?"

"I'll never be done talking, you know."

He gave her the last word, stealing the rest of them with a kiss so tender, so full of longing, that speaking became unnecessary. There was so much intensity in the embrace, Candace thought she might burn from the inside out.

But he didn't stop there.

His hands, calloused from hard work, slid up under her shirt, removing it and tossing it aside. His lips traveled down her neck as he unhooked her bra. It too fell away, followed by the rest of her clothing. When she met his gaze, flames danced in his eyes, a smoldering hunger that was only for her. She peeled away the fabric clinging to his hardened muscles, intent on learning every inch of him, every curve, every dip, every surface.

Jackson pressed against her. The shelves of the bookcase dug into her back, but she barely noticed. When she lifted up, he carried her away, laying her down on cool sheets that held his scent, earthy and warm. His mouth and hands explored her body; each kiss a silent prayer, every touch a blessing. She gasped when his lips met the center of her desire. His tongue danced across her flesh, a whirlwind of sensation igniting inside her. Her back arched, her head spun, unable to see straight from the delicious waves of pleasure wrenching his name from her throat as she came for him.

He worked his way back to her, slowly, giving her time to catch her breath. When his eyes came into focus, she touched his face but couldn't speak.

When he slipped inside her, it was so gentle she nearly cried. Each movement was so careful, so calculated, she couldn't fathom how he could be so in control.

"You saved me, Candace," he whispered into her hair. "You saved me from myself."

She clung to him. Everything about him was open to her in that moment. Anything she wanted, needed from him, she could take and he would give.

She ran her hands through his hair. "It was nothing you haven't done for me, and nothing I wouldn't do again in a heartbeat."

He rested his forehead against hers, fighting to draw out the moment. "Why, Candace? Why would you risk that for me?"

She sucked in a sharp breath as he pulsed inside her. Thoughts and feelings swirled together, creating a force that tore down her walls and dragged her below the surface.

"Because…" She pulled him close, rising up on a current of uncontrolled passion. "Because I love you."

His release was immediate, intense, filling up the cracks in her heart with light and warmth and absolute trust.

He didn't need words to express how total his surrender was: she felt it in the tears that slid down his cheeks and onto the pillow beside her. She held him, allowing him to take it in, to know that she was there, that nothing, nothing would ever make her let him go.

Not even if the world around them burned to the ground.

CHAPTER 17

MOST AWKWARD entrance ever.

Everyone stared at them. News of what happened during the Mirror test spread like wildfire. The moment they walked into the dining hall, every eye was on them, waiting for visual confirmation of the rumors.

"Jesus," she mumbled under her breath as she turned towards the serving line. "What's the big deal, anyway?"

Jackson chuckled behind her. "Well, it's pretty much a one-eighty from what it was this morning, Sugar Plum. But I think it'll be old news before either one of us is used to it."

She frowned as she took her plate of food. "Thanks for the vote of confidence."

"Don't get all sensitive on me now, Candy Cane," he whispered in her ear. "You'll wreck your reputation."

She snorted a laugh. "Don't even go there."

Gabe didn't try to hide his grin when they sat down across from him. "So it's true then, huh?"

She gave him a blank look. "I have no idea what you're talking about."

He shifted his focus to Jackson. "It's probably too late to warn you, but you should know my cousin here might be the most stubborn person on the planet."

Jackson took a bite of pasta and swallowed. "You don't say. Well, I'm sure I can give her a run for her money on the title."

"You know I'll kill you if you fuck this up, right?"

Candace gaped at him, but Jackson didn't even flinch. "I'm aware. I think I can handle that baggage."

"Okay, Candy Cane. You can keep him," Gabe said, winking at her.

Her eyebrows lifted. "I didn't know I needed your permission."

"Just looking out for you."

She rolled her eyes. "Didn't we decide you were going to stop meddling?"

"I have no recollection of agreeing to such an arrangement."

Before she could fire back another smart reply, True and Amir slid in beside Gabe.

"There's never a dull moment with you, is there, sugar?" True said.

"I like to keep things interesting," she replied, shrugging.

Amir chuckled. "Well, you've given everyone enough to talk about for the next year in the course of a week. That's an accomplishment."

Candace stopped and watched the three remaining members of the Pavo Team. "I was wondering…" Maybe she shouldn't say anything.

Amir looked up at her with a sad smile. "Ask, Candy," he said.

She fidgeted with her fork. "I was wondering if you do anything, you know, like a memorial or anything."

They were quiet for a minute, then Gabe spoke.

"Nothing official, but we were going to go out tonight for our own send-off."

She chewed her lip. She didn't want to intrude on their grief, but part of her wanted to be there.

"You're welcome to come along if you want," True said. "You fought with him. You earned it." She glanced at Jackson. "You too, Sunshine."

He made a face, but Candace nudged his shoulder, easing the expression.

"There are a few others joining us, too," Amir said. "We're leaving right after dinner."

She nodded and lapsed into silence. They ate the rest of the meal without much conversation. Jackson's presence steadied her, and she felt ready to say her farewells to their fallen friend.

Six others joined them after the meal, including Tobias and Ella. Tobias was in the same training group as Allen, and Ella was there to support him.

Ella took one look at her and Jackson and grinned enigmatically. She didn't comment, however, sticking with Tobias and following him down the path away from the compound.

They kept to the back of the pack, and Jackson lit the way for the two of them with a small ball of flame in the palm of one hand, the other holding hers. It was strange. He barely broke contact with her since that afternoon. Was he making up for lost time, or did he need it as much as she did? His presence was a comfort, though she hadn't expected it to be. Not like that. Not so completely.

They walked for twenty minutes before they came to the place. A dried up creek ran between two small hills, a few trees on either side. Amir frowned at it.

"Damn," he said. "This used to run steady. What the hell?"

Candace knelt and set her hand against the damp earth. She saw the problem right away. A fallen tree a mile away cut off the supply. Forcing the built up water against one end of it, the log came free, sending a torrent downstream, but it would take a while to reach them.

"Give it a minute," she said as she stood. "It'll be back shortly."

The group sat on the hillside and waited, sharing stories about Allen. She didn't have much to say, but listened as each person spoke. Jackson even recounted the fight that got him rolled back in training his first week at the compound. There wasn't all that much to it, mostly Allen knocking Jackson on in his ass three times before soldiers stepped in and carted Jackson off to the clinic to recuperate.

Before too long, the creek ran smoothly in front of them, and Amir rummaged around in his backpack, passing tiny paper boats to everyone. Candace took one and used a pencil to inscribe a message on its hull.

I will be better because of you.

As they set their boats in the stream, Candace spoke to

the water, asking it to carry the vessels as far as it could. The little creek spoke of the sea, and would empty out into the ocean miles and miles away. She lingered after most of the mourners drifted away, watching the tiny boats sail off into the night. When only her, Jackson, and the Pavo Team remained, she felt it was time. Those three were closer than she had been to Allen. They needed their own moment to say goodbye.

She met Jackson at the top of the hill and headed back with him. Exhaustion seeped into her bones the closer they got to the compound. He didn't press for conversation, understanding that she needed to adjust to the new absence in her life.

There were too many of them recently.

At least, with Jackson beside her, they might be easier to handle.

SHE LAID in his arms, soaking up his ever-present warmth. Sleep was closing in fast.

"Can I ask you something?" Jackson asked, his fingers trailing up and down her arm.

"Sure," she said, yawning. She hoped it wasn't the beginning of a deep conversation.

"Why don't you wear your hair down anymore?"

Well that was about the last question she expected. She propped herself up on an elbow and looked at him. "My hair?"

"You used to wear it down when you weren't training.

Why did you stop?"

"Aside from the fact that I'm almost always training now?"

He nodded.

Her cheeks heated. She still had a residual knee-jerk reaction to telling him things, like she expected him to make fun of her for sharing the silliest details about herself. "It's… well, it's difficult to contain if I don't."

He raised an eyebrow. "Difficult to contain?"

It was really dumb. She shouldn't be embarrassed about it. Reaching up, she pulled out the pins securing the bun in place. Candace sat and combed it out with her fingers, then shook her head to give him a demonstration. The pale strands drifted up, away from her shoulders, as though they were suspended in water that wasn't there.

She bit her lip and looked away. "It floats. It's too weird even for me."

Jackson sat up and ran his fingers through it, watching it as it moved. "It's…"

She grimaced. "Weird."

He smiled and shook his head. "Not what I was going to say."

"Then what were you going to say?"

He held her face and leaned in to kiss her, so soft her eyelids fluttered closed.

"Beautiful," he said, resting his forehead against hers. "I'm not going to hurt you, Sugar Plum."

She swallowed. "I never said —"

"But you're acting like you think I might. It's okay. I know that's how it was. That was our thing."

"I'm sorry. It's hard to stop playing visceral sarcasm tennis once you start."

He chuckled. "Visceral sarcasm tennis?"

"Felt fitting at the time."

"Yeah, it has a certain ring to it," he said, then wrapped his arms around her, holding her against his chest. "Don't apologize to me though, okay? I know I was a total ass most of the time. You expect that from me."

"I wasn't much nicer to you."

Jackson sighed into her hair. "I never gave you a reason to be nicer. That's not how it's going to be any more." He pulled away and held her face between his hands. "You're safe with me."

She wanted to believe him. She wanted more than anything to trust him. "You really don't think it's weird?"

"I'm going to have to prove this to you, aren't I?"

She frowned. "Prove that you think my hair is beautiful? How could you—"

"Not that," he interrupted. "The other part."

"Oh," she said. "I don't know that it's something you can flip a switch on, Jackson. I mean, I believe you, I do, but…"

"Then let me offer you a trade. That's also kind of our thing, isn't it?"

Was it? The more she considered it, the more it felt true. "Trade how?"

He touched her hair again. "Well, you shared something about your ability, so ask me about mine."

She giggled. "How many questions do I get?"

"For tonight? One. It's already late and if I let you loose we'll never get any sleep."

She made a face at him. "Fine. How do you move so fast?"

Jackson grinned. "How long have you been wanting to ask me that?"

S.A. HUCHTON

"You can't answer a question with a question."

She blinked and he was gone. The faucet turned on in the bathroom and ran for a minute. When it shut off, she blinked again and there he was, offering her a glass of water.

"Show off," she said, accepting the offering.

"What is fire?" he asked her. "In the most basic terms."

Candace frowned. "Uh... fire results when matter combusts, releasing heat, light, and various by-products and oh my God you travel at the speed of light?" The answer washed over her even as she talked through it. "That's unbelievable!"

He laughed. "You really are pretty smart when you want to be. You're right. That's exactly what it is, but I can't do it for long. Short bursts only. I have to stop and release the heat as well."

Her mind jumped from one thing to the next as the revelation sank in. "That's why you were burning up in San Jose. You held on to the heat, right?"

"Which you helped me out with," he said. "I don't think I said thank you for that, did I?"

Candace snorted and grinned at him. "You didn't say thank you for a lot of things. We'll be here for the next week if you start now." She lifted the glass to her lips and took a long drink.

"Wow," he whispered, touching her hair. "Do that again."

She giggled. "You think that's cool, wait until you see what happens when I get dehydrated and have to refill the tank."

He pulled the glass away before she could take another sip. "What happens?"

"Nothing I can do in public, now give me back the glass."

As she reached for it, he pulled it away. "Oh really? I

think I'm going to need a demonstration."

"Give me back my water."

"First tell me what happens."

She laughed. "No. It's embarrassing."

"That's what you said about your hair, too." He set the glass on the nightstand. "Can I have a hint?"

Still laughing, she shook her head. "You're going to blow this way out of proportion, you know. Then you'll be all disappointed when you see it for yourself."

"Won't happen," he said. The shift in his tone was almost palpable. "Everything about you is always more than I expect."

"Better than the imitation, then?" She winced the moment it was out of her mouth. "Sorry, I didn't mean —"

He cut her off with a long, slow kiss that left her breathless.

"That wasn't fair," he whispered against her mouth. "I never asked her to do that, you know. I didn't think anything of it until the minute she turned into you. That was when I knew, Candace. I knew no one would ever be what you are to me. Ella paid the price for that, but there wasn't a thing I could do to change it. You were with someone else, and I needed —"

She placed a hand over his mouth. "I know. I'm sorry I brought it up. Everyone has history, Jackson. I'm not mad. I remember. I remember that a single touch from you sent me running the other way to keep from getting hurt. I know exactly what that's like. You don't have to apologize or make excuses for it."

His fingers wrapped around hers and he pulled them away from his face. "I'm not. I wanted to tell you."

She kissed him again and smiled. "I can deal with that."

They settled back into bed and she curled up against his side, listening to his heartbeat.

"You won't even give me a hint?"

Candace giggled and snuggled in closer. "Maybe I'll wake you up in the morning so you can find out for yourself."

He grumbled in response, but she was too exhausted to bait him further. Within seconds, she was sound asleep in his arms.

F O R T H E first time in weeks, the nightmares left her alone. Candace awoke slowly, cherishing the feel of the body beside her.

"Good morning, Sugar Plum." The sound of his voice rumbled through her, and she smiled.

Not ready to submit to the sun yet, she pulled the covers up over her head. "Shh. I'm enjoying this."

Jackson chuckled. "You slept like a rock last night. You can't still be tired."

"I didn't say I was tired," she giggled, her fingers creeping lower, over those amazing abs of his.

"That's dangerous territory, Candy Cane," he said.

She peeked out at his face and grinned mischievously. "Danger is my middle name."

"Right. What exactly are you planning down there? Because I've got a few ideas of my own if you need some suggestions."

"If I told you, it wouldn't be a surprise," she said. She giggled and hid again, sliding on top of him.

Candace started at his chest, leaving a trail of kisses along his skin. She teased each nipple, listening to his breathing quicken the lower she explored. By the time she found the waistband of his boxers, he was more than ready for her.

When her mouth closed over him, he spasmed in response, emitting a low, deep growl of pleasure. She took her time, batting his hands away whenever he'd try to touch her. The heat level under the blankets rose exponentially, making it hard to breathe, and eventually she gave in, emerging from the covers flushed and gasping.

He didn't give her time to recover, grabbing her and crushing his lips against hers. Jackson scrambled to relieve her of his t-shirt that she slept in. As it dropped to the floor, she straddled his legs and plunged him inside her, as desperate as he was to complete their coupling. She moaned against his mouth and ground her hips against him. He leaned her back, running a hand over her breasts, her stomach, down to the heat between her thighs. He held her there, teetering on the brink of bliss. She threw her head back, begging for release.

Jackson sat up, pulling her against him, his fingers in her hair, mouth against her neck. "Say it again."

Candace couldn't think. Her thoughts obliterated as quickly as they formed.

"Tell me you love me."

That was what he wanted? She stilled in his arms, gathering his face between her hands. His eyes were on fire, burning with need.

"I love you, Jackson."

He kissed her. "Again," he breathed as pushed into her, deeper, harder.

She gasped. "I love you."

Over and over she repeated it, each time bringing him closer to completion. When he came, he shuddered, gripping her tightly as she whispered it one last time.

"I love you. I will say it forever. As many times as you need me to."

He was silent, panting as he struggled for air.

Candace smoothed his hair as he rested in her arms. "Even if you never say it to me, it's all right."

"Candace…" He hugged her, burrowing deeper in her embrace.

"It's fine. Really. They're only words, Jackson."

He lifted his head and gazed at her, sweeping aside her unruly hair. "Thank you."

She brushed a kiss across his nose and smiled. "You're welcome."

As she extricated herself and pulled the t-shirt back on, she considered what she told him. It was the truth. His feelings were clear even if he didn't say it. She had her own hangups. That one was his.

Turning on the bathroom faucet, she braced herself for a drinking binge. Between the Mirror test and everything else that happened yesterday, she hadn't drunk enough water.

When the first glass went down, so did she, sinking to her knees and gasping.

Loud laughter startled her. "That's what happens?" Jackson said, kneeling down next to her.

Her cheeks burned. "I told you it was embarrassing."

"Embarrassing?" he touched her chin. "If I'd have known about that, I wouldn't have brought all that water out with me to clean up our pool mess. I doubt much would've gotten done after that, though."

She rolled her eyes. "Right, because I would've died on the spot."

"No, because I wouldn't have been able to keep from kissing you the rest of the day."

She giggled. "I would've beaten you within an inch of your life for it."

"I doubt it," he said, grinning. "I stopped pulling my punches after you ambushed me."

Halfway to kissing him, Candace stopped. "Wait. What did you just say?"

Jackson blinked. "Hmm?"

She backed up and frowned at him. "You stopped pulling your punches after I ambushed you. Meaning you were before." Her mind rewound to hand-to-hand combat training. "Did you throw that fight on the ballfield?"

The smile disappeared from his face. "I... no, of course I—"

"Don't bullshit me. You gave up, didn't you? You let me get that last hit in. Why?"

He sat back and propped himself up in the doorframe, closing his eyes. "Because I knew how badly I'd hurt you, and I knew you'd keep fighting if I didn't go down."

Candace gaped at him, at a loss of what to think. He threw the fight because he didn't want to hurt her more? He cared about her that much even then?

She crawled towards him and wrapped her arms around his neck. Jackson didn't move for a moment, searching her face to decipher her emotions.

"You're right," she said. "I would have. I wasn't about to lose to you, no matter what it cost me. And while I sort of hate that it wasn't an honest win, you probably saved my life." She grinned at him. "For the second time."

His relief was palpable as he let out a puff of air. "Holy hell, I thought you were going to clock me for a second."

She giggled. "I thought about it, but then I thought about your reasons for doing what you did. I'm not completely irrational, you know." She kissed his cheek and stood to refill her glass. "Besides, I like to save kicking your ass for our sparring sessions."

She shooed him out so she could refill the tank in private. Four glasses down, she finally felt in control of her faculties again. After washing her face, she opened the door to see him standing there in his swim trunks.

"You read my mind," she said. "But, I have to run to my room to change first."

Eventually she managed to get dressed. no thanks to his grabby hands doing their best to change her mind. Wearing clothes from the day before was a little gross, but she'd be out of them soon enough. Outside his door, she turned towards her room, but he pulled her back for one last kiss.

She smiled against his mouth. "I'm going to see you again in like five minutes. Are you going to do this every time I go somewhere without you?"

"Seems like as good an excuse as any." He chuckled.

Candace gave him a playful shove and stepped away. "Not sick of me yet?"

"Not yet, no," he said, winking.

She shook her head and backed away. "Well, at least I know you can't fake lose against me in the pool."

"Is that a challenge?"

Candace turned and grinned at him over her shoulder. "Always."

CHAPTER 18

AFTER THE swim, she showered and headed for the dining hall. While he couldn't beat her in a race, he did beat her to breakfast.

Jackson was already seated across from Gabe, True, and Amir when she set her tray down. She couldn't help but grin a little. All of a sudden, Jackson was Mr. Sociable.

Her grin faded when she took in the serious expressions at the table. "What's going on? Did something happen?"

"There's an all-hands meeting at nine," Amir said. "Another situation briefing."

She sighed and closed her eyes. Likely that meant more ANGELs had died, probably out east. "Great. Can't wait."

True grimaced and nodded. "I think that's the general consensus."

Candace decided to change the topic. "How's the leg,

cuz? Still need more rearranging?"

Gabe shook his head. "Nope. They gave me the green light to get back to business. Or, rather, to begin round two of treatments."

Her jaw fell open. "Already? They only just finished with us."

"They seem fine with the results. I heard they're moving up when the newest recruits are arriving too," he said.

Amir nodded. "Yep. They're trying to beef up the reserves. Normally a new group wouldn't come in until March, but they're moving them up to February first. I think the plan is to put a group through every three months instead of every six now. They told the team leaders to prepare everyone to take on extra mentoring duties."

"On top of the new treatments? Great," Jackson said. "Because we don't have enough to do already."

Candace bit back a laugh, not wanting to hurt his feelings, but he caught it.

"What's so funny?"

"Nothing," she choked. "I'm just trying to picture you mentoring anyone. The clinic would be full up in a week."

He snorted. "Like you could do any better."

In an attempt to avoid his eyes, she tucked into her food while True, Gabe, and Amir hid their laughter. Poorly.

"I seem to be missing out on the joke."

Candace quietly slipped her hand into his under the table. "We'll discuss it later, Sunshine." She winked at him.

After giving her a look that told her there would be all kinds of discussion later, he gently pulled his hand away to eat his meal.

She sighed and shot the Pavo Team a displeased grimace.

When breakfast was over, it was nearly time for the briefing, and they headed to Auditorium B, a larger room than the other auditorium. The entire science and medical staff was on hand in addition to the ANGELs. Dr. Poznanski took the stage promptly at nine.

"Good morning, everyone. Thank you for being on time," he said. "I've gathered you all here to disseminate a few changes to the ANGEL Project. In light of recent events, we're doing a bit of shuffling and reorganizing."

Shuffling? That didn't sound good.

"The first matter is one you may already be aware of. As of now, we're adjusting our intake schedule to every three months. The next batch of trainees will arrive February first, then again in May, August, and November. This will affect all personnel at the compound. Not only will ANGELs be expected to take up more of the burden in training, but with the influx of candidates, some of you will be required to double up on rooms. There's a plan for expansion of the compound in the works, but until such plans are completed, you'll have to bear with us."

Crap. Did that mean they were going to stick her with another girl? Or would she be able to choose her own roommate? It was a petty concern, in light of everything, but really, it would affect her everyday life quite a bit. Even more worrisome, if they could choose their own roommates, would Jackson welcome that sort of invasion of his space?

"As to the shuffling, you are all aware of the losses taken here. I've mentioned the hits taken by the Eastern teams, but since that briefing, there have been more. In order to fill up some of these holes, some of you will be transferring to the Virginia facility."

There was a collective intake of breath, Candace included. Surely after her little show of force at the Mirror test, they wouldn't separate her from Jackson, would they? Not when they were finally so close to each other.

"Two of our SAGEs will be a part of this transfer, Mr. Aiza and Mr. Nguyen. We've not yet decided who amongst the first stage ANGELs will go, but they will be notified in the next few days."

Candace released her held breath. Thank God.

"There are some ideas for trading some of you as well, in order to balance out the remaining teams. This may be on a temporary basis, or for certain missions, or possibly even permanent moves. In any case, be prepared for changes."

Damn. That wasn't going to go over well.

"We're also the only facility capable of implementing the secondary enhancement for ANGELs, so others will come and go as required. The first of these will arrive in February as well. SAGEs will note this is where they will be most needed as far as mentorship goes. Do not expect to spar with non-SAGEs at any point, though you may be required to provide verbal guidance for that."

Yay for pulling double duty.

"At this time, non-ANGEL personnel may leave."

The room cleared of all but Dr. Poznanski and the Supers. When everything settled, he spoke again, calling up images on the screen behind him.

"I'd like to take a moment to apologize to you all. I know these new demands and changes will be difficult to adjust to. You've all given so much of yourselves already, I feel I need to explain why these new sacrifices are necessary."

A picture came up on screen. Two people in lab coats

hovered over a work table: a woman and a version of Dr. Poznanski that looked about twenty years younger.

"This is a photograph taken while GEF was being developed sixteen years ago," he explained. "At the time, I was working with a partner, Dr. Emily Ferdinand. Together, we created the basis for the formula used in the ANGEL Project today."

He studied the picture, a sad, wistful expression flitting across his face. "When we hit upon the multiple birth genetic marker, we realized our work was finally ready to be unveiled. However, there was a... disagreement over how we should go about it. Given the nature of what GEF does, I insisted we take our findings to the US military. She felt it was better to recoup our financial losses by selling our research to private companies. As you know, I prevailed in this, but Dr. Ferdinand didn't take it well. Before the government took possession of our data and equipment, she chose to use herself as the first human test case."

He changed the picture to that of a destroyed office building. The damage was unbelievable, exceeding that of any Candace had seen in the field.

"She did this unbeknownst to me. What you see is the aftermath of her reported clash with authorities. I wasn't present to witness this, but I was told she was killed during the attempt at capture."

The picture changed again, displaying the woman alone.

"It's my belief that Dr. Ferdinand is behind the sudden appearance of these HEX operatives. She initially referred to our proposed project as Human Evolution Experiments and it stands to reason she would hold on to that name. All indications point to her being at the heart of this matter.

Either she was not killed as I was told, or she escaped from wherever she was being held."

Dr. Poznanski rubbed his face and looked back at the screen. "She is the only person outside of the ANGEL Project that possesses the knowledge to duplicate our original formula. After my time working with her, there have been more developments on the serum, along with creating the rigorous screening process, that results in greater stability. As she was not privy to these advancements, she's arrived at a different point in her research, creating powerful individuals who lack key traits we look for in candidates. Her treatments result in volatile and destructive creatures who choose to hurt rather than help. As I said before, I believe this is intentional; it's a means for revenge. That, of course, is speculation on my part, but knowing her as I did, I wouldn't doubt it."

He turned back to the ANGELs, looking very tired. "You need to know what you're up against and why. This is the reason we must take these HEX operatives alive. They must be questioned. Until we can find Dr. Ferdinand, these attacks will continue and likely become more frequent and harmful to all involved."

Not good. What that could mean for the world…

"That is your situation brief. You'll all receive individual briefings on your new duties and whether or not you can expect a transfer. Until then, please continue on as you have been. As always, thank you for your service. Stay safe."

SAFE. WAS there such a thing in her life?

Candace considered that as they wandered out of Auditorium B. There was very little about her existence as a superhero that came without great risks. Even her new relationship with Jackson felt uncertain after everything Dr. Poznanski told them.

"Where you headed?" Jackson leaned into her ear and whispered.

"Hmm?" she asked as his hand brushed across the small of her back. "Well, I have some reading to do, so I suppose back to my room."

"Reading what?"

"Medical textbooks."

He stopped walking for a moment, then caught back up. "Did you say medical textbooks?"

She nodded. "Long story. I can tell you about it if you like, but it's not all that exciting, really."

"You don't mind if I tag along then?"

Candace looked at him. "Tag along? Why would I mind?"

Shoving his hands in his pockets, he shrugged. "Oh, I dunno. Not sick of me yet, then?"

Candace giggled and threaded her arm through his. "Not yet, Sunshine. Come on. I'll even let you snoop around in my stuff if you want."

When they got to her room, he hesitated in the doorway, looking uncomfortable.

She picked up one of the anatomy books and cocked her head to the side. "What's the matter?"

Jackson shut the door. "Oh, nothing."

"You don't have to stay if you don't want to." she said, sitting on the bed and taking off her shoes. "You'll probably be bored out of your mind anyway."

He got as far as her desk and studied the stack of books Deborah delivered a few weeks ago. "What are all these for?"

Candace propped up her pillow and leaned against the headboard. "For me to read, duh." She tossed him a wink.

"Well, *duh*," he shot back. "Of course to read, but why?"

She cracked open the anatomy book to where she left off the other day. "My ability has medical applications. Dr. Poznanski thought it would be a good idea if I started studying how the human body is put together before I go messing around in it."

"Messing around in it?"

So much for reading. She closed the book and set it on her nightstand. "Yes. Messing around in it. I can move muscles and such by forcing the water in them to shift. It's how I've been fixing Gabe's leg."

"You've been fixing Gabe's leg?"

"You're just full of questions, aren't you?" She smiled at him. "Yes, I've been fixing Gabe's leg. That's why I missed that sparring session and why I told you I was in the clinic. That was my first attempt at…" She frowned, not really sure what to call it. "Hmm. Therapeutic manipulation? Something like that. Basically, I can feel out how things want to go together and put them back that way."

"Really?"

"Mmm hmm. I give a damned good massage too." She giggled. "If you behave, maybe I'll let you find out for yourself."

He didn't reply, fixated on her bookshelf.

"Jackson?"

"Hmm?" he murmured, brushing the spines of her books

with his fingertips.

Something was off with him. Not that it was unusual for that to be the case, but she never had the occasion to ask him about it before. "Is something wrong?"

He blinked a few times and turned his head toward her. "Wrong? No, not really."

Candace studied him for a moment, then patted the mattress beside her. "Sit."

When he perched next to her, she poked his arm. "Whatever you want to say, just do it, okay?"

It took him a long moment of thinking before he said anything.

"You don't have a lot of stuff."

"Huh? Uh, no. I don't, really. Why?"

He stood up and headed for the door.

"Where are you going?"

Without answering her, Jackson left.

What the hell? Was he mad about something? Had she used some mysterious trigger word to upset him? Jesus. Just when she thought she was starting to figure him out, that happens. Whatever. He'd be back. After everything between them, his bizarre behavior would be explained eventually. She picked up the anatomy book and continued reading, casting the occasional peeved glance at the door.

An hour later, there was a knock. She didn't need to look through the peephole to know who it was. Candace yanked the door open and prepared to lecture him, but stopped.

Jackson was holding several empty, broken down boxes.

She closed her eyes and took a deep breath. "Are you going to explain, or what?"

He glanced up and down the hall. "Can I come in first?"

Candace gave him a look.

Jackson grumbled. "Are you trying to make this as difficult for me as possible?"

"Am I…" She gaped at him, completely confused. "What the hell is wrong with you? You left with no explanation, pissed off for all I knew, and now you're standing here, demanding I let you in, and you tell me *I'm* making this difficult? I don't even know what *this* is!"

"It's me offering to help you pack your stuff, but if you don't want me to…" He leaned the boxes against the wall and turned away.

"Pack my…" She looked down at the flattened containers. It took her a moment, but she finally understood. "Is this your ass backwards version of a romantic gesture? Because you really ought to work on that, if so."

He backtracked and leaned up against the doorframe. "Sorry, Sugar Plum. I figured actions spoke louder than words."

She rolled her eyes. "Actions without context are confusing at best. You could have asked you know."

"I thought you'd prefer the straightforward approach."

"And what makes you think I'd agree to this?" She leaned back and crossed her arms. "Maybe I don't want to live with a smelly boy."

Propping himself on the doorframe behind her head, Jackson grinned at her and bent down until he was in her face. "Didn't seem to bother you much last night."

Candace decided to press her luck. "I'm not going anywhere until you ask nicely."

He turned his face to the side, his lips brushing her ear. "Please." The word tickled as he breathed it against her skin.

and her eyelids fluttered closed.

"Please what?"

"Please let me keep you where I keep the rest of my things."

Her eyes popped open. That was not what she'd been angling for. "The rest of your..." She ducked away from him, back into her room. "Referring to me as one of your things is so not the way to get what you want here, Sunshine."

Even as she shut the door, his hand came up to stop it. "Why are you fighting me? I don't believe for a second that you don't want to."

She grimaced. "What I want is for you to ask before assuming things. I don't want to be told what I'm going to do, Jackson. I get enough of that already. I don't want you to give me the moon, just a little courtesy. Until you can show me that, then the answer to your *unasked* question is no."

Surprised at her reaction, he lost his hold on the door, and she closed it in his face.

Candace sank to the floor, leaning against cold metal and waiting for him to leave.

He didn't.

Fifteen minutes later, he was still out there, pacing. She tried not to laugh. Her pride and indignation at being ordered around refused to let him win that one, but her resolve was slipping. Attempting to take her mind off of it, she went to the bathroom for a drink of water.

During her second refill, she heard it: the distinct unlocking of the door from the outside. What? How?

Jackson strode in, looking smug. He held up his badge. "Guess they made some assumptions and gave me an all-access pass."

She set the cup down and glared at him. "This changes nothing, you know. I'm still mad at you."

Without missing a beat, he closed the distance between them and kissed her. God damn it. She couldn't not kiss him back. Her body responded to him no matter how much she didn't want it to.

"Please move your stuff into my room, Candy Cane."

She decided to try again. "Why?"

He gathered her up in his arms, pulling her to his chest. "Because up until last night, it felt empty without you. Because I want to know you're not going anywhere, or, if you do, that you'll always be coming back to me."

She sighed and snuggled into him. "You're so dumb sometimes. Where else would I go? You couldn't get rid of me if you wanted to."

Jackson chuckled. "Oh, I'm sure I could find a way if I put my mind to it."

Tilting her head back to look at him, she made a face. "I think we've already established that nothing short of killing one another is going to make this relationship avoidable."

"Well, we attempt that on a semi-regular basis, and neither of us has managed it yet," he said.

She snorted. "Oh honey, if I try to hurt you for real, you'll totally know it. Those were only love taps."

"Is that right?" His grin was that dangerous one that usually meant she was in for a workout.

"Absolutely."

He went to kiss her again, but stopped shy of making contact. "You didn't answer my question."

"What question?"

"Woman, do not toy with me."

She couldn't help giggling. "Oh, all right. Yes, Sunshine. You can absolutely help me invade your inner sanctum."

"It sounds dirty when you say it like that."

"Should be right up your alley then, hmm?"

His laughter came out as a growl laced with desire as his lips closed in on hers. "You already know me so well."

"EVER THINK that maybe you might have a little addiction?" Jackson said, waving around the binder with her ANGEL collector cards.

"What?" she said, leaning out of her closet. When she saw what he held, she rolled her eyes. "Whatever. That's nothing. My room back home was all superheroes, all the time. Ask Gabe if you don't believe me."

"Yeah, but you brought them with?" He shook his head and grinned at her.

Candace sighed and returned to packing. "Well, I thought maybe I'd get them signed or something, but it seems kind of weird to do that now."

She heard the plastic pages flipping in the other room. "Good lord. How many of these do you have?"

"All of them," she replied. "Well, all of them except for the new ones. The new series just came out when I left, and I didn't get them all beforehand."

He murmured something she couldn't quite make out.

"What was that?"

The binder thumped into the bottom of the box. "Nothing.

You about done in there?"

She emerged from her closet, wheeling the suitcase behind her. "Just finished. What's left?"

Jackson motioned to the shelf of books. "Those and anything you've got stashed in your nightstand. I didn't want to pry in case there was something there you didn't want me to find." He winked at her mischievously.

Candace snorted a laugh. "Seriously? What do you think I'm hiding in there, whips and chains?" She strode to the nightstand and opened the drawer, removing the only thing inside it. "It's just a photo album."

Sitting on the bed, she ran her fingers over the faded red leather cover. She couldn't remember the last time she looked through it. Flipping open to the first page, she was struck by a pang of homesickness. Funny, as she barely had time to think about her old life recently. Her mom smiled back at her from the photograph, holding the camera out with one arm, the other around Candace as they posed on the dock. It was their last summer vacation together, and they spent a week sunning by Lake Okoboji, doing nothing but reading and talking about inconsequential things.

"You look just like her," Jackson said as he sat beside her.

"She has better hair. And I got my dad's eyes." Tears blurred her vision. It had been a while since she thought about her mom, and all she wanted in that moment was to hear her voice again.

"You can send an email, you know," Jackson said softly, slipping an arm around her waist.

Candace stared at him. "I can?"

He smiled. "Sure. There's a computer in the library they'll let you use, but everything's screened before it goes out, just so you're aware."

She flung her arms around his shoulders. "Thank you!"

Squeezing her tightly, he chuckled. "Someone wasn't paying attention in the intake brief, I guess. I thought you knew."

"I was paying attention!" She pulled away and pouted. "They didn't tell us."

Jackson shrugged, standing up and pulling her to her feet. "Maybe they decided to keep the new recruits from hogging the screen. I don't know. Why don't we finish this up, and I'll show you where it is?"

Giving him a nod, she left him to pack up the bookshelf and made a last pass over all the drawers and cabinets to make sure nothing was missed. When she emerged from the bathroom, Jackson was all done, save for one book.

He was holding the fourth book of *The Morania Chronicles*. Her throat constricted as she watched him.

"You haven't read it yet, have you?"

She shook her head and looked away.

He carefully tucked it into the box, but didn't say anything else. Grateful for the small reprieve, she finished up her last pass and grabbed her pillow.

"What's that for?"

Taking her suitcase handle, she grinned at him. "For me. You're kind of a pillow hog, Sunshine."

Jackson picked up both boxes of her meager belongings. "Are you complaining, Sugar Plum?"

As she opened the door, she grinned at him. "Not really. Just don't be surprised if I kick your ass to the floor tonight."

"Are you one of those difficult roommates? I'm not going to be rethinking this whole thing in twenty-four hours, am I?"

Candace turned and brushed a kiss against his lips. "Maybe, but I promise to make it worth the effort."

CANDACE ENJOYED a whole week before the nightmares returned.

She awoke to her own terrified shouts and arms closing around her. Frozen in fear, it took her a moment to realize it was Jackson, and not one of her ghastly visions that held her. When rational thought returned, she crumpled into his embrace, shaking as she tried to get a grip on reality.

"Shh," he whispered. "You're safe now."

Candace shuddered. "I'm sorry I woke you."

"Don't be."

Shivering, she picked up the water from their clothing and the soaked bedding, and sent it off to the bathroom. She sat up and pulled her knees to her chest, trying to rid herself of the remnants of the nightmare. "I thought it was getting better. I haven't had one of those since before the Mirror test."

He rubbed her back, his warmth chasing away most of the chill. "Guess I need to do a better job of wearing you out at night."

Candace tried to smile at the joke, but her terror was still too fresh. "I don't know that you can do any more than you already are, Sunshine."

He sat up and kissed the back of her neck. "Maybe, but I'd like to give it a shot all the same."

"I appreciate the thought, but you'll have to forgive me

if I'm not really up for that right now."

His heat disappeared and the bathroom faucet turned on. Jackson reappeared a moment later, bearing a cup for her. As she took it, he caressed the side of her face. "I didn't say right now, Sugar Plum. I'm not that much of an insensitive ass."

She closed her eyes and leaned into his touch. "You're not an insensitive ass at all. Thank you."

"You're welcome. Drink your water."

When she finished, he brought her another, and her terror subsided.

"Better?"

"Much."

He grinned slyly. "I kinda wish I hadn't done that. Seeing you refill the tank is always the highlight of my day."

"Ha ha."

"I wasn't joking." His grin widened. "There isn't anything hotter than watching you when you're—"

"Easy, tiger," she said. "Don't get yourself all worked up now."

He ran gentle fingers through her hair, sending shivers through her. "With you, I don't think I have an off switch."

"So what you're telling me is that I'm a walking, talking centerfold?" She laughed. "That's ridiculous."

"It's true," he said. "Has been since day one, whether or not I wanted to admit it."

"Then you admit to spying on me in the pool?"

"Depends on if you're going to get mad at me again."

She chuckled at the memory. "I hope you don't expect me to apologize for that. You scared the hell out of me."

He looked genuinely surprised. "I did?"

Candace folded her arms on top of her knees and rested

her chin. "You have to understand, Jackson. I didn't want to get close to anyone again. It wasn't just you I was afraid of. It was me, too. Even the thought of it..." She sighed. "So, yeah, that whole situation was brutal. You're probably lucky all you needed was an ice pack."

"In my defense, I was hoping it would push you over the edge the other way, more like in the sparring room."

"To your credit, you almost did," she said, meeting his gaze. "Though at the time I couldn't figure out if you were trying to make me hate you more or what."

Jackson crawled back under the covers and yawned. "Well, I figured after you attacked me outside, you were looking for more. I've been wrong before, I suppose."

Candace winced.

"Candace?"

"Um, well, about that..."

He stopped mid-stretch and propped himself up. "What about that?"

"That, uh, may not have been entirely my idea."

Frowning, he angled her face toward him. "Explain."

"Ambushing you was sort of Amir's advice on how to..." Damn.

"On how to what?"

She took a deep breath and turned to him. "After the accuracy demonstration in the Showcase, Dr. Poznanski 'suggested' I mentor three of our cohort: Hector, Andrew, and..." She closed her eyes and braced. "You."

He was dead silent, and she peeked at him. "It wasn't something I asked for, you know. I don't know why he told me to, and I didn't really want to, but —"

"Candace."

"Are you mad?"

Slowly, a smile turned up a corner of his mouth. "Has anyone ever told you how damned manipulative you are?"

Her forehead pinched in confusion. "Wait, so you aren't mad?"

"I'm willing to let you make it up to me."

Her shoulders relaxed. "I can do that." When she glanced at the clock on the nightstand, she groaned. "Pending you'll take a raincheck."

Jackson pulled her into his arms and kissed her softly. "Absolutely."

CHAPTER 19

ANOTHER ATTACK.

That time, they specifically called for her and Jackson along with the Corvus Team.

As the shuttle landed near the Hoover Dam, Candace told herself it would be different.

No one would die that day.

"It's a water bug, people," Andreas Turner, the team leader, said after conferring with the authorities. "Candace, we'll need you to counteract whatever they try. You'll know their tricks better than anyone, so we need to use that to our advantage."

She nodded, her thoughts already switching to battle mode.

"We have a hostage situation, also," he continued, flipping a chocolate curl of hair away from his forehead. "A school group was getting a tour at the time of attack, and there's about 30 kids and adults trapped in one of the Penstock viewing towers. If Candace can keep the enemy occupied, Leigh, you and I can get them out."

Leigh Grady was a defense power house. She was short, but as fast as Tobias and insanely strong, rivaling Trevor in all but size. Completely unassuming, if her face hadn't been plastered all over trading cards and news articles, you could easily miss her in a crowd.

Andreas was a duplicator. He could produce temporary carbon copies of himself, each a little weaker than the last. He possessed some extra strength, but nothing in comparison to Leigh. On top of that, he was an excellent strategist, seeing the plays of the game before the pieces were even in place.

"Jackson, you'll be with Candace on offense. Stay out of sight until you're needed. You've got a good idea of their capabilities too, but we have to take this one alive if at all possible."

Jackson nodded once, thankfully not mentioning that it had been Candace who took out the last three. Permanently.

"So I'll just hang back for cleanup duty then, shall I?" The last member of the Corvus Team, Sarah Urban, sighed and crossed her arms.

"Stay out of the way, but be on alert," Andreas said. "If any of these structures start to go, you need to be on it for the rewind the second it happens."

Candace looked at Sarah, confused. "The rewind?"

She snorted. "Will wonders never cease. The Superhero Encyclopedia doesn't know my ability?"

Candace grimaced. "I've had a few things going on

lately, in case you didn't know. You'll forgive me if I didn't study up on your stats."

"Sarah has the ability to temporally reverse damage done to inanimate objects," Jackson explained. "But not living things."

Candace started to thank him, but Sarah interrupted. "Nice job, Mr. Sensitive, but I think she'd have figured it out eventually."

Wow. The girl had a serious chip on her shoulder. What was her deal?

"Enough," Andreas said. "We're wasting time. Last report had the perpetrator outside the towers. You two head out that way. Sarah, find a good vantage point. Leigh, with me."

They split off, Candace and Jackson following the road as they ducked behind overturned cars washed aside by the attack. Most of the vehicles were empty, but several bore unmoving bodies, still strapped into their seats. When they reached a lower parking lot, they crouched behind a minivan.

"I'm going to draw them out," Candace told him. "The others need time to get the hostages to safety."

"I'm not going to tell you I like that idea," he grumbled.

She smiled and kissed his cheek. "Don't get all over-protective on me, Sunshine. I got this. You just keep your pretty face out of sight until I take care of business."

As she went to make her move, Jackson yanked her back into a passionate embrace. Time stopped whenever he held her that way, but they couldn't afford more than a second or two of indulgence.

Candace eased away and touched his face. "I'm far more

worried about you than me. Jackson. Don't get caught, okay?"

"Be careful," he said.

With a brief nod, she darted a few cars down, then between them. At the edge of the parking lot, she emerged from cover and surveyed the scene. Nothing moved.

Putting a few fingers in her mouth, she let out a shrill whistle. "I heard a rumor someone wanted to splash a bit of water my way! Where you at, happy fun ball?"

There was nothing for a moment, then she felt the water stir. She waited, keeping her cards close to her chest until her opposition was in sight. At the base of the nearest tower, there was a ripple. It spread outwards, growing in intensity until it was a wave over fifteen feet high. She didn't flinch. There — a shadow behind the crest. Perfect.

It arced high, towering over her head, before she made her move. The will holding the wave together was weak, and it didn't take much to turn the tide and reverse the curl. The water shifted and lunged backwards, taking the enemy with it.

Riding an attack? Big mistake.

The panic was palpable when her opponent hit the surface, the water absorbing the tirade of emotions. There was flailing, confusion…

And then, anger.

Good. Anger meant loss of control. Anger meant they would be sloppy. Of course, anger also meant stronger attacks, but she was stronger than the gen-evo.

A giant spout of water rose into the air, a howling woman atop it. Candace watched as it curved over to a rock plateau to the left. The woman landed in a crouch.

"Who are you?" Her voice carried over the tops of the

parked cars. She stared out from behind limp, dripping strands of wet hair that draped across her face.

"Your opponent, unless you'd rather just surrender now. Either way, I'm good."

The woman stretched out a hand and pulled, attempting to summon the water within Candace's body.

She giggled at the small jerks and spasms in her abdomen. "That kinda tickles, sweetheart. But it's not gonna work, sorry."

The hand dropped, along with her jaw. "You're like me..."

"Took you long enough. What's the matter? Weren't you smart enough to pass the ANGEL entrance exam?"

"I'd rather die than be an ANGEL," she hissed.

Confused, it wasn't the answer she expected.

The distraction cost her, and a hard blast struck her in the stomach, knocking her into the windshield of one of the vehicles behind her. She cursed the moment she was able to breathe again, then rolled off hood and back to the pavement.

"You're the one that killed my brothers, aren't you?"

Candace jerked to a halt before she reached the end of the car. Her brothers?

"They told me it was another like me, only working for the other side. I didn't believe it. Water would never betray me!"

Clearing her head, Candace stepped back out into the open, closer to the HEX operative. "Water doesn't choose sides, kitten. It flows where it will. You've got some funny ideas, but you're right about one thing. If your brothers were the ones who slaughtered all those people in San Jose, then, yes. I did. And I would do it again in a heartbeat."

The woman screamed with rage and flooded her system, turning the hydraulics on full blast as she leapt over the edge of the rock ledge and barreled towards Candace.

Too easy.

Candace snapped the rope taut.

The woman twitched, fighting fiercely for control over her own body. It wouldn't work. Candace was too strong. It was different, however. Her command over the woman wasn't as complete as it was in others.

Strained screeches burbled up from her throat. Candace circled around her, considering what to do next. She couldn't hold her that way indefinitely. They needed to transport her back to the compound for questioning.

"Need any help, Sugar Plum?" Jackson said. He leaned up against one of the cars, looking bored.

"You were supposed to stay out of sight," she said, frowning.

"Seemed safe enough to—" He jerked forward, the water in his body responding to the pull of the enemy.

Candace tore her eyes away and back to the woman, gripping her jaw painfully. "Don't you even fucking think about it."

An angry right hook to the jaw and her head drooped forward, a few drops of blood splattering on the pavement below. Unconscious, the woman was no longer a threat.

Candace rushed to the doubled over Jackson, dropping the paralysis on the woman to check him over for damage. Gently, she pushed back on the water that was nearly ripped from his body, sending a soothing massage after to ease his pain. He laid in her lap, eyes closed and breathing shallow while she smoothed his hair.

"Go ahead and say you told me so," he said, coughing.

"Please don't scare me like that again, Jackson. I don't want you getting hurt because you wanted to feel useful. In this case, I'd rather you be useful when we get home."

He opened his eyes and looked up at her. "Sorry. I thought you had her."

"Only her body. I was still working out what to do with her. Maybe talk to her if I could. Her mind was still functioning, and that's all she really needs for her ability."

"Forgot that part."

She leaned down and placed a kiss on his forehead. "Take your time. When you have your strength back, I'll let you carry her back to the shuttle."

"Gee, thanks."

Candace giggled at him. "I thought you wanted to feel useful?"

"Not really what I meant."

After a minute or two, and a few more of her massages, Jackson was ready to go. As they hiked back, Candace kept her senses tuned to the unconscious woman, following behind and watching for any signs of movement. While she had the time, she wandered around inside the woman's body, seeking out physical indications of abuse or violence. There was nothing of note until she got to her brain and encountered signs of trauma, likely from when Candace struck her. Locating the spot keeping her sedated, she focused on it, making sure it didn't clear up on its own and cause her to wake inconveniently. It was entirely possible to keep her in that state, so long as Candace kept the pressure there.

"You'll have to explain to them what happened," she said as they walked. "I need to stay focused on her until we get back to the compound."

"Does that mean I'm on my own for conversation?" He chuckled.

"Not a good time for jokes. Keep walking. We don't want this one awake until they can restrain her. She's going to be pissed."

Candace fell silent on the trek back to the shuttle. Jackson dumped the HEX woman on the floor, hesitated a moment, then went to report to Andreas.

It was a victory, she knew, but something about the whole incident felt off. It was too easy. Every time she went up against HEX, it was more difficult than the time before. They needed to question her, true, but should they be doing it at the compound? Was it wise to bring an enemy into the stronghold?

Even more concerning, how did they intend to go about the interrogation? If they were desperate to get to the source of it all…

They had been willing to "neutralize" Jackson at the Mirror test when it got out of hand. How far would they go in the current situation?

She remembered the bodies in the cars along the road. The woman killed indiscriminately. Certainly she couldn't be allowed to live.

But did she deserve to be tortured?

Andreas returned to the shuttle with Jackson, who strapped himself in after helping to restrain the woman.

"Beautifully done, Candace," he said. "I'm sending you back with Jackson while we clean up here."

She gave him a nod of acknowledgement, but it was all she could spare. Things were stirring in the woman's head, and she needed to keep it under control. Even her own thoughts fell by the wayside as she poured her focus into pressurizing specific points. The shuttle rose into the air and blasted back towards the California compound. Fifteen minutes dragged by as she fought to keep the woman under control. Landing was a relief, and she hung on until a team ran in to relieve her. The HEX operative was secured to a gurney and Bradley Pryor stepped up, his red aura immediately surrounding the captive, rendering her nearly powerless.

One of the soldiers touched Cándace's shoulder. "All secure. We'll take it from here."

Exhausted, Candace dropped the link to her connection. They wheeled the woman out as she started to stir.

Jackson rested a hand against her back and guided her out of the hangar. "Come on, Sugar Plum. You look like you could use a nap."

INTENSE PAIN wracked her body, jarring her from sleep. Candace couldn't scream, couldn't breathe. Even thinking was impossible through the sudden torment.

Jackson's voice broke through the haze, in between waves of agony.

"Candace? Candace! What's going on?"

God, she couldn't even answer. It was all she could do to suck in one ragged gasp of air and squeak out a whimpering cry.

As he lifted her, every place the two of them touched stabbed into her like a white hot knife. Jackson ran with her in his arms, not stopping until they reached the clinic.

The whirlwind of activity around her went by in a blur, each moment excruciating. The first time she screamed was when they hooked an IV into her arm. But as the saline solution entered her system, the new fluids eased the pain. It took an hour before she could focus her vision on anything.

The first thing she saw was Dr. Poznanski's concerned expression.

"Still with us, Miss Bristol?"

"Still here. Better now," she replied.

"Any idea what happened?"

Candace closed her eyes and tried to breathe normally. The pain remained, but was fading. "No. It just hurt everywhere. That's all."

"Can you describe the pain? Burning? Achy? Stabbing?"

She considered the question, trying to narrow down a proper descriptor. In the end, she settled on the only thing she could. "All of them. All at once. Am I dying?"

His expression deepened into a scowl. "I don't think so. All indications tell us you're stable. We can't find a physical cause for your discomfort."

Discomfort? Could he have understated it any more than that?

"Did you take any damage during the fight today?"

"My butt went through a windshield, but that's it. I didn't take any damage from that as far as I can tell."

"And you were asleep when this business started?"

"Correct."

"How is your ability? Any changes?"

Pushing past the pain, she closed her eyes and focused inward. Her connection was there, but something was different. Following it, she explored the change. It led away, somewhere else in the compound.

Deeper still. The source was close. Where was it?

Candace gasped and sat up.

That woman. That HEX woman was on the other end. She could feel her. The pain, it was her pain, brought on by something being done to her.

What had been a suspicion a few hours ago, turned into a certainty.

"Miss Bristol?"

She didn't know what to say. If she told him what she knew, what would they do?

"It's still there. No changes. It just hurts." Candace lied, unsure of what else to do.

"Well, I think we'll do a full checkup, to be on the safe side. You seem to be doing better with the IV. Perhaps you were only dehydrated?"

She frowned. "Maybe, but it doesn't feel that way. The fluids are helping though."

They put her through the normal blood draws and scans but, as she thought, they found nothing that would cause the crippling pain she experienced. Shortly before dinner, they released her with orders to return the moment any signs of her "discomfort" reappeared.

Jackson stayed through the entire process, refusing to leave even when she insisted she'd be fine. He walked with her to the dining hall, always remaining in constant contact with her. Submitting to his concerns, she took his hand and squeezed it gently.

"Thank you for being my ambulance."

"Apparently 'female transport' is my new job title," he said, squeezing back, but his smile wasn't convincing.

"I'm fine now, Sunshine. Stop worrying."

"Do they have any idea what happened?"

Candace shook her head, not meeting his gaze.

He pulled her to a halt and lifted her chin. "You're not telling me something."

She looked away. "You want to take a walk? I could use some fresh air."

After collecting their jackets, they headed out. They were barely on the Quad before he questioned her again. Candace refused to answer him until they were further out, away from anyone who might overhear.

"I think I know what happened, but I can't really prove it," she said when they sat down on a rock a mile from the compound.

"Can't prove it? Why? What's wrong?"

She put her elbows on her knees and rubbed her eyes with the palms of her hands. "I think the pain I was feeling wasn't mine. It was that woman we brought back earlier."

"What? How?"

"Because our ability is the same, I think we got tangled up, linked by the water maybe. It was better once I got new fluids in my system, like that flushed out the old water, but it's disturbing regardless."

"Disturbing to be linked to her that way? Yeah, I would think so."

Candace shook her head. "Not so much that. Think about it. What I felt is what she was feeling. Someone was doing that to her — someone *here*. Torture, Jackson. They're using torture."

He had no response to that. She glanced at him, trying to read his expression.

"Did you tell them?"

Shaking her head, she sighed. "How could I? I have no idea what they'd do if they found out I know. I mean, they might lay off her if they thought they'd affect me, but, God, Jackson. That they're doing it at all... How am I supposed to feel about that?"

"She killed people," he said flatly. "Why shouldn't they?"

His response shocked her. "What? Why would you say that? I've killed people too. Would you have them do the same to me?"

"That was different. You were protecting others." When he touched her face, she jerked away.

"That doesn't make it right," she said, standing. "That isn't equal punishment. Making someone else suffer for the sake of making them suffer? We're supposed to be the good guys. Last time I checked, torture didn't fall under the umbrella of heroism."

He leaned forward on his knees, frowning. "How else would you suggest getting answers from her?"

"Oh, I don't know, maybe try talking to her?" That Jackson was actually defending it... The whole thing made her sick. "We have empaths. I know what Deborah can do. At the very least, putting the woman at ease, calming her, might help develop trust. If this woman was made to change her mind about the ANGEL Project, wouldn't she help us willingly? Torturing her is only going to make her hate us more."

Jackson sighed and hefted himself to his feet. "Candace, you can't let yourself get invested in —"

As his hands reached out, she brushed them away and turned. "I'm already invested. So are you, in case you forgot. What do you think would've happened if I hadn't stepped in on your Mirror test? The word 'neutralized' was thrown out there, Sunshine. That's government speak for 'they would have killed you,' if you need clarification. And that's the best case scenario. We don't know that they wouldn't have dumped you in some cell to rot. This involves us as much as anyone."

"You're right," he said, his arms wrapping around her. "Please don't be angry with me. I can't force myself to feel bad for her, though. She put herself in this situation by attacking innocent people."

Candace closed her eyes. "She said it was her brothers I killed, Jackson. Her brothers. If it was me, I'd probably have done the same thing."

His lips brushed her neck, leaving a gentle kiss below her ear. "No, you wouldn't have. You wouldn't make the innocent pay for someone else's crime."

"But if it was the only way to find the person at fault?"

"Stop, Sugar Plum." Jackson turned her around and hugged her to his chest. "You can't compare yourself to those people."

Candace buried her face in his shirt. "Yes, I can. If it had been you or Gabe that had been —"

"Stop. Don't think that way," he said. "Don't let yourself go down that road. Even if it was me, I wouldn't want you to go that far. Gabe wouldn't either. You're better than that."

"Then you understand why I can't stand this now that I

know about it, right?"

He kissed the top of her head and tightened his hold. "I do. But there's nothing you can do here, Sugar Plum."

"I could say something."

Jackson pulled back and held her at arms length. "Don't. Please don't. If they know, they might try to use you, and I don't want you anywhere near that."

"I don't know how to do nothing. I can't live with this. It's not right."

"It isn't up to us to decide what's right in this case."

Her scowl deepened. "There's no way I can't think about this. It's going to eat at me until I do something about it."

His hands drifted up and over her shoulders, coming to rest below her face. "I think I can find some way to distract you."

The kiss was warm and soft, easing her tension as she let herself fall into the feel of it. Jackson was insistent, drawing her closer into his embrace. Each touch warmed her a little more, until she was completely caught up in the moment.

"Hungry?" he whispered against her mouth.

She giggled. "Isn't it a little chilly to be cashing that raincheck?"

"I meant dinner," he said. "But if you'd rather pass on food…"

"Tempting," she said and ran her fingers through his hair. "We should probably eat, though. Growling stomachs tend to ruin the mood."

Jackson led her back towards the compound, looking pleased with himself.

"This isn't the end of it, you know." She bumped her shoulder against his arm. "No matter how many temporary distractions you throw at me."

"That sounds like a challenge." He grinned.

"While I look forward to seeing what you come up with, I'm not going to forget, Jackson. I can't. I'm going to do something about this."

"We'll see."

She shook her head and smiled. "You're incorrigible."

He draped an arm across her shoulders. "I've been called worse."

CHAPTER 20

SHE WAITED until he was asleep.

Candace made good on the raincheck, putting Jackson through his paces in bed that night. She needed him completely exhausted for what she was going to do. If he knew what she decided over dinner, he never would've closed his eyes.

It was probably the dumbest thing she ever thought to do, and that included streaking through a cornfield at two in the morning. That decision only meant the possibility of scars and years of embarrassment, but this? It was in its own category of stupid.

It was entirely possible they'd kill her.

She could still feel traces of the woman, though it was no longer painful. As she walked through the halls of the compound, Candace followed where the feeling led, playing an internal version of hot and cold. Her search led her past the training rooms, to a hall she'd never been down, and to an elevator she'd never used before. Descending until it felt right, she got off at the fourth subfloor, then hooked right, left, and another right. Five doors down, she stopped.

One last barrier stood between her and her quarry. But how to get in? If she swiped her badge in the card reader, would it work? Then again, no one had come running yet, and there was surveillance equipment everywhere. She looked at the wall to her left and glared into the camera.

"Open it," she said, loud enough she knew they would hear.

A moment passed, and then the lock hummed and disengaged.

Candace opened the door and stepped into the room.

The smell hit her first. The stench of vomit forced her to cover her face, but she pressed forward, not about to be dissuaded.

The woman was still strapped to the cot, unmoving, her breathing shallow. Candace approached, weighing the single bottle of water she brought with her. She held her breath as she unscrewed the lid and directed the liquid outward, cleaning the worst of the mess off the prisoner. It wasn't a perfect solution, but it made the smell tolerable.

Candace held back a small amount, enough to offer a little to drink. It was clear the woman was very dehydrated. From the dark circles under her eyes to the pallor of her skin, it was every bit of how Candace felt following her treatments, but the feelings coming from the woman were nothing like the pain of GEF plus radiation. It was so much worse than that, and never ending. What did they pump into her system to do that? What would cause her to dehydrate so rapidly, not to mention induce vomiting? Although, the pain alone could have been enough to make her sick.

"The ANGEL returns," she said, her voice raspy. "My hero."

Candace fidgeted with the cap to the water bottle. "I didn't know what they would do. It probably doesn't mean much, but I'm sorry about what happened."

"You're right. It doesn't mean much."

"I have a little water left if you'll accept it. It's only a sip or two, but I can't risk giving you more than that now."

"Come to poison me some more then?"

Candace shook her head. She stepped up to the nearest side of the cot and studied the captive. She couldn't be a day older than eighteen. Slowly, Candace reached up and brushed the tangled strands of dark hair out of her face. "You have no reason to trust me, but I promise I'm not here to hurt you. I only wanted to talk."

"Right," she hissed. "That's what they said too."

Realizing there wasn't anything she could do to convince her otherwise, Candace poured out a capful of water and put it to her own lips, swallowing it quickly. "See? Totally safe."

The woman set her mouth in a hard line, but looked like she was considering it. Not waiting for a reply, Candace poured another capful and held it to the woman's parched lips. Her wild aqua eyes fluttered closed as the first drops seeped into her mouth.

"I know the feeling." Candace twitched a smile. She continued dealing it out by the capful until every last drop was gone.

"I'm not going to say thank you."

"I wouldn't expect you to. I didn't do it to earn praise."

She narrowed her eyes. "Then why bother?"

Candace exhaled slowly. "Because when I found out what they were doing to you, I had to do something. I don't think I can stop them, but I needed to act. This... this isn't right. What you did was awful, but no one deserves this."

"Didn't keep you from dragging me back here, now did it?"

"I told you, I didn't know."

"Would it have stopped you if you did?"

"Maybe. I'd have been more likely to kill you first."

She coughed out a hoarse laugh. "Right, because that's what you do, isn't it?"

Candace winced. "Sometimes death is the greatest mercy you can grant another person," she said. "If I had given you the choice, which would you have wanted?"

Silence was the reply.

"What's your name?"

Still nothing.

Frowning, Candace considered what more she could do. Was there anything? Maybe the woman was still too dehydrated to think clearly, but the bottle was empty. If she brought more...

"Kristie."

Candace blinked. "Kristie?"

"My name. You asked."

It wasn't much, but she'd take it. "Kristie, I'm Candace."

"Good for you."

She sighed. "Look, I can't promise you anything, but I'll see if I can make this easier for you, okay? They know I'm in here, and probably aren't very happy with me right now, so they're not likely to listen to me, but I'll try."

"Yippee."

"I'll know if they hurt you again. Well, pending the link holds."

Kristie snorted. "Link? We got linked? That's fantastic."

"I'll need to strengthen it again to monitor you. I'm not really sure how it happened in the first place, so if you've got any ideas…"

"Seriously? You don't even know how it happened? That's hilarious. What the fuck are they teaching you guys out here in the sticks?"

She bristled, defensive. "There aren't any other water manipulators in the program. Who would you suggest I ask about it, if not you?"

Kristie grimaced. "Fine. Pool some of your water in your hand and give it to me. That's the quickest way. At least then you'll suffer too."

Candace frowned at her. It didn't occur to her that she could do that, although it made sense given what happened to her before she got her ability under control. She never tried to *purposely* leak fluids.

"Hurry up before I change my mind."

Candace closed her eyes and focused inward, finding the water inside her body. Concentrating on the palm of her left hand, she eased it out through her pores, collecting maybe a quarter of a cup. "Open wide."

Kristie rolled her eyes, but let her jaw fall open. Candace fed it to her in a steady stream.

"Interesting flavor," Kristie said. "Do I detect a hint of boyfriend in the aftertaste?"

Her cheeks reddened. "That's none of your business."

Kristie gave a throaty laugh. "I didn't say it was a bad thing. I take it that was him I nearly—"

"Don't," Candace said, temper flaring. "You make any threats to me or the people I care about, and we're done here, understand?" Her anger simmered below her forced calm. "I want to help you, but I won't tolerate it if you so much as hint at hurting them."

Kristie glared at her, but said nothing more.

That single reminder of nearly losing Jackson was all it took to obliterate her desire to do anything else that night. Candace turned away and headed for the door.

"Get some sleep, if you can," she said over a shoulder. "Until they know that hurting you hurts me, I make no promises about their actions."

She left, slamming the door behind her.

A rather irritated Dr. Poznanski and four soldiers met her in the hall. "It seems we need to have another conversation, Miss Bristol."

Candace scowled at him. "I agree. Tea and biscuits by the fireplace then?"

"I'm not in the mood for sarcasm at one in the morning. Be in my office at seven on the dot. Try not to pull any more stunts on your way to bed."

She stomped away. The lecture meant no morning swim. A few feet away, she turned back. "Oh, if I were you, I'd leave Kristie be for a while. Whatever it is you did to her today, you also did to me. That's not likely to change in the near future."

Candace didn't wait for a reply. She would already have to explain it to Jackson, and she'd be lucky to get four hours of sleep tonight.

EVEN BEFORE her badge hit the card reader, the door swung open.

Jackson stood there, glaring. "Where the hell have you been?"

"Causing trouble, like I do. You gonna let me in or what?"

"Don't get pissy with me. I thought we settled that issue. And yet, I wake up and find you gone. You lied to me."

"I didn't," she said, crossing her arms. "I told you I wasn't going to forget about it, Sunshine. I never lied to you. Now let me in if you want to hear about it. If not, let me get my stuff and I'll go."

Still fuming, he let her by. She stood in the middle of the room, waiting for him to make his choice.

"You knew I didn't want you to go, but you went anyway," Jackson said. He kept his hand on the doorknob.

"Yes."

"Why?"

She took a deep breath, trying not to be angry with him. Why couldn't he understand? "I had to. It's not right. She's still a human being."

"Yes, a psychotic one that kills the defenseless without a second thought."

"But she doesn't torture, which, in my opinion, is a step above what they put her through today. I felt it firsthand. I'd rather die than spend the rest of whatever is left of my life that way."

He closed his eyes, the muscles in his jaw clenching and unclenching as he tried to rein in his temper. "What did you do, exactly?"

"I talked to her. I cleaned the puke off her. I gave her a few sips of water."

"That's it?"

She nodded. "That's it."

His shoulders relaxed and he let go of the door, closing the distance between them in two large steps as he swept her up in his arms.

Candace winced, suddenly realizing what he probably feared she would do. She couldn't return the embrace. "You thought I was going to kill her, didn't you?"

Jackson didn't say a word. He didn't have to.

Tears stung her eyes. She pushed away from him and swallowed hard. With a nod of her head, she headed for the door.

"Wait. Where are you going?" he asked as she pulled it open.

"You think it's that easy for me? You think I'd make a decision like that over the course of a few hours? I..." She stepped into the hallway. "I don't even know where to start with how completely fucked up that is, Jackson."

"Candace, I just —"

"No," she said. "That one isn't going to go away with an apology. You should know better. An 'I'm sorry' isn't going to fix it." She let the door close and walked down the hall. Maybe she could still get into her old room.

C A N D A C E T O S S E D and turned for hours, unable to sleep after the events of the night. On top of seeing what they did to Kristie, Jackson apparently thought she was capable of premeditated murder, too. How could he? After everything he'd seen, everything he knew about her, why would he think killing another person would be that easy for her? Especially when doing so might land her in a cell like Kristie's.

She rolled out of bed and took a few handfuls of water from the sink in the bathroom, then cleaned up as best she could. If she had the forethought to grab her suit, she'd be in the pool already. As it was, the best she could do was roll up her pants and sit on the edge, soaking her feet. It was better than nothing.

An hour passed with her laying there, legs dangling in the water. It wasn't the same, but it helped a bit. Sick of thinking about Jackson, she returned to Kristie, analyzing every second of their conversation. What could she tell Dr. Poznanski about the girl that might convince him to ease up?

At six, she got up and headed for breakfast. The only people in the dining hall were the serving line workers. That was fine with her. She was in no mood for company that morning. Around six forty-five, about the time she was finishing, others filtered in. Jackson was one of them. He looked as though he had as much sleep as she had, but she wasn't anywhere close to ready to deal with him. Even if she didn't have somewhere to be, she needed more time to figure out what to do about the whole mess. She dumped her dishes and left.

Dr. Poznanski was unlocking his door when she walked up. "At least you're punctual, Miss Bristol. Come on then," he said, showing her in.

She took a seat and waited for the lecture.

"You neglected to mention last night how it was you knew what was happening to her. How long were you aware of it?"

Candace swallowed. "When we spoke in the clinic. You asked me if my ability felt okay. When I explored it, I felt Kristie at the other end. Our abilities got tangled in the initial fight because we share an element."

"And why did you hold on to that information?"

"I…" she began, then stopped, trying to find a way to phrase it that didn't make her look bad. "I was confused, and a little afraid. It's not something I would have thought the ANGEL Project capable of. I needed time to process it."

He stared at her for a while, drumming his fingers on his desk and studying her. Whatever was going on in his head, it wasn't readable on his face. "You got her name?"

The question caught her off guard. "What?"

"She told you her name?"

Did that mean she was in less trouble? If he was asking, it meant they didn't get as much from her. "Only her first name: Kristie. That's all she told me."

Dr. Poznanski took another long moment to think it over. "Would you be willing to speak to her again?"

That wasn't how she saw the conversation going, but it was possible her punishment was forthcoming. "As an alternative to torturing her? Yes."

He sighed and rubbed his forehead. "That… was not my idea. There are certain things here I have little say over. That's one. They didn't see any other alternative, and I had none to offer as rebuttal. However, if you think you can get the information we need from her —"

"I don't know that I can get anything from her." Candace flinched. The lack of sleep made her cranky. She needed to be careful. "I got her name because I attempted to treat her like a human being instead of... I don't know what. I can't tell you I can get what you want from her, or, if I can, on what sort of schedule. She doesn't trust me, and I don't blame her. She's convinced the ANGEL Project is the enemy. Getting her to betray her core beliefs isn't something I'm trained to do, and I'm not sure I want to learn how."

Dr. Poznanski rubbed his tired eyes. "Miss Bristol, you got more out of her in five minutes than we did all day with the General's methods."

"You made me look good, more than likely."

"Regardless," he said, giving her a look that meant she should think very carefully before interrupting again. "I think we should let you try."

Candace grimaced. "Even if I can't promise anything? How long would you be willing to wait? Trust isn't built overnight, and it can be destroyed in seconds. Besides, I'm not going to do that if you're just going to turn around and kill her once she gives up the information. Can you make that trade? Sparing her life for whatever she knows?"

He was quiet for too long.

"I can't go in there with nothing to offer her as incentive," she continued. "I can tell from our conversation last night that she's rewards based. You give, she gives. She gets, you get. It confused the hell out of her that I was so nice. That's probably why she told me her name. I gave her a drink, so she gave me something in return. Water balances. I know. We seek equilibrium even when there's no water involved. We can't help it."

"Interesting insight," he said. "I hadn't considered the effect of an ability on personality. You may be correct."

"I *am* correct," she said flatly. "It's not a guess."

He thought about it some more before reaching a decision. "I'll have to discuss this with General Jacobs and let you know. You didn't sleep last night, did you?"

"Did you?"

"A fair point," he said. "Go get some rest, Miss Bristol. I'll send for you later when I have news."

There was nothing more to be done. Candace left the office, wondering where she should head next. Dealing with Jackson was the last thing she wanted. She'd have to talk to him eventually, but, as tired as she was, it wouldn't go well if she attempted it. If she crashed in her room, he could corner her and force the issue, again, not a pleasant thought. She settled on a third option.

Gabe was leaving his room when she got there.

"I need a favor," she said.

"What's up, Candy Cane?" He looked at her and his forehead wrinkled. "What's wrong?"

She covered a yawn. "Can I crash here for a few hours? I'll explain later, but I had a rough night."

"Too much Action Jackson?" he asked, the slightest hint of a grin curving the corners of his mouth.

Candace frowned. "Something like that. So can I or not? I'm exhausted."

Sensing it wasn't a good time for jokes, Gabe relented and let her in. "Should I be prepared for a blowout between you two?" he said as she kicked off her shoes. "No offense, but you two aren't known for uneventful confrontations."

She crawled up onto the pillow and under the covers. "Tell him I'll talk to him later if he comes looking for me. Or lie and say you haven't seen me. I don't know. Whatever. I'm not moving until noon at the earliest, never mind dealing with him. I can't even think straight I'm so tired. If you're really feeling pushy, by all means, ask *him* why I'm upset."

"If it's all the same to you, I think I'd rather not," he said. "We're not quite to the heart-to-heart stage of our relationship yet."

She snorted. "Then maybe this is your golden opportunity." Candace yawned again and looked at her cousin. "Thanks for this, by the way."

Gabe sat down on the edge of the bed and pushed a stray hair back behind her ear. "You're welcome, but we're going to talk about this later."

Closing her eyes, she nodded. "Later."

She was asleep before he even shut the door.

CHAPTER 21

CANDACE NEARLY fell out of bed when the banging on the door blasted her awake. She bolted upright, trying to place her surroundings.

"I know you're in there," Jackson yelled from the hallway. "You've been hiding long enough."

Right. Gabe's room. So he finally tracked her down. What time was it? Nearly dinner. Damn. She really had been tired.

"Candace," Jackson said. "Let me in."

Her stomach rumbled as she threw her feet out onto the carpet and put on her shoes.

"Come on. You don't want to be responsible for me liquifying this door, do you?" he said.

She rolled her eyes and went to the bathroom for a drink. Sure he could hear the water running, she took her time with two full glasses before she opened the door. He was about to pound on it again, and almost punched her in the face. She took advantage of his unbalanced moment and stepped around him, heading for their room. If nothing else, she could get a fresh change of clothes, and maybe a shower if she was lucky.

He fell into step behind her and followed her inside. Candace rifled through the drawers for clean everything, but didn't say a word.

"Candace, you have to talk to me about this."

She finished getting what she needed and headed for the bathroom. Jackson grabbed her arm as she tried to pass him.

"How long am I going to get the silent treatment, Sugar Plum?"

She pinched her eyes shut. As she slept, the whole mess had clarified in her mind. She knew exactly why she'd been so short with him, and she knew that only one thing could fix it. "Until you can tell me why I should stay with someone who thinks I'm capable of premeditated murder."

"You know I don't think that," he said.

She shook her arm free. "That's exactly what you thought of me last night, and that isn't the answer I'm looking for." Not waiting for him to try again, she got to the bathroom and locked the door behind her.

She'd been telling herself that it didn't matter, that he'd come around to it eventually. She thought she believed it. They were just words, after all.

Three little words.

Words she hadn't said to Adrian until it was too late.

It was a mistake she wasn't going to make again. The lives they led were too uncertain to leave the important things unsaid. Either one of them could die tonight, and not in the vague sense of mortality that most people understood. Every hour held the absolute possibility of being their last.

The shower took away the grime, but not the gloom. She pulled her hair into a loose braid, letting it fall over her shoulder, and dressed. Jackson was sitting on the bed when she emerged, his forehead resting in his hands.

She didn't understand why it was so hard for him, but there was more to it than his own stubborn pride. After a moment of waiting for him, she took a deep breath and went to the closet, pulling out her suitcase.

She rested her hand against the handle and looked at him. "Last chance, Sunshine," she said quietly. "Why should I stay?"

"You know why."

"Do I? I know you enjoy having me in your bed. I think you like me a whole lot. But that isn't enough for me, Jackson. Neither of us has the luxury of putting what's important off until tomorrow, because there might not be one. I love you, and I know I said it didn't matter if you said as much, but it does. It matters a lot. I need to know, and I need to know right now if I'm wasting my time with someone who is never going to feel the same way. I can't. I can't do that to myself."

He looked so vulnerable sitting there, like she could prick him and he'd shatter into a billion little pieces. "You're not wasting your time."

Releasing the suitcase, Candace approached and knelt in front of him. "Why is this so horrible for you? I don't know how to make it better when I don't know what's wrong. Anything you've ever asked me, I've told you honestly. So now I'm asking you, why are you willing to let me walk out that door before you'll give me the one thing that will ensure my presence for as long as I'm breathing?"

He took a long, shaky breath. "Because the only people I've ever said that to died because of me."

What could she say to that? She couldn't tell him it wasn't true when she had no idea what the circumstances were.

Candace reached out and pulled his hands away from his face, hanging on to them tightly, like he might try to run if she didn't. "Tell me what happened."

A shadow of deep hurt haunted his eyes. "I can't."

"You can. You have to," she said. "I'm not trying to trick you, Sunshine." Releasing one of his hands, she set her palm against his cheek. "I want to know you. This thing, whatever it is, is a major part of who you are. Without it, I'm no different than anyone else outside of these walls. But if you tell me, that makes me important. Even if I'm only important to you, that's all that matters. Do you see that? I need to know that what you are to me, I'm that for you, too."

Jackson was quiet for a long moment, his eyes closed and breathing deep. Finally, he gave a single nod of his head.

Rather than make him stare at her as he spoke, Candace moved to the bed and sat beside him, waiting patiently. She was eager to hear this story, but wasn't about to rush him.

"I told you I didn't have any family," he said, so low she had to strain to hear him. "From the time I was eight on, I bounced around in the foster system, each place worse than the last. The case workers would throw around words like survivors' guilt and PTSD, but they didn't know the truth of what happened."

Candace stayed silent, giving him all the time he needed to get through it.

"I was angry with them for some reason," he continued. "Something stupid and small. I don't remember what. As I laid in bed that night, I decided to burn the family pictures. When they were all asleep, my mom, my dad, my little sister, my older brother… I snuck out to the garage. My dad kept cigarettes and a lighter out there. I took the lighter and the photos, and I lit them."

His head drooped until his chin nearly rested on his chest. "I don't know what my dad was working on, but something on the bench caught fire. I panicked and ran. Instead of yelling, screaming, warning them, I bolted out the back of the garage and hid in the trees behind our house. It spread so fast… They never had a chance."

That was what he'd meant by "join the club." She closed her eyes, trying to imagine what kind of torment a kid would put themselves through after something like that. "You were only eight, Jackson. You couldn't know what would happen."

His hands balled into fists. "I killed my family. Kid or not, I'm respons—"

She grabbed his face and forced him to look at her. "It was an accident. A terrible accident, but still an accident." She let out a slow breath and brushed the hair away from his forehead. "I'm sorry. I can't fathom what that kind of loss is like. That you're here at all, Jackson…" Candace dropped her hands and looked away. "I'm sorry I was such a bitch to you. You deserve better. I shouldn't have pushed you like that."

"Candy," he said, turning her chin towards him. "I

understand why you were upset. And you're right. We need to tell each other these things while we have the chance. I've never thought of you as someone with so little regard for life that you would kill without a very good reason. I've never met someone so thoroughly committed to doing the right thing. The first time we spoke, I didn't know what to make of you. I thought you were trying to build up some sort of image for yourself, to make everyone think you were perfect. I spent hours, days, trying to find a chink in your armor, some kind of flaw, but I never could. At least, not until that night in the locker room. Everything I heard and saw... Candace, what happened that night showed me that you were human, still capable of making mistakes, but you didn't run away from it. You tried to help him. You tried to talk him down. And when you couldn't, you did the only thing you could have. Your choice saved more lives than we'll ever know. You saved *me*. And you never asked for anything in return for that— from me or anyone else. I know how badly you wanted to follow him, but I couldn't let you. That's why I carried you away from there that night. Seeing him after... You never would have slept again. It would've been too much."

Tears stung her eyes, and Candace looked away. Somewhere deep inside, she knew it was him that had taken her away from there. How had she looked that night? How broken? "It isn't the same, you know. I did what I did knowing the consequences. You were a kid. You never could have known or expected what happened to your family. I don't know which is worse to live with." She took a deep breath. "I'm still sorry for how I've been acting. I won't force you into anything. If you want me to stay..." She reached out and threaded her fingers through his. "I'll stay without asking any more of you."

"Do you remember what I said to you when they sent me into your room that day?"

Of course she did. She remembered nearly every word he ever spoke. "Which part?"

"You can either drown in it, or accept that it's part of who you are."

She nodded, staring at their joined hands.

"Maybe it's time I took my own advice."

Candace met his eyes, searching for any hint of doubt or hesitation. "I meant what I said, Jackson. You don't have to do this because of a stupid ultimatum from me. It's not fair, and I don't want it if you —"

His kiss was so warm, so pure, that she couldn't breathe. Everything from the gentle caress of his fingers along her neck to the tenderness of his lips against her own reached into the deepest places of her soul and filled them with light. Jackson held nothing back, giving every bit of himself in that singular moment.

"I love you, Candace," he whispered.

Overwhelmed by his unquestionable devotion, the first tears spilled down her cheeks as she struggled for air. She slowly opened her eyes, trying to find words for the amazing gift he gave her.

His eyebrows bunched together as he watched her, and he looked uncertain. "You haven't said anything yet."

Candace held his face and smoothed out the worried look. "Say it again."

Jackson frowned. "But —"

"I want to make sure I'm not dreaming," she interrupted.

"I don't think I've ever had such a perfect moment in all my life."

A soft smile eased its way onto his mouth. "I love you."

Candace threw herself into his arms, almost knocking him over as she kissed him for all she was worth. He chuckled at her unstoppable embrace, breaking her concentration.

"I love you, too," she said from his lap, her forehead pressed against his. "Thank you."

"For what?" he said. "Being completely defenseless when it comes to your charms?"

She giggled. "My charms? I had no idea being a demanding, relentless harpy was so irresistible."

"Demanding and relentless, maybe, but never a harpy, Sugar Plum."

Candace sighed and held him to her chest. "You're sweet, but wrong. I have no clue why you put up with me sometimes."

"It certainly helps that you have an excellent set of—"

"Choose your words carefully."

"Personality traits to offset your moments of unpleasantness."

She snorted and pulled back. "Right."

"What?" he said, winking. "I'm a great admirer of your personality traits."

Sliding her arms around his neck, Candace kissed him again, slowly. "I am totally willing to give you another opportunity to admire those particular personality traits as closely as you like right now."

"Is that so?" Laughter rumbled in his throat. "How generous of you."

"Mmm," she murmured and ran her fingers through his

hair. "I'm a very giving person."

Jackson growled as she captured his lower lip with her teeth. "I think I'm going to need some proof of that," he said.

"Ask and ye shall receive," Candace said, continuing to leave little kisses along his jaw and neck.

He opened his mouth to speak, but was interrupted by knocking at the door. She sagged in his arms and muttered a curse. Jackson held her, locking eyes with her. "Don't answer it."

Candace grimaced. "As much as I hate to, we have to. They know we're in here."

"We have ways of making them go away."

The knocking continued, insistent.

"Tell you what," she said, putting a finger to his lips. "I'll go see who it is and you sit here and think of how you're going to make me prove exactly how giving I can be, okay?"

Jackson caught her hand and grinned. "Oh, I've already got plenty of ideas about that."

She giggled and extricated herself, sliding off of his lap. "Then make a list."

Her good mood faded the moment she opened the door.

"Miss Bristol," the soldier said. "Dr. Poznanski needs to see you."

"Now?"

The soldier nodded.

Realizing she hadn't told Jackson about her meeting that morning, she turned to him, trying to look as apologetic as she possibly could. "Raincheck?"

Jackson's face was tight, clearly displeased. She looked at the soldier. "Just one minute."

After closing the door, Candace walked back to the bed

and tried to coax the pout off of Jackson's face. "I don't have a choice. I promise to make it up to you, though."

He stood and pulled her against him. "Did you get plenty of sleep today?"

She shrugged. "Enough. Why?"

Jackson bent low and whispered in her ear, "Because my list just got a lot longer."

Giggling, she turned her face and brushed her lips against his cheek. "You won't get any complaints from me, Sunshine."

He turned the quick kiss into one that set her pulse racing. Another impatient knock cut him short, and he took a deep breath to calm himself. "You'd better go see what Poznanski wants."

She sighed and released him. "I'm pretty sure I already know, but I'll tell you about it later, okay?"

When he reluctantly let her go, she cast him one last longing look and headed out.

ONCE AGAIN, SHE found herself on the receiving end of General Jacobs' disapproving stare. Candace couldn't care less. Knowing it was his idea to use torture on Kristie did nothing to endear the man to her.

"One week," he said.

Candace frowned at him from the other side of Dr. Poznanski's desk. "One week for what?"

"I'm giving you one week to get information out of that girl. That's it."

Her jaw sagged open. "You're joking. You expect me to build a trusting relationship in seven days with someone who hated us even before you tortured her?"

The General's eyes narrowed. "I'm not going to waste my time coddling the enemy when I have more direct methods of making her talk."

Candace couldn't believe it. Anger and disgust churned her stomach, coating her tongue with the taste of bile. "Because your methods worked so well yesterday, is that it?"

"Miss Bristol," Dr. Poznanski said, his tone soothing. "You must understand the position we're in. People are dying. We can't afford to—"

"We can't afford to make any more enemies, or fuel the ones we already have," Candace said. She could barely control her temper. "Did you not listen to anything I told you this morning? You won't get what you want from her doing it your way. She'll die before she gives up any information on HEX while she thinks we're the bad guys. I don't know what they told her, or how they convinced her we're so terrible, but she bought it completely. Until I felt firsthand what you were doing to her, I would have argued that we were the good guys. You go forward with this despicable plan, and I'll kill her myself to save her from you."

General Jacobs rose up to his full height. "If I were you, I'd watch what you say, Miss Bristol. You wouldn't want us questioning your loyalty."

Candace jumped to her feet, instantly on the defense. "My loyalty is to preserving human life and creating a better world than the one we have now. Resorting to torture makes you no better than the people we're fighting against. I won't tolerate needless suffering, not when there's a better way. I thought that was the side the ANGEL Project was on, too. Was I wrong?"

"I suggest you sit down right now, Miss Bristol," Dr. Poznanski said. His voice held an edge, a warning she was in dangerous territory.

Giving the General one last look of defiance, she lowered herself back into her seat.

"Better," he continued. "While I understand your position, you must understand ours as well. General Jacobs is correct in that time is of the essence. However, I do disagree with the methods he seems to think are necessary. That said, I would like to propose a compromise."

She waited, doubtful that she would make any concession when it came to the subject.

"I believe we should let you attempt to build a relationship with the prisoner. We'll go forward with a one-week trial period and reassess the situation at that time. If significant progress has been made, you'll continue to work with her. At any time, if she ceases to be cooperative, we'll abandon the experiment, you'll allow your connection with her to expire, and you will no longer be involved in the interrogation process."

"You mean torture," she said, sneering.

"Those are the terms," Dr. Poznanski said. "Do you accept?"

Candace thought long and hard about what she was agreeing to. Essentially, the woman's life rested in Candace's ability to weasel information out of her. "What if she cooperates? Then what?"

Both men remained silent.

"I told you, she won't be willing to give up what she

knows with nothing in it for her. There has to be something on the table she'll want. If it means enough to her, you'll get what you're after. If she thinks she's dead no matter what she does, she won't give up the others and you may as well kill her now."

Dr. Poznanski turned to the General, waiting for his response.

"What would you have me do, Miss Bristol?" he asked. "I won't release her back into enemy hands, and with her modified DNA, she can't be integrated back into the general population."

"Rehabilitation, if she responds to my outreach," Candace said. "She might not ever be fit for combat with the ANGEL Project, but someone with a water ability could be useful in a humanitarian crisis or natural disaster. Don't throw away a potential resource before we know if it's even feasible."

"We could always farm her out to other nations," Dr. Poznanski suggested. "Pending she can be turned to our side."

It gave Candace hope that maybe all was not lost for Kristie. Surely it would be a better alternative than death, wouldn't it?

"I admire the idea, but there's no guarantee you'll be successful in your endeavors," General Jacobs said. At least he didn't look hostile anymore. "I can't promise you that until I see results."

"But it's a possibility?" Candace asked.

"I'm willing to entertain the idea."

It was the most she would get out of him, and she nodded. "Then tomorrow is day one," she said. "If I'm not needed in the clinic, or called to the field, I'll do everything I can to sway her." She stood to leave.

"For her sake, I hope you're successful," General Jacobs said as Candace walked to the office door.

She gave him a last look and a nod, not betraying her thoughts.

But she knew, without a doubt, that if she couldn't turn Kristie, she would kill her to save her.

CHAPTER 22

CANDACE BROODED through most of dinner. It took Jackson tickling her knee before she realized she was all but ignoring the conversation around her. Four heads jerked in her direction when she let out a little giggle. Her cheeks heated, and she shot Jackson a peeved look.

"So anyway," Amir resumed what he was saying before her outburst. "It looks like they're running the new batch of ANGELS through right after they start up the next round of SAGE treatments."

Candace brushed Jackson's hand off of her thigh and kicked him lightly under the table. "Have they picked the next SAGEs then? Aside from Gabe."

Amir nodded. "Tobias Sokol. Leigh Grady, and Valerie Rhodes."

Candace flipped through her mental index. "Valerie does

a momentum reversal thing, right?"

True nodded. "It's more of a polarity shift, actually. She changes the direction of movement on a molecular level. It works with magnetic fields as well as motion."

"You forgot about the outsiders, Amir," Gabe said, waving his fork around.

"Outsiders?" Candace asked.

Amir sighed and rubbed at his forehead. "I'm trying not to think about it."

"It's not that bad, sugar," True said. "It's been years since we've seen them. Maybe he's calmed down."

He looked at her as though she lost her mind. "Are you talking about the same Christian I am? It would take a nuclear bomb to deflate that guy's ego."

Candace's spine went rigid. "Christian Markov? Coming here?" Holy crap. Her old fangirl habits flew into overdrive.

"And Marissa Hayden, too." Gabe gave her a knowing look. "They want to put their poster children out on display again."

Her mouth went dry. They would both be there at the same time? The ANGELs that saved her four years ago would be standing right in front of her and she could finally thank them.

"Close your mouth, Candy Cane," Gabe smirked.

Amir groaned. "Tell me you aren't a member of Christian's fan club, Candace."

Words refused to form in her brain.

"In her defense," Gabe said. "She has good reason to be, since the two of them saved her life once."

Candace swallowed hard and stared at the table, sure her face was crimson. No one there, outside of her cousin, knew about that incident.

"Is that so?" Jackson said. He stared at her so intensely, Candace worried she might burst into flames.

"Yep. There was an attack during their PR tour stop in Des Moines four years ago, and we were there for a school trip. Candy Cane wandered off and ended up in the middle of the action. Christian got to the guy before he laid a finger on Candace, and Marissa whisked her down the street. She's been starry-eyed ever since. Well, not that she wasn't before that, but afterwards she was totally done."

She shot a hateful look at Gabe. "So much for familial loyalty."

"Pff. Like they weren't going to find out eventually."

"Jesus." Amir said, pinching the bridge of his nose. "He's going to be unbearable when he finds out."

Jackson was eerily silent. She peeked at him out of the corner of her eye, but his face was stony and unreadable. God damn it.

"No one has to tell him, I suppose," True said. "But I think I'm going to agree with Amir on this one. If he's the same jerk he was the last time we saw him, then yeah. When Christian finds out he inspired one of the strongest ANGELs to date to become a superhero, yep, there'll be no living with him."

Sheepish, Candace ducked into her shoulders. "He can't be that bad, can he?"

True and Amir leveled her with flat looks. Ouch.

"Guess we'll find out next week," Gabe said, shoving food into his mouth.

"Next week?" Candace squeaked. Good lord, she sounded like those swooning girls outside the capitol that day.

Jackson bit into his bread a little more violently than she thought was necessary.

She cleared her throat and resumed eating. "I mean, I guess if they want to start the next batch of SAGEs up before the new recruits get here, that probably makes sense."

"It also means Hector and Andrew will be taking their places out east," True said.

Candace paused. Damn. What about Chloe? She'd been with Andrew since the beginning. What was it going to do to her? "Did they make any decisions on who else was going to Virginia?"

Amir shook his head. "They haven't said yet."

She glanced around him to the table at the back. Chloe and Andrew were sitting so close, Candace wondered how they had room to eat their meals. If they didn't send the two of them together, would they be able to function? The mere thought of being separated from Jackson terrified her. Had they been split up, she knew she wouldn't able to cope.

It bothered her all the way through the remainder of dinner and on the walk back to the room. Jackson was also quiet, but for a different reason.

"You never mentioned that stuff about Markov and Hayden before."

"Huh?" she said, blinking at him.

He leaned up against the desk, frowning. "You know, the whole reason you decided to become a superhero? Slip your mind a bit?"

Candace took her hair down and unbuttoned her collar. "No, but you never asked. Did I miss the memo about that homework assignment?"

His frown deepened to a scowl. "It seems like one of those important details you should offer up to your significant other."

She watched him for a moment, studying his expression. When she realized what was bothering him, she fought back a grin. Candace took him by the hand and led him over to the bed to sit.

"Are you jealous?"

Jackson snorted.

"That's not an answer."

He continued glaring at the floor.

Intent on getting his full attention, Candace peeled off her shirt and stood, slowly removing her pants. Jackson watched her, his scowl softening some, but it wasn't enough of an improvement for her. Letting him take a good, long look at her in nothing but her underclothes, Candace sashayed to the light switch and flipped it off, throwing the deadbolt on the door at the same time. Her return was slow and deliberate, and she kept her gaze trained on him the entire time.

She eased into his lap, straddling his legs. "Christian Markov has nothing on you, Sunshine. Nothing. And I fully intend to prove it to you."

His hands glided up her bare back, unhooking her bra with suspiciously practiced ease. "And how are you going to do that?"

She tossed away the undergarment. "Did you make that list?"

The corner of his mouth curved upward. "I've had that list for months, Sugar Plum."

"That's a little twisted, you know that, right?"

"Are you surprised?"

She giggled. "Not really, no. So, tell me. What's on your list?"

He paused, thoughtful. "Do you trust me?"

What kind of a question was that? Of course she did. "With my life."

"And you swear you're mine?"

She frowned. "I don't like that question. I'm not a thing. I'm a person."

Jackson touched her face. "Don't do that. You know what I mean. Do you belong to me as much as I belong to you?"

She nodded.

"Say it."

Candace rested her hands against his chest and kissed him softly. "I belong to you, Jackson."

"Give me permission," he said. His hands drifted up over her shoulderblades, coming to a rest on the meat of her upper arms.

"For what?"

"To mark you."

She stilled in his grasp. "Mark me?" What was that about? Confused and a little nervous, Candace waited for him to explain.

He released her left shoulder and held up his palm. A symbol glowed in the center of it, two backwards, intertwined letters on fire, scrolls of flame looping out from their edges.

C and J.

She swallowed. When she started the game, that wasn't what she intended. That looked like it would hurt. A lot. It would scar for sure, but that was his intention. It was his way of ensuring her commitment to him, the way hearing him admit he loved her was so crucial for her. Forever branded. Forever his.

As she tore her gaze away from the burning symbol, she met his eyes. Her doubts died in that moment.

Forever wasn't long enough. Not for a superhero.

Candace held his face and kissed him again. "Permission granted."

Pain flared to life on her right arm, shooting through the nerves as she bit back a scream. The water in her body responded immediately, rushing to the site of the injury, quenching the burn as the endorphins kicked in. The scent of charred flesh accosted her nostrils, conjuring memories of Portland. Jackson pulled her to his chest, stroking her hair as she worked through the pain. It was nothing compared to treatments or what she felt through Kristie, though.

Kristie.

Candace straightened, worried about what conclusions the woman might draw from the connection Candace shared with her.

"Something wrong?" Jackson asked, brushing her hair aside. "Was it too much? I'm sorry. I tried not to—"

"No." Candace shook her head. "I'm fine." She glanced down at her arm and cringed. "Well, mostly. Damn, that stings."

"Suppose I should find out for myself," he said, pulling off his shirt.

She gaped at him. "You're doing it too?"

Jackson chuckled and kissed her. "Of course. Did you think I was going to put you through that without me getting one to match? That hardly seems fair."

"So you made me go first?"

He shrugged. "I didn't want to freak you out if you weren't down for it. Besides," he held up his palm again, rotating the symbol a little. "There are two letters here, not just mine. Ours. Both."

Candace gave him a doubtful look. "Is that even going to work on you? Aren't you impervious or something?"

"Are you impervious to water?"

"No."

"It's the same with fire for me. I don't get burned because I tell it not to."

Jackson moved to place the white-hot symbol over his left arm, but she stopped him.

"Hold on," she said, closing her eyes. Candace reached for her connection, locating the water within his body. "Okay. I'm ready."

He gritted his teeth against the agony, and as soon as he pulled his hand away, she rushed fluids to the burn, keeping the damage restricted to the intended design. As she worked, he leaned his forehead against hers, taking slow, steady breaths.

She smiled softly, ignoring the discomfort in her arm. "Are the rest of the things on your list that sadistic?"

Jackson laughed. "Sadistic? I thought it was romantic."

"I think you need to re-evaluate your definition of that word." She giggled and tweaked his nose. "So let me rephrase. Are the other items on your list going to result in permanent marks on my body?"

"Do you trust me?"

"You're answering my questions with questions again."

He ran his hands up her neck and into her hair. "Do you

trust me?"

"Of course."

"Then you have nothing to worry about."

When he kissed her, any remaining concerns vanished, lost to the abyss of desire.

SHE BALANCED the tray of food in one arm as she swiped her badge through the card reader. The cell door opened and Candace walked inside, noting little had changed since her last visit. Kristie was still strapped to the cot, her wrists rubbed raw from struggling against the restraints.

Candace set the tray on the floor and shrugged out of the backpack she brought with her. The first thing she did was free the prisoner from the leather straps; after all, there wasn't anything the woman could do that Candace couldn't defend against. Kristie's sigh of relief was audible.

"I'm here to talk, but not until you've eaten and had some water," Candace said.

Kristie kept quiet, refusing to say a word until she was given food and drink. She all but inhaled the massive bowl of beef stew, nearly choking on a piece of bread.

"Slow down." Candace chuckled. "We have plenty of time, and you'll make yourself sick if you eat too fast."

"Yes, Mom," Kristie said, rolling her eyes.

As she ate, Candace returned to the hall and grabbed the bucket of warm, soapy water. It might not be a hot shower, but it would do. Kristie watched her through narrowed eyes.

"You can't beat me in a water fight. I'm far stronger than you are, so I wouldn't waste your energy."

Kristie snorted. "How much stronger could you possibly be? You're just like me."

Candace shook her head. "No, not exactly. I've had a secondary round of treatments. You can't win against me. But. I'm not here to fight."

"You're wasting your time," she said. "I won't give up my family."

Family. Did she mean HEX? Candace debated on telling her about the one week ultimatum, but decided against it. "They're your family, huh? I think I understand why you were so angry with me, then. You should know, however, that I did what I did to protect *my* family. HEX attacked. They killed people. They killed my friends, the people I serve with, people I've lived with every day for months. I didn't go looking for them, but I won't stand by while innocent life is destroyed. I became an ANGEL to protect others."

Kristie snorted again. "Boy, did you pick a winner. You have no idea how many secrets your precious ANGEL Project keeps from you. They aren't nearly as perfect as you think they are."

"Maybe not, but at least they don't send me out to wipe out masses of defenseless people going about their everyday lives."

Kristie's faced pinched together. "They didn't send me out. I… I ran away."

"What?" Candace said. "You attacked the dam of your own free will?"

Her expression contorted into something Candace couldn't quite define. "I was trying to lure you out. I wanted revenge for my brothers and they wouldn't let me go. They told me I wasn't ready yet, but I thought... I thought..." Her words stuck in her throat.

"You thought that water would never betray you, right?" Candace finished for her. "You thought it was your trump card."

She nodded, staring glumly into her stew.

Candace removed the tray and passed her a bottle of water in its place. As Kristie drank, Candace bent down and rifled through the bag, looking for the first aid kit she stashed in the bottom. Kristie made a valiant effort to fight off the effects of rehydration, but couldn't completely cover up her whimpers of pleasure. When the first bottle was gone, Candace took one of Kristie's arms and gently sponged off the grime, applying antiseptic ointment and gauze wrap when the wound was clean. She did the same with the other arm and handed over another bottle of water.

Candace didn't press for conversation. She was processing Kristie's words, trying to decide how next to proceed. Pulling a fresh set of clothes out of the backpack, she set them on the end of the cot.

"You can clean up as best you can with the bucket and then change. If you want to keep your old clothes, I can have them washed and hang on to them for you if you like."

Kristie eyed the sweatpants and t-shirt warily. "I thought you had a boyfriend. Now you want to watch me take a sponge bath?"

Candace sighed. "I don't want to watch anything, but I don't really have a choice. I have zero reassurance you won't try something dumb and make them change their minds about letting me in here."

"How do I know you won't try something with me?"

"Seriously?" Candace said. "If that's what I was after I think I have other ways of getting the job done aside from being nice to you."

"Maybe you like your victims clean."

Candace threw up her hands. "You're right. I've lulled you into a false sense of security so I could get you to take a bath in front of me. That's exactly how I get my jollies. Sorry, sweetheart. You're not really my type. If you don't want to wash up, I'm not going to make you."

Kristie's gaze strayed to the security camera above the door. "What about them?"

Candace considered, then strode over to it. Using a handful of water, she crafted a filter to cover the lens, effectively obscuring its view. "Happy now?" she said when she turned back to the cot.

Reluctantly, Kristie slid her legs over the side of the bed and undressed.

Candace spent the next twenty minutes studying her nails, the walls, the ceiling— anything to keep her eyes averted. She didn't need to look to keep tabs on where the water was and what Kristie did with it anyway. When the woman let out a small sigh of relief as she settled back on the bed, it felt like a major victory to Candace.

The third and final water bottle emptied down Kristie's throat.

"I have a question," Candace said.

Kristie's expression soured. "And here we go."

Candace ignored her. "Were you forced to get the treatments, or was it your choice?"

She paused, apparently expecting something else entirely.

"What? It was my choice, of course."

"Why?"

"So I could save people that couldn't save themselves."

Not commenting on the irony of that statement, Candace nodded and collected all the things she brought in. "What's your last name?"

"Burke."

As Candace headed out, Kristie called to her. "Wait, that's it?"

Shrugging, Candace lingered in the doorway. "I'll be back at dinner. Oh," she said, setting everything down on the floor of the hall and rummaging through the pack again. When she found the book, she tossed it inside and smiled. "So you have something to do. I didn't know what you'd like, so I took a guess."

Kristie retrieved the paperback and studied it, curious. Her eyes drifted up to meet Candace's, all traces of hostility gone. "Thank you. I haven't read this one before."

"You're welcome," Candace said with a smile. "I'll see you later."

The door closed and locked behind her as she left.

She chuckled to herself. Sexy aliens. How could you go wrong with that?

CHAPTER 23

CANDACE TOSSED the backpack on the floor of her room and stretched. Maybe she hadn't gotten the exact information they wanted, but it was progress. Eventually, she wanted to get Kristie to a point where it was safe to bring another ANGEL into the holding cell, likely an empath like Deborah or Chloe. As she debated on which to approach with the matter, someone pounded on the door.

"Clinic. Now," Gabe said when she opened it. "It's Trevor."

Candace's heart raced as they ran down the corridors. She heard the howls of pain before they reached his room in the ICU.

"He's finally awake?" she asked. "What's going on? Why all the yelling?"

Dr. Poznanski and a group of soldiers waited outside the

door.

"We need you to paralyze him, Miss Bristol," Dr. Poznanski said. "His system was impervious to the first anesthesia we tried and he had a bad reaction. We need to get him still to administer stronger drugs to induce a coma while his body continues the healing process."

There was a crash as something slammed into a wall, followed by more howling. Candace flinched. "Is he okay? Aside from the burn damage?"

Dr. Poznanski shook his head. "We don't know. It's possible the electricity he was exposed to caused neural damage, but we can't get close enough to find out."

Deeply worried about that possibility, Candace tried to ignore the noise and focus on her connection. She located each individual standing with her, then explored further out, into the room beyond. Well-hydrated from IV fluids and with his massive size, Trevor was easy to find. She waited until he threw whatever he was holding before snapping the cord taut, stopping his movements instantly.

Cracking the door, she looked inside, making sure the room was safe. Trevor was frozen by the side of the bed, his face contorted in a mask of anguish. His eyes locked on to her, both angry and pleading for her help. Candace slowly stepped through the doorway, over a shattered monitor, hands raised.

"I'm here to help," she said in the most soothing tone possible. Candace tried not to stare at the torn open skin grafts and bandages hanging on to his face by bits of flesh. "I know you're scared and in pain, so let's go slow, okay?"

Closing her eyes and releasing a deep breath, she guided his body back down onto the cot, resting him on the side without damage. Carefully, she dodged broken and overturned things to stand beside him, and bent down to his eye level. "I'm going to try to ease some of your pain, but I'll have to release you to do that. Are you with me, Trevor? Will you stay calm while I try?"

She eased up on her hold enough to let him speak.

"C-Candace?" His formerly strong, steady voice cracked over the word.

She smiled and nodded. "That's right, Trevor. Candy Cane is here to help. Can you hang on while I do this? You're so strong, there's no way I can fight you physically, and I don't want to get hurt. Will you trust me?"

His eyes were wide, searching hers. "I don't know what's happening. It hurts."

"You don't remember what happened in Portland?"

"Portland?"

She frowned as she thought of where to start. "What's the last thing you remember?"

"You were fighting with Jackson on the field. I carried you here, right?"

Jesus. That was months ago. She sighed. "That's right, but that was in the fall. It's halfway through January now, Trevor. You don't remember anything since then?"

He squinted his eyes, struggling for memory. "You flew in the shuttle."

Better, but so far his recollections were only about her. Maybe he needed a visual prompt to get his synapses firing. "Do you remember what happened with Adrian?"

Trevor blinked at her, scanning every inch of her face. "He... he died?"

She nodded slowly, pushing past the ghosts calling to

her. "That's right. He died. Okay, I think you'll be all right and that things will come back to you little by little, but it'll take time. Now, you swear you won't try to hurt me if I let you go?"

"I won't hurt you, Candy Cane," he said with a small, pained smile.

Candace gradually released her hold on him, replacing paralysis with a soothing massage. Guiding gathered water away from swollen tissue, she took some of the pressure off of his wounds and stabilized the flow of blood throughout his body. At some point, Dr. Poznanski and a corpsman entered and started patching up the places he tore away during his outburst. They ran a new IV line into his undamaged arm, the doctor giving her a nod when they were ready with the new drugs.

Again, she crouched to his level. "Trevor, they want to put you to sleep for a while, so you can heal and not be in pain. I wish there was more I could do for you, but I can't keep you comfortable indefinitely. The relief isn't permanent. What I've done will help you, though. I've coaxed some of your damaged tissue back to the way it's meant to be, so it will heal faster and with less scarring. I don't know when we'll talk again, but try to hang in there, okay? People here miss you."

"You got it, Candy Cane," he said, already sleepy. "Tell Allen I'll be ready to pound him again soon."

She fought back a flinch. He didn't know about Allen, or Gil, either, for that matter. "Trevor?" she said.

"Hmm?"

She'd better not tell him yet. "Thank you for not dying. I know this sucks, but I'm glad you're still with us."

"Mmm…" he mumbled, his eyelids drooping closed.

Candace passed one last ripple through his body and left the room, hoping he'd come out on the other side less upset.

"How is he?" Gabe asked as she emerged.

Candace rubbed her forehead and walked down the hall with him. "He didn't remember anything about Portland, but once I started talking to him, I think seeing me brought back a few memories. There's definitely some brain damage. I don't have a clue how much or how severe or how permanent it is, though."

They stopped outside of Dr. Poznanski's office. "But you think he'll be okay eventually?" Gabe asked.

"I really have no idea," she said, tired. "I'll need to tell Dr. P about the medical things, though, and see how he wants to proceed. If you see Jackson, could you let him know where I am? I don't know how long I'll be, and I don't want him to worry."

Gabe frowned. "Worry? What, like he has to know where you are every second of the day?"

She shook her head. "It's not that, it's… something else. I had another thing this afternoon, and I don't want him to think it didn't go well."

"Another thing? That's suspiciously vague. Does this have to do with whatever fight you guys had yesterday?"

Candace waved it off. "Yes and no. It's a long story. Just let him know where I am, okay?"

"Sure thing, cuz," Gabe said, lightly punching her right shoulder.

Biting down on her lip, she gasped as the soft tap ignited pain from Jackson's brand.

Gabe jerked, startled by her reaction. "What the hell?

Are you hurt?" He grabbed her arm and lifted the sleeve of her polo before she could stop him, revealing the gauze-covered burn. "What happened?"

She pulled her arm away and gave him her best "I'm not a kid anymore" look. "It's nothing. I'm a superhero. We get hurt. I'm fine."

"That's not nothing and you didn't say what happened. You weren't out in the field yesterday or I'd know about it." He lowered his voice and stepped in close. "Did he do something? Because you can tell me, Candace. It's okay."

Good lord, did he think Jackson was abusing her? "What? No. Well, yes, but not like you think. We…" Hmm. The explanation of what adorned her shoulder sounded really stupid saying it out loud. "He didn't do anything I didn't give him permission to do."

Gabe's stare was piercing. "If this is some weird sex thing, you need to cut it out right now. I've got nothing against a good spanking or whatever, but if he's leaving marks—"

"Oh my God," she groaned, covering her face with a hand. "No, it's nothing like that. Yuck. But, fine. Since you're not going to drop it, I'll show you." She looked up and down the hall, checking for eavesdroppers. Seeing no one, she pulled the sleeve of her shirt up and over the bandage, rolling it on top of her shoulder. Carefully, she pulled away one side of the adhesive to show him the product of Jackson's artistic side. "See? That's all it is. He has one too. That's it. Happy?"

Gabe winced when he saw the burned flesh. "Christ, Candy Cane. That's disgusting. You let him do that?"

She nodded.

He blew out a breath and ran a hand through his hair. "Your mom is going to hate that, you know."

She choked back a laugh. "Seriously? I've had my DNA altered twice in the last six months and you think *this* is the thing that'll push her over the edge? Besides, she said 'no tattoos.' This isn't a tattoo."

"He branded you like cattle," he said flatly.

With a sigh, she realized it wasn't a battle she was going to win. "Whatever. It was my choice, the same way *he's* my choice. Anyway, it's done, regardless of your feelings on it." She put the bandage back in place and lowered her sleeve. "But, I do appreciate your concern. Believe it or not, he probably puts up with way more of my shit than I do of his. You'd be surprised how sweet he can be." Try as she might, she couldn't keep the smile off her face. "He's very careful with me. He knows what I can take and doesn't ask for more than that. And he always asks for permission. Always."

Gabe had the strangest expression on his face. "So, it is possible, then?"

"Is what possible?"

He swallowed, staring at the floor. "Finding someone else."

She touched his face, then pulled him into a hug when he looked at her. "Definitely possible," she whispered to him. "Don't give up on yourself."

He squeezed her tightly, sucking in a deep breath. "Thank you, Candy Cane."

"You're welcome," she said, pulling away. "Now, about passing that message..."

Gabe grinned. "I'll go find him and let him know."

As he strode off down the hall, Candace watched him.

With SAGE treatments fast approaching for her cousin, all she could hope for was that someone really fantastic would arrive with the new batch of ANGELs. If anyone deserved a chance at love, it was Gabe.

JACKSON WAS pacing the room when she returned from the clinic.

"How was it? Did it go okay? Are you all right?" he asked, bombarding her with questions the moment the door closed.

Candace smiled at him. "It was fine. I'm going back at dinner to talk to her again."

He frowned, displeased with the situation.

"What's the matter?" Candace asked.

"Isn't there someone else that can do this? I don't like you going in there by yourself."

She set her hands on her hips. "By myself? Really, Sunshine, it's not like she can hurt me. No one else can defend against her ability. It's probably safer for me to be in that room with her than it is to be sparring with you."

"Not the same," he growled. "I'd never hurt you intentionally."

"Don't be silly. I know it's not the same." She slipped her arms around his waist and looked up at him. "But she can't hurt me, intentionally *or* accidentally. Seriously. It's a matter of strength. Not only is she still really dehydrated, but with the SAGE treatment it's no contest. Now that she's aware of that, she knows better than to even try."

Jackson stared at her. "You told her about the second round of treatments?"

"I wasn't specific about anything, but, yes, I told her."

"Why? You're giving up information to the enemy."

She shook her head. "For one, she's not going anywhere. Who's she going to tell? For two, everything is a trade-off with her. I have to give to get. If there's nothing in it for her, I don't get a single thing. And, really, nothing I said was specific, so even if HEX knew, they couldn't replicate it. It's not like I have formulas to give her or anything."

He sighed and pulled her close. "I still don't understand what you're hoping to accomplish here."

Candace snuggled into his embrace, doing her best to be patient with him. "It's a matter of trust. We may have started off on opposite sides, but I don't think it's out of the question to reach an understanding, at least between the two of us. She doesn't like the ANGEL Project, that much is for sure. Still, I think I'm making progress."

"So you think you'll get her to talk?"

Pulling away, she stretched and yawned, then made her way to the bathroom. "At this point, I have no idea. I'm working on the trust part first before I try to get anything substantive out of her. So far all I've gotten is her name and that she decided to become a superhero to help people that couldn't help themselves, which is more than they got out of her the other way. And going by some of her comments, HEX works really hard to make their members feel like family, rather than teammates. It's a psychological tactic. Especially if you give a feeling of belonging to people that didn't have that before, it can inspire almost kamikaze loyalty in members." She filled a glass with water and leaned up in the doorway to watch him as she drank. "Cults work the same way. They offer something the broader world doesn't, and that's the draw for people who get sucked in. They don't see the crazy side of it; they're too dependent on what they're being given."

"Basically, you have to un-brainwash her?" he said, crossing his arms.

Candace shrugged. "I dunno. Some of what she said…" She frowned, unsure it was the right place to voice her concerns. "I'm not sure she's entirely backwards in her thinking, but I don't know enough yet to say either way."

Fiddling with things on the desk, Jackson continued frowning. "I don't like the sound of that."

She took a drink and considered him. A new idea took hold, but it was probably a terrible idea. Still, the more she thought about it, the more she liked it. It would give Kristie the chance to see her as a real person, rather than the enemy.

"Do you want to meet her?"

He looked at her, confused. "What?"

"Kristie," she said. "Do you want to meet her? She actually reminds me a little of you. Snarky, reticent, untrusting, violent tendencies…"

"Flatterer."

She laughed. "I'm sure she has redeeming qualities too." Setting the glass down, Candace walked back to him and wound her arms around his neck. "It might go a long way in showing her I trust her if I bring someone in that's important to me. If you don't give people a chance to be better, they never will be."

Jackson gazed at her, a bemused smile curving his lips. "Sounds like a philosophy you've used before."

"I'm sure I have no idea what you're talking about," she said, batting her eyelashes. "So, what do you think?"

"Just to be clear, you want me to go meet the woman that tried to kill me so she'll be your friend?"

Candace played with the hair at the base of his skull, twirling it between her fingers. "Basically, yes."

"What's in it for me?"

"Hmm," she murmured. "My undying devotion and gratitude?"

He grinned. "Already got that."

Her hands drifted down to the front of his shirt, gripping his collar and pulling his face down to hers. "Maybe a few more items checked off this list of yours?"

"I'm listening."

She held him there, eyes never straying from his. "Do this for me, and I give you free reign, Sunshine."

"Anything I want?"

"Anything."

It took him a moment, but he nodded, a devilish gleam in his eyes. "Okay, Sugar Plum, but no takebacks."

Candace leaned up and kissed him. "Well, we still have an hour until dinner, so..."

"Hate to disappoint you," he said, a chuckle rumbling in his chest. "But that's not enough time for what I have in mind."

"Oh, really?" she said. "Now I'm curious. Wanna give me a hint?"

"Not a chance."

She pouted. "Please?"

Jackson laughed and released her, picking up his coat. "Nope. Think I'll go for a walk. Want to come with?"

She wrinkled her nose. "Pass. Too cold out there for me."

"Even if I promise to keep you warm?"

Giggling, she relented. "Fine, but my clothes stay on."

S H E   L E F T Jackson in the hall outside the cell. Kristie was reading when Candace walked in.

"Good book?" she asked.

Kristie looked up. "Hmm? Oh, yeah. Not bad. Is this a series or a standalone?"

"A series," Candace said, setting the tray of food in Kristie's lap. "So, I thought you might be getting sick of my face by now, but I need you to promise me you won't hurt anyone else I bring in here."

Folding the corner of the page back, Kristie closed the book and set it aside in favor of the meal. Candace winced, but couldn't help being amused at yet another similarity to Jackson.

"Depends," she said. "Is it your precious Dr. Poznanski coming in to torture me again?"

Candace sighed. "No. It's my boyfriend. The one you already tried to kill once."

Kristie choked on a bite of carrot, washing it down with a big gulp of water. "You want to unleash someone on me that I tried to... I don't think I'm okay with that," she said after she recovered.

"He's not here to hurt you," Candace said. "He's here because I asked him to be. He worries about me, and I want him to know I'm safe. But, I'm not going to bring him in if you're going to try something. So can I have your word that you'll behave, or not?"

"As you've already said you'll leave me to rot if I don't, I think he's safe." She rolled her eyes and stuffed another bite in her mouth.

Candace grimaced and went back to the door, opening it to let him in. Jackson entered, his expression dubious as he handed Candace her dinner tray. "I don't see why we had to eat down here."

"Stop complaining, Sunshine," she said, brushing a kiss against his cheek. "Consider it community service if you like. Have a seat."

When she glanced back at Kristie, the girl's head whipped back down to her food, purposely avoiding looking at them. What the hell?

"Kristie Burke, this is Jackson Lawrence. Jackson, Kristie," she said. "There. Now we're all friends." Plopping down on the floor, Candace tossed him a wink.

"So you're a firebug then, huh?" Kristie said, still focused on her food.

Jackson snorted. "What, did she tell you that, too?"

Kristie shrugged. "It was in the water she gave me. She didn't need to."

Candace's cheeks heated. "You could tell from that?"

"What's she talking about?" Jackson said.

The look of "don't you know anything?" on Kristie's face spoke volumes. "Yeah, I could tell from that. The aftertaste of smoke gave it away. You'd be surprised what you can learn about a person that way."

Candace made a face. "Well, I don't generally go around drinking other people, so—"

"Drinking people? What the hell have you been doing down here?" Jackson interrupted.

"Calm down, Sunshine," Candace said. "I gave her a little of my water to keep our connection intact."

He raised an eyebrow. "Is that so?" He grinned. "I think I just added something to the list then."

"That wasn't part of the deal."

"You said free reign."

"I meant of the existing list."

He chuckled. "Too late now. No takebacks, no addendums."

She brandished her fork at him. "So not the time or place to discuss this."

Kristie cleared her throat. "So, as entertaining as it is to listen to your verbal foreplay, can we maybe change the subject?"

"Sure," Candace said, giving Jackson a look of warning. "Anything on your mind?"

Kristie tapped a piece of bread against her lips, thinking. "How long have you been an ANGEL?"

"I got here in August," Candace replied. "What about you? When did you start with... um, them?"

She shrugged. "About a year ago. HEX approached me after my brother died."

Candace swallowed. "Can I ask what happened? If you don't want to tell me —"

"He was collateral damage in an ANGEL rescue," she said, eyes fixed firmly on Candace. "They didn't get there in time."

Candace flinched. That was one of the hazards of deploying from a central location. There were always casualties, no matter how fast the shuttle was. "I'm sorry," she said, though it was a hollow sentiment. Once she knew what she was fighting against, turning her to their side seemed impossible. Because of the delay, Kristie lost her brother. Candace could never make up for that.

"HEX is different," Kristie continued. "They can be anywhere and everywhere in seconds. And when we have problems, we don't shove them away in some dark corner. We show the world how imperfect the process is. Only the truly special can be superheroes."

Suspicion gnawed at her insides. "What do you mean, you show the world? Show them how?"

Kristie shrugged again. "Maybe you heard about them. Miami, Myrtle Beach, Portland. They were mistakes."

"Mistakes?" Candace's voice was barely above a whisper. "Portland was one of your *mistakes*?"

"Some ANGELs cleaned it up. You should know since that one was West Coast."

God, she wanted to puke. Candace pushed aside her meal, unable to stomach another bite. "So HEX just dumps their fuck ups in the middle of populated areas and leaves them for others to deal with?" She pinched her eyes closed, shaking with anger. Jackson was beside her in an instant, an arm around her shoulders.

"I think it's time to go, Sugar Plum," he whispered in her ear. "You can't take it out on her. You know that."

She looked at him, tears brimming in her eyes. "You weren't there. You didn't see what he did. Everyone he killed, all those people, plus Gil, and Trevor... I saw him today, Jackson. He's never going to be the same. Never."

"You..." Kristie said, hesitant. "You were in Portland?"

Candace stood, scooping up her tray. She glared at the

girl; the stupid, naïve, completely brainwashed girl. "I'm the one that cleaned up that mistake," she spat. "I snapped his neck after he killed the team leader and severely wounded another. And that was after your *mistake* massacred over twenty-five innocent people. Do you think that's right, making other people pay for your screw ups?"

Kristie stared at her, mouth gaping.

Candace didn't wait for a reply. She snatched the rest of the meal away from her and headed for the door. Jackson was already there, holding it open as she marched out into the hallway, trying not to cry.

CHAPTER 24

CANDACE HELD it together long enough to give her daily report to Dr. Poznanski and General Jacobs, though how she managed it was a small miracle. Afterwards, Jackson brought her back to the room and held her while she cried herself out.

"I'm sorry it went like that today, Candy Cane," he said as the last of her sniffles abated. "But if it means anything, I think you had a lot of really good insights about HEX in your report."

"I should have let her finish her meal," she said, miserable. "It's not her fault HEX does what they do with unstables."

"You can apologize to her in the morning. Maybe bring her something special for breakfast?"

She nodded and snuggled into his arms. "And more

books." Exhausted, her eyes started to close, but they popped open again when she realized she had a debt to pay, and she propped herself up to look at him. "I... Don't I owe you —"

Jackson set a finger to her lips. "Don't worry about that right now. Sugar Plum. Get some sleep."

Candace closed her eyes and settled back into his embrace. "You know I love you, right?"

"Shh," he whispered. "I love you, too."

It was still dark when she woke, cold and alone. Candace sat up, confused, and looked at the clock. Where would Jackson go at three in the morning? When she saw her swim suit and a towel draped over the back of a chair, she immediately knew: the pool.

After changing, Candace headed out, pausing at the sign on the inner locker room door that said "Closed for Maintenance." She reached out with her connection, to the water in the next room. It was no surprise when she sensed him already swimming.

What might be on his list that involved the pool? Candace grinned. She had a guess, but it was one of several possibilities. Guiding the water surrounding him, she did what she'd done twice before, albeit with different intentions. Without hesitation, she began her aquatic exploration of his body. Powerful arms. Chiseled chest. Those amazing abs of his.

Lower still.

Over his back as the muscles rippled with each stroke. Down his legs. Back up his thighs...

"You should really come and join me, Sugar Plum," Jackson called from beyond the doors.

Thoroughly pleased with herself, Candace pushed open the door, only to be knocked back by a cloud of steam. The room was completely filled with fog, obscuring the windows and anything beyond a foot in front of her. She tossed her towel on a chair and felt her way to the edge, slipping beneath the surface and cloaking herself immediately. The game was afoot.

She prowled along the edges for a while, watching him as he searched for her. He found her last time, but not with his eyes. As heated as the water was, she couldn't stay down for long.

Jackson stopped in the center of the pool and sank down to the bottom. Even though the goal of the game was to get caught, her heart raced as he focused and searched for her. When he locked in on her position, she scrambled upwards, but barely got a hand over the ledge before he was on her.

"Took me longer this time, sorry," he said as he pinned her against the side. "Wasn't as easy to find your heat signature with the pool so warm."

His fingers brushed the side of her face, breaking through the aquatic camouflage. Dropping the barrier, she waited for further instruction. It was part of his list, his fantasy.

Pressed against her back, he leaned in to her ear. "I've wanted you like this since the first time I saw you in the water, Sugar Plum. The way you move here, it's magic. Did you know? Watching you swim that first time was the sexiest damn thing I'd ever seen."

Candace closed her eyes, feeling his breath against her skin.

"Last time we were here," he continued. "You asked me

to stop. It took every ounce of strength I had, but I did. I can't do that again, Candace. I can't anymore. Because I need you. I need you, and that's never going to go away."

Unable to hold out another moment, she turned in his arms and kissed him, desperate for the taste of him, to share her overwhelming desire with him. She whispered his name as his hands stripped away her suit, touching every inch of her bare flesh as he went. A strong current was all it took to tear away his trunks. Not wasting another second, Jackson crushed her against the wall of the pool, pushing inside her with a need as great as her own. The ecstasy of each thrust compounded by the sensation of water against her skin, surrounding her, surrounding him. Her bliss rippled out from her in waves, overloading her senses. She clutched at him, clinging to him. Every time he said her name was more beautiful than the last. Every movement was in sync. Every sensation shared. She succumbed to the total pleasure of the moment, and he followed her, overcome as the climax took them both.

Jackson held her there, his breathing labored. "Magic," he whispered.

Candace kept him close, relishing the beat of his heart in time with hers, and unwilling to let go of the feeling. They were the same, two halves of a whole, their energies intertwining. Slowly, she opened her eyes and released a held breath. Steam puffed out from her lungs, adding to the cloud already surrounding them. She stared.

"Oh my God," she said, disbelieving what stirred inside her.

Her connection exploded outwards, into the air, filling the room. New voices, ones that held the ghosts of liquidity, echoed in her head, speaking to her, welcoming her to their fold.

"Jackson will do fine, Sugar Plum," he said, chuckling as he nuzzled her neck. "But you can call me that when we're alone if you really want to."

"No," she said, tapping him on the back absentmindedly. "I mean, yeah, maybe that too, but look."

When he lifted his head, he followed her gaze to the open air. Candace focused, shaping the vapor into recognizable shapes: spheres, pyramids, rings. The condensed gases floated lazily over the pool, dripping slightly as the water molecules cooled and combined.

"What the hell?" Jackson said, jerking away and breaking their contact.

Candace giggled. "Guess you're rubbing off on me, Sunshine. I think I just leveled up."

"That's hardly fair," he grumbled. "How come you got the upgrade?"

She swam the short distance between them and poked at his ribs. "So, what? You're saying if you don't get a power up, you're not getting anything out of this? Because if that's the case, you can go celibate if you like."

He caught her, treading water for the both of them. "You really think I'm capable of that?"

She giggled again. "No, but it's silly to be jealous over some stupid clouds. How is that even useful? It's a parlor trick and nothing more."

"You say that now." He nipped at her earlobe. "But wait until they start asking you to make it rain."

At that, she burst out laughing.

"Are you perpetually thirteen or something?" he chided.

Candace floated up and caught his bottom lip between her teeth, sucking at it gently before breaking away. "How about you make it rain, Sunshine?" She dove under the water, Jackson at her heels. It was a race he'd definitely win.

JACKSON WENT with her to see Kristie that morning.

More standoffish than last time, the girl completely refused to meet her eyes, and even flushed when she glanced at Jackson. Weird.

"I owe you an apology," Candace said, handing over the breakfast tray. She went the extra mile that morning and made sure to get the Belgian waffles with strawberries and whipped cream from the serving line. They always went fast on Wednesdays. "I got upset yesterday and took it out on you. What happened in Portland wasn't directly your fault, but you need to know that what HEX does has serious consequences. Just because you don't see it, doesn't mean that other people don't suffer because of their callousness."

"Pot, meet kettle," Kristie mumbled into her orange juice.

Candace sighed. "Okay, I get it. HEX has its ugly side, and maybe so does the ANGEL Project. But I don't get why you hate us so much. Is it only because of your brother? Or is it something more than that?"

Kristie met her eyes, seriously considering her. "You don't get out much, do you?"

"Is that a serious question, or commentary on my naïveté?"

"A serious question."

Candace unpinned her hair and shook it out. "Look at this and look at my eyes and you tell me: do I look like I'd blend in anywhere?"

Kristie took it all in and shrugged. "HEX lets us out all the time. But, then again, they don't whore us out to parties and propaganda so no one would know us anyway."

"You just walk around the streets being superheroes?" Jackson said. "I think we'd have heard about that if—"

"No," she interrupted. "We don't do anything. We just live. You know, like real people do."

Candace couldn't wrap her head around it. "Wait, let me get this straight. You have your DNA altered to make you superhuman and then go back to your normal lives?"

"Well, no, not exactly," Kristie said. "We live in groups, and when we're asked to do stuff, we do it unobtrusively and make sure no one sees us. But we come and go as we please so long as we don't bother anybody. Mostly."

"Asked to do stuff?" Candace said. "What stuff?"

Kristie poked at a strawberry. "Stuff. Mostly bother you guys, but I've put out a house fire or two. That kind of stuff."

"Why?" Jackson asked. "What's the point?"

She shot him a dull look. "To prove we don't need Big Brother watching over our shoulder every single minute of every day. But now that you guys kidnapped me, they're gonna be pissed."

Candace wasn't buying it. The whole thing sounded too good to be true. "I thought you ran away. If it's so wonderful, why would you leave? To avenge two guys that went off the rails and started killing people in San Jose? I call bullshit."

She frowned at her food. "I don't like snow. It makes me

slow. Demetri and Caleb didn't like it either. They said no."

"Huh?" Candace said. That answer didn't even make sense.

Kristie chewed on her lip, deep in thought.

Jackson stepped up beside the bed, his shoulders relaxed, eyes soft. Candace paused, watching him. What was he doing?

He reached out and gently tilted the girl's chin up to him. "Did they ask you to do something you didn't want to?"

Kristie's gaze went fuzzy and the flush in her cheeks was unmistakable. When Candace realized what he was doing, she bristled, but tried to get a handle on it. How had he known he'd have that effect on her?

Kristie nodded ever so slightly, her eyes tearing up.

As Jackson bent lower, closer to Kristie's face. Candace clamped down on her jealousy, but also her sense of absolute wrongness. He was manipulating the poor girl.

"What did they want you to do?"

When Kristie spoke, it was barely a whisper. "Hit the X-Games on Saturday. I didn't want to hurt anyone."

Holy shit. What just happened? Candace put the brakes on her urge to run out of the room. She needed to let it play out, as much as she hated it.

Jackson's fingers drifted away from her chin, brushing against her jawline as he pulled away. "Smart girl. I wouldn't want that on my conscience, either."

Kristie's eyelids fluttered as he backed up, then she balked, her hands covering her mouth, horrified at what she said. "Oh my God. I just… I mean…"

"Calm down, Princess," he said, chuckling. "I'm not going to hurt you. And neither will they. You did the right thing.

You saved people that won't be able to save themselves."

Jesus H. Christ. Candace never knew Jackson could be so manipulative. What he got Kristie to confess, never mind how at ease she looked, it was scary. It also made her wonder what else he might've used that particular skill of his to accomplish.

"How's your breakfast?" he asked, completely ignoring everything that transpired a moment ago.

Kristie blinked a few times then stared down at her meal, stupefied. "It's really good."

Jackson glanced at Candace, indicating it was her turn. What was she supposed to do? "Oh, right," she said, trying to sound as nonchalant as he apparently was about the whole thing. They were definitely going to talk about it later. "I brought you more books," she said. Candace dug through her backpack and pulled out the other three volumes of the sexy alien series. "I wasn't sure how fast you read, but I wanted to make sure you had these in case I get called away or busy in the clinic and can't make a meal. I mean, you'll still get food and all, but I'd miss it if you finished a book and needed another."

She set them on the floor, then fished out a two-liter bottle of water and handed it over.

Kristie grinned and took it, not even trying to hide the effects of rehydration. God. That wasn't at all obvious, and it definitely wasn't meant for Candace. After taking a shaky breath, Kristie smiled coyly at Jackson then put on a friendly expression for Candace. "Any chance for another sponge bath today?"

Candace had enough for one day, and nodded. "Sure. When I drop by at lunch, I'll make sure you have what you need."

"Just you?" Kristie said, pouting as she glanced at Jackson, who grinned like a cat. Damn him.

Before he could get a word out, Candace answered for him. "Just me, sorry. Sunshine here has other things going on this afternoon." She shouldered the backpack, then stopped before she turned to go. Doing her best not to frown, she collected a handful of her own water and offered it to the prisoner. "Time for a recharge."

Kristie slowly closed her eyes, leaned forward, and parted her lips, waiting for an offering. Remaining calm, Candace directed the water accordingly, making sure not to send it up the girl's nose like she really wanted to.

That done, she hooked an arm through Jackson's and pulled him away. He tossed Kristie a little wave as they left.

Candace didn't say a word as they wound their way out of the underground passages and up into the main complex. It was stupid to get jealous. Really, he was playing mind games with the poor girl. She should be appalled. Instead, she stewed all the way back to their room. She wanted to drop off the backpack. They should be reporting to Poznanski and Jacobs. Plans needed to be made and they should be running to tell them.

When the bag hit the floor and the door closed, Candace spun on him. Her planned diatribe was cut off before it began, replaced by Jackson's unrelenting kiss. Even when she tried to break away, he wouldn't let her. Only when she relaxed and gave way to his affection did he ease up.

"Just in case you were worried," he said against her mouth. "You don't have to be, Sugar Plum. Not ever. Don't even think it."

She grimaced. "I dunno, Sunshine. You were awfully damn convincing down there. I had no idea you were an actor on top of being an artist."

He winced, then wrapped his arms around her, totally enveloping her in his warmth. "I would never, ever, give you up. I love you too much, but I saw an opportunity and I had to take it. I wanted to help you. You want her to live, and I want to help you get that."

Candace closed her eyes and breathed in his scent: warm, smoky earth. "What opportunity? How did you know she would react that way?"

Pulling back a little, he met her gaze. "You didn't see it when we walked in?"

She frowned.

"Candace, she barely looked at you, and she was redder than a tomato with one glance at me. You can't think of why?" He chuckled, further irritating her.

"No."

He brushed the floating hair away from her face. "Think for a second. What was the last thing you did before we left her cell?"

"Tried not to look pissed off," she grumbled.

"To Kristie," he said with a sigh. "Use your brain. I know you've got one in there."

Candace stepped back and crossed her arms, still pouting a little. "I gave her water."

"To what end?"

"To make sure we stay—" When it hit her, she slapped a hand over her mouth. "Connected," she whispered through her fingers. "Holy shit. I didn't even consider…"

Jackson laughed. "Guess you weren't the only one

saying 'oh my God' last night."

Candace buried her face in her hands, completely mortified both at what she shared with Kristie and that she'd been so blind to it. "Damn it all."

Taking her back up in his arms, Jackson kissed the top of her head. "Well, if nothing else, it only reaffirms my own suspicion."

She tilted her face up to his. "Oh, really? And what might that be?"

When his lips brushed against hers, she shivered. "That you are totally, undoubtedly, one-hundred percent mine."

"Was there ever a question?"

"Mmm," he murmured. "Not really, but it's nice to get the affirmation."

"And how would you know that means I'm yours?"

"If you weren't, she wouldn't have been that convinced I'm amazing. If even a little of what you feel transferred to her, the whole of it is more than I can imagine."

When he kissed her again, she didn't fight it. He was right. Candace was irrevocably his, and she would tell him that every day if she needed to.

CHAPTER 25

"I LOOK like a strawberry marshmallow," Candace grumbled as she tried to disappear into the puffy pink coat.

Jackson laughed. "It's not that bad, Sugar Plum." He took her white-mittened hand and pulled her down the street, away from the bus stop. "It's kind of nice to see your feminine side."

She dragged her feet across the packed snow as they followed the crush of people headed toward the X-Games festival grounds. "Just because I'm a girl doesn't mean they have to douse me in cotton candy pink. This coat is ridiculous, and don't even get me started on this hat. How many rabbits died to make this fuzzy monstrosity possible?"

Chuckling lightly, he tucked her arm into his and leaned in to her ear. "I dunno. I think the snow bunny thing kind of works for you."

"You're hilarious."

"It's one of my better qualities, I think," he said. "Now, are you going to whine about your clothes or help me look for these guys?"

"Would be easier if I didn't have to crane my neck around all this fluff," she muttered.

Jackson rolled his eyes, then turned his attention back to the crowd. Sighing, Candace gave up complaining and took to scanning the faces around them. Standing barely five-foot-two didn't do her any favors, as most everyone was taller than her.

After they made it through the crush of people at the main gate, they headed to their assigned post at the Slopestyle area. Jackson cut through the spectators easily enough, leading them up the left side of the viewing area.

"SAGE Team Alpha in position," a voice said over the tiny speaker in her left ear. Candace tried not to show surprise at the reminder of its presence.

But when the alarm sounded to indicate a snowboarder was starting his run, she jumped. Her eyes turned to the massive screen across from them, above the heads of those on the other end of the half-moon spectator area, and watched the man's opening few seconds. Though she would have liked to see the whole thing, that wasn't her role that day. No, that afternoon she was playing the part of someone's girlfriend who was dragged to the event by her boyfriend. Stupid gender stereotypes. As such, it wasn't a stretch to look a little peeved at the situation, but she kept it in check while she surveyed the scene.

No one looked out of place or obviously plotting something. If they were going by what Kristie said about

HEX, it wasn't surprising. Candace pushed the sunglasses up her face. Dear God, even they were tinted pink. With another sigh, she decided to try a different tactic. So long as they were waiting anyway, she had time to experiment.

Her discovery of her new connection to steam got her thinking. At first glance, it seemed pretty useless. It wasn't like she could create steam any more than she could liquid water, only manipulate it. There was more to it, however. It wasn't mere manipulation. Her connection was communication, and communication was a two-way street. If she could talk to steam, maybe it would tell her something she could use.

The voice of the gaseous state of water was different from the liquid one. It was faster, wispy, and harder to understand. As it required more concentration, Candace needed a fixed point to stare at, rather than a person. How obvious would she be if she was going one by one through the crowd with intense scrutiny? Instead, she pinned her gaze on the signage above the widescreen showing the event in real time and pulled herself inward, reaching out to the elusive voices of steam.

With most of the water around her frozen, there was little to distract her from the cloudy breaths coming from the spectators. Unsure of what she was looking for, she tapped into the molecular memory within the energy of each particle. More than one spoke of alcohol, but that wasn't a shocker given where she was. Nothing felt out of the ordinary. Still, she needed a baseline to judge it against. Jackson's breath drifted up into the air beside her and she turned to that to see if anything stuck out. Sure enough, there was a distinct difference. There was strength, there was heat, but something else too; something she couldn't quite define that made it feel different. Satisfied that it was the unidentified element she should be looking for, she went back to her search.

About halfway through reading the crowd, Candace stopped. There it was. That unusual something she couldn't quite describe. It came with the feel of distance, of being misplaced somehow, instead of heat like Jackson. She frowned impatiently at the screen as another boarder geared up for his run, and visually made her way around the crowd until she found the source.

If he noticed her, she couldn't tell. He wasn't particularly tall or broad, but his spiked blond hair, the tips tinted red, added an extra three inches to his height. He was singularly focused on the contestant ready to come down the course.

Candace turned to Jackson and tugged on his sleeve. She looked up at him with plaintive eyes when she had his attention.

"I'm bored. I want hot chocolate."

It was their code for spotting a potential enemy. Jackson's eyebrows lifted slightly and he lowered his face to hers. "Do we have to go right now?"

"I'm bored. Hot chocolate calls to me. Please?" She batted her eyelashes. "There's that one tent nearby so it shouldn't take long to check it out."

"That one?" he said, clarifying he understood her code. "I thought you'd have them all mapped out by now."

Were there any more, or was the guy alone? She frowned and withdrew to quickly continue the search. Nothing else in the immediate area presented itself. "I suppose I can check out the tent by myself since you can't be bothered," she said. "But I'm only coming back with one cup then."

"SAGE Team Alpha detects one hostile. Request visual identification," the voice in her earpiece said.

"Which tent?" Jackson said, touching her nose.

Candace shrugged. "The one kind of in the middle back there. Nothing special to look at except for some colored business going on up top. Red on white."

"Target sighted. Male, blond with red highlights, early twenties, five-ten, one-hundred eighty pounds. Jeans, red shoes, black parka."

"You want to leave before the real action starts?" Jackson said. "You might miss something good."

"I'm not missing a thing, Sunshine," she said, grinning. "I'll only be gone a minute."

"SAGE Team Alpha go for closer inspection. Proceed with caution."

"Be careful," Jackson said, kissing her quickly. "You never know who's lurking around this place, waiting to abscond with a cute little snow bunny."

She tried not to punch him, instead settling for nipping his lip with her teeth to demonstrate her displeasure at the reminder of her current fluffiness. "Maybe if you're nice to me, I'll share," she said. Tossing him a grin and a giggle, Candace edged her way out of the area, angling for a closer look at the man she picked out. Tugging down on her hat, she reinforced her courage for a close pass. If she could spot something obvious, like the edges of the HEX brand maybe, they could confirm it was who they were looking for. The problem was in not knowing how many enemy operatives were scattered around the area. That guy might be the only one there, but surely there were others. Kristie didn't know any particulars about who would be there or where, and not much more than the attack would come around lunchtime.

As Candace squeezed between a group of rowdy guys, one of them grabbed her arm, slurring an indecent proposal at her. Damn it. The last thing she wanted was to call attention to herself, and especially not six feet away from the person she was stalking. There was no easy answer. If she caused a commotion, she'd be spotted. While her sunglasses might disguise her eyes some, if a person looked closely enough they'd notice a difference.

"No, thank you. A bit early to be falling all over yourself drunk, isn't it?" she said, shaking her arm free.

He sloppily reached out for her again, but she dodged it. When he called out curses after her, she pretended to ignore it, but it was hard to hide her grin when he crumpled to the ground.

It was probably all the packed snow that caused him to fall and sprain his ankle.

Probably.

Pleased at how she handled the situation, she pressed forward, but when she looked around, the HEX guy was gone. Biting back panic, she continued on, only allowing herself the slightest opportunity to search for anyone retreating from the crowd. There was no sign of him. The guy had disappeared into thin air. Damn it.

With no other recourse, she consulted her mental map of the event grounds. She could either head towards the VIP suite where Gabe was perched on the rooftop, or backtrack towards the entrance and concert area, then to the end past the downhill ski route. Deciding she could get a better read on any potential HEX operatives the further she strayed,

Candace started for the concert area.

The music was incredibly loud and there were too many people crammed together to get an accurate result, but the slightest hint of that intangible something else hung in the air over the audience. For a moment, she caught the faint feeling of heat, like Jackson's but not Jackson. It was so fleeting she couldn't be sure. It wasn't a singular person, however. There was at least one other there as well.

"Hmm," she mumbled. "There's gotta be hot chocolate around here somewhere. One or two of these tents should have it."

"SAGE Team Beta, be on alert. Suspected hostiles in your AOR. Two possible. Request visual identification."

She sighed. "Nothin'. It's warmer in there though." Making a face, she continued towards the ski area. They probably wouldn't catch her meaning about the heat manipulator, but she had to say something. Hector and Sarah were flying blind.

"Cannot identify hostiles. Remain on alert."

She didn't dawdle, but Candace didn't rush getting to the concession tent behind the ski run. Constant scans revealed nothing, however, and she returned to Jackson before too long, but with two cocoas instead of one.

"Find what you were looking for?" he asked.

"Yes and no," she shrugged. "There was more than one tent, but further out than I thought. What did I miss?"

Screams from an event behind them cut off Jackson's reply. They spun, facing back towards the downhill ski area and beyond. Candace gasped as a snowmobile went flying through the air, three others close behind, their drivers barely hanging on as they sailed through open space.

Jackson grabbed her hand and pulled as the first landed, the vehicle cartwheeling across the snow, headed directly for them. People rushed toward the exit, pushing each other violently to get out of the way of the oncoming disaster.

At the last second, the unmanned snowmobile was thrust aside, crashing sideways against an event jump ramp. She let out a sigh of relief. Andrew caught that one in time.

"Enemy sighted at the snowmobile course! Identified suspect and two others. Material manipulation verified. SAGE Team Alpha en route to SAGE Lone Wolf."

Jumping the metal barricades, Jackson ran towards the disturbance, Candace on his heels for a moment, but she paused.

"Wait!" she yelled at him. "This could be a distraction!"

Jackson skidded to a halt and backtracked. "Explain."

"There are at least two more at the stage. One of them is a fire bug."

"How much ammo do you need?"

Candace took a visual inventory of all the giant snowbanks devoid of people nearby. Five, not including the immaculately groomed Slopestyle course. "Light up whatever's free," she said.

She blinked, and he was gone. Within seconds, newly freed liquid water poured down the mountainside. She collected it before it made a mess of the grounds below where people ran, trying to escape the chaos of the out of control snowmobiles.

"Full evacuation in process."

Candace ran towards the stage, keeping the torrent of water collected at her back, but moving to keep it from freezing. As she reached the outskirts of the concert area, more cries of alarm went up. A fireball rocketed into the sky, decimating half of the stage. Entering the warzone, she sent a burst of water at the flames, dousing them instantly and revealing several charred corpses in its wake. Another blast of heat hurtled towards her, straight from the hands of a tall, black woman, hair cropped close to her scalp. A waif of a girl huddled beside her, looking terrified beyond words. Candace doused the attack with little more than a flick of her wrist. There was no sign of Hector or Sarah. Had they been caught up in the crowd and pushed out?

"Look, Mindy." The woman chuckled. "It's a soggy Easter Bunny."

Say what? Screw that noise. Candace ripped off her hat and tossed it to the side. "I might look cute and cuddly," she said, unzipping her coat to reveal her skinsuit. "But this bunny has a nasty bite."

When the HEX woman's next attack came, the pink marshmallow horror show served as a sacrifice. Good riddance. No longer hindered by the wretched thing, Candace dodged and doused everything that came her way, relishing the freedom of movement. Let that one tire herself out first.

When Candace finally struck, however, it didn't have the intended effect. Every blast of water she sent at them bounced away harmlessly. She sent another, skidding to the side on the slushy ground to get a look from another angle. Something shimmered as the water hit; a forcefield? Candace ran behind the row of tents for a moment to think of how to proceed.

"Need a hand, Candy Cane?" Gabe said, meeting her once she was out of sight.

"Where is everyone?" she asked, catching her breath.

"Hector and Sarah are MIA," her cousin said. "They were here one minute, gone the next. We don't know what happened. Jackson and Andrew have two guys pinned down between the snowboarding and ski run and the snowmobile track. They're having trouble getting a hit in, though. One of those guys has some slick trick up his sleeve. What's going on here?"

"Fire bug, for one," she explained while they ran further down the line of tents, the one behind them bursting into flame. "The other, I'm not sure. I think it's some sort of forcefield thing going on. I'm not sure how to get past it."

"Can't get close?"

Candace shook her head. "Not if I want to keep my eyebrows."

Gabe smirked. "Why don't you try something more subtle than power-washing?"

Putting out the flames of the tents down the line, Candace risked a glance through a small opening. "Well, where they're standing is still mostly frozen. If I could get them to move into the slushy areas, I could definitely do something with whatever water gets trapped inside their protective bubble. But, damn, Gabe. The defense here is just a kid. Seriously. She can't be more than fourteen. Why would they do that to someone so young?"

"Ours is not to question why—"

"Spare me the boot camp chant. Anyone could see she's scared shitless. That kid doesn't belong here."

Gabe sighed. "Okay, I get it. You don't want to hurt her. Try this. The support beams on the stage are ready to give. Hit 'em right and it'll collapse. They'll either get buried in the rubble or move away to where you can get to them. When that's done, I'll run a diversion, and you take out the fire bug."

"A diversion?"

"I think if I panic them enough, we can get some space between them."

A fireball took out the second to last of the tents. His plan was as good as any. "Okay, cuz, but it's your fault if they get pissed about the stage."

He snorted. "Tell them to charge it to my account."

Candace rolled her eyes, then set off down the row of ruined tents, which were little more than scantily clad skeletons after the hits of fire. The tips of her hair singed as an attack came in closer than she expected. Rounding the corner, she called up everything that remained of the liquid water, sending it spiraling into the bent support columns of the stage. Direct hit.

The resulting collapse was far more powerful than she anticipated, and pushed the HEX women away, nearer to the center of the concert space. She had them right where she wanted them, pending Gabe could distract them.

Whatever he did, he did it quickly. Both of the HEX women immediately shifted into full-on panic mode. The younger one flailed blindly, batting at imaginary things and drifting from her partner. The other yelled for the girl, spinning and throwing flames in all directions.

It was her chance.

Candace hesitated. All it would take is a drop of water and it would be over. More blood on her hands. Another face haunting her dreams.

The woman was screeching, flailing, firing off huge burst

of flame. "I will kill all of you!" she screamed.

They wouldn't stop. HEX was set on bringing death, and doing so indiscriminately.

She hesitated in Portland. Gil died.

She hesitated in San Jose. Allen died.

How many more had to die before she learned her lesson?

She closed her eyes.

Breathe in. Breathe out.

A single shot and the woman crumpled to the ground. Blood seeped from the tiny hole in her forehead, dripping down her face.

Candace bit back the urge to vomit. Those two hadn't stood a chance against her and her cousin combined.

"Stephanie?" The younger girl, Mindy, rushed to the side of her fallen comrade. Gabe's illusion no longer needed, it was replaced by something even more horrific. "Stephanie!"

Candace's heart broke as Mindy wailed and sobbed over the dead woman. What could she do? No comfort would come from her apology and nothing could erase what was done.

"She died fighting," Gabe said, emerging from his hiding place to stand beside the girl. "I don't know if she was fighting for something good, but it was something she believed in. But now, you have a choice to make."

Candace watched, transfixed by the girl's wide brown eyes and fearful gaze.

"A choice?" she whispered.

Gabe knelt down to her level. "We don't want to hurt you, but we can't let you go. You can choose what happens next. If you come with us, you'll be safe. If you go back to

HEX, we can't protect you. You know this one's ability." He flicked his head at Candace. "You can't defend against what she can do."

Mindy gulped and nodded once. At that, bile rose in Candace's throat. Gabe just used her as a death threat.

"You need to choose." He held out his hand, waiting.

The girl's mouth moved, trying to form verbal arguments, but coming up empty. After a minute or two, she slipped a tiny hand into his, tears spilling down her cheeks.

Gabe looked up in the direction of the VIP suites, the building towering over the wreckage of the stage. "One in custody. Area secure."

AFTER A small platoon of soldiers rushed in to take charge of Mindy, Candace and Gabe made their way toward the rest of the fighting. Between the wrecked snowmobiles and the injured or dead, it was slow going. Past the ski area, then around and up behind the athlete housing and additional VIP area, they tried to stay out of sight as much as they could. When they hit the first slushy puddles, Candace knew they were close.

Too close. A flaming piece of wreckage that might have been a ramp at one time hurtled towards them. Candace threw herself over to one side, Gabe to another as it crashed down precisely where they stood not seconds before. Pain flared to life in her right shoulder, the impact of her fall knocking something out of place. Gritting her teeth, she stood, focused, and wrenched it back into its socket with a gasp of agony. She glared at the smoldering wreckage hatefully. Was Andrew so busy that he couldn't keep the heavy structure from nearly killing them?

Gabe found her again, looking concerned. "You okay?"

"Super as always. What the hell is going on? Do you think Andrew missed that, or something else?"

"I don't have a clue. There's a lot of confusion about what's going on up there," he said. "They can't get a clear visual and there's no contact from the guys. They must have lost their mics."

Candace peeked out from their position behind a port-o-potty. A steady stream of water flowed from further up the mountain. She tapped into her connection and followed the trail up into the event area. Whatever Jackson was doing, he was doing a lot of it. Checking her connection with him, she wasn't getting any emotional extremes, so he must be okay, right?

"So we don't know anyone's position?" she asked. "I could potentially flood the area, but I won't risk our people."

"If we head that way," he pointed to the right, past a large tent with "Podium Club" signage. "We can cut up through the snowmobile course and use some of that as cover. Maybe flank them. If nothing else, we can at least see what's happening."

They hurried down the line of toilets and tents, dashing across to the edge of the course where they were shielded from sight by an undamaged slope. Gabe set a finger to his lips before shimmering and then vanishing altogether. Candace followed his movements by the tracks he left in the half-melted snow. When he disappeared around the corner, she held her breath. With his ability to bend light waves,

Gabe was completely invisible.

Several minutes passed and he didn't return. Every second that went by ratcheted up her tension level until she was borderline panicking. Her nails dug into her palms as she tried to keep from dashing out to follow him. The sudden onslaught of new explosions did nothing to ease her worry. Unable to stand another moment of inactivity, Candace eased around the side of the ramp, searching for the source of the sounds of battle.

Her jaw dropped. It was chaos. Jackson and Andrew were fighting both each other and an unknown man, as well as defending against Gabe as he popped in and out of visibility, throwing punches when he rematerialized before them. It was insanity! What was going on? They were all under some strange spell that caused them to fight everyone within sight, as though they couldn't trust their own senses. Her gaze drifted further up the mountain to another figure, a female. Dark blonde hair spilled down her back and she wavered the way asphalt looked on a hot summer day. That woman was causing it, but how? Everyone was disoriented, but only within a radius Candace couldn't determine.

Angry at the sight of her friends turning on one another, Candace closed her eyes and prepared for a long range attack. On the far side of the course, down into the ski area, she collected as much water as she could, building it up, churning it, whipping it into a frenzy. Ready, she emerged from hiding and stepped around the edge of the ramp, ripping the water upwards, over the top of the wall dividing the events, washing the two HEX operatives down from the high ground and into the low areas of the course.

Candace raced around a collapsed ramp, seeking out her

targets. She needed to take out the woman causing the confusion. If she missed her chance...

A fireball decimated the structure to her left and she was launched forward. Candace skidded through the slush on her already weakened right side, coming to a stop against an embankment. That was one of Jackson's attacks.

Scrambling to her feet, she searched for the HEX woman, finding the enemy also recovering and starting up the assault again. As everything warped around her, Candace struggled to focus.

One shot. That was all she had.

As she flung her arm out towards the wavering woman, Candace poured everything she had into a single bullet.

Before she could confirm the hit, she was ripped off of her feet by an explosion behind her. The world slipped into slow motion as she left the ground. Her body contorted, spinning in mid-air as she grasped for anything to hold on to. In a heartbeat, reality caught up, and she crashed to the ground, her head slamming against something with the clang of metal.

Was someone yelling her name?

She couldn't breathe, couldn't think. The ringing in her ears drowned out everything else and her vision blurred and darkened.

The shadow shifted and a face came into view: the man from the snowboarding crowd, the one who disappeared before she could get to him.

He said something she couldn't understand and lifted her, slinging her over a shoulder. Candace's forehead smacked against his back, jarring her further, but at least there was sound again.

"Candace!" Jackson was yelling, screaming her name.

Sudden brightness blinded her, sending her senses reeling. Her mind exploded, expanded, shifted, even as she heard him call to her one last time.

And then…

Nothing.

ABOUT STARLA—

A GEEK of all trades, Starla Huchton has been crafting stories in various genres since 2007. She is a three-time finalist for Parsec Awards for her podcast fiction work, and was the first place winner for Science Fiction & Fantasy in the Sandy competition in 2012. Her work spans Science Fiction, Fantasy, New Adult Romance, Young Adult titles, Steampunk, Contemporary, and various other varieties of stories. She is greedy and likes all the genres!

When not writing, Starla trains three minions, a black lab, and a military husband whilst designing book covers for independent authors and publishers at www.designedby starla.com.

Connect with the author on the Starla Huchton Author
Page on Facebook, @starlahuchton on Twitter,
or at www.starlahuchton.com. To be notified
only for new releases, sign up for the mailing list at
https://tinyletter.com/SAHuchton.

OTHER BOOKS BY STARLA

AS STARLA HUCHTON

THE ANTIGONE'S WRATH SERIES
Master of Myth

FLIPPED FAIRY TALES
Shadows on Snow
The Stillness of the Sky

My Bittersweet Summer (standalone)

AS S. A. HUCHTON

THE ENDURE SERIES
Maven
Nemesis
Progeny

THE EVOLUTION SERIES
Evolution: ANGEL
Evolution: SAGE
Evolution: HEX

Lex Talionis (standalone)

CPSIA information can be obtained
at www.ICGtesting.com
Printed in the USA
LVOW08s1910040517
533268LV00010B/1142/P